THE ELUSIVE EARL

THE BAD HEIR DAY TALES

BOOK THREE

GRACE BURROWES

GRACE BURROWES PUBLISHING

DEDICATION

To all who have been banished—from a family, a marriage, a career, or a home of any sort. May you thrive anew wherever you are loved and cherished.

CHAPTER ONE

"How is it possible that London reeks even more intensely than it did eight years ago?" Graham MacNeil hung his hat on a wall hook, nodded to the harried tavern maid, and took a seat. "You're looking well, St. Didier."

Leopold St. Didier, always a considerate sort, had chosen a corner table, meaning both he and Graham could sit with their backs to the wall.

"We're to believe that reek is the smell of progress." St. Didier had been nursing a small pint, or pretending to, based on the amount still remaining in his tankard. "One might say you're looking robust, MacNeil, and rather formidable. Please stop glowering as if you'd delight in starting a melee."

"No melees until I've had a drink."

St. Didier had dressed for the occasion, meaning the hat on the chair beside him was a dusty, low-crowned beaver, his cuffs were frayed, and his jacket was worn at the elbows. He smelled faintly of horse, suggesting the jacket had been stored in a stable by design. All the careful costuming in the world could not disguise the watchful look in St. Didier's dark eyes, the slight looseness of boots that allowed for a knife or three to be kept discreetly from sight.

He was leaner than Graham recalled him being, and his features were more sharply defined. Of all Graham's London acquaintances, St. Didier alone might have fared well in the Antipodes.

Not necessarily a compliment, given that St. Didier was an English gentleman of aristocratic origins.

"Is the ale drinkable?" Graham asked.

"Of course. I would not poison you after spending two years trying to lure you home."

Engaging in polite blackmail, more like. Dropping hints, letter by letter, and leaving innuendo between each line and the next.

Graham's drink arrived. He set a coin on the tavern maid's tray, then another. She'd give them privacy, or what passed for privacy in this malodorous dockside hole. St. Didier watched that transaction with unreadable eyes.

"I am not home," Graham said, blowing the head off his ale. "Home is a good four hundred and fifty miles north. Perthshire is ever so much more fragrant, and one encounters a lot fewer English aristos there."

Not the most diplomatic comment Graham could have made. St. Didier's family had boasted of a viscountcy in his uncle's day, but no male heir of the body, anywhere, of any description, had been available to succeed the old boy, and the title—along with a significant pile of wealth—had reverted to the crown.

"No aristos here, MacNeil. Perhaps your travels affected your eyesight."

His travels. Hilarious. "My travels damned near put an end to me, St. Didier. New South Wales boasts a wee spider that can kill you with one bite. The denizens of Sydney Harbour include a jellyfish that can literally sting you out of your mind the pain is so unbearable, and then you die of the shock. The crocodiles up north delight in snacking on human bones, and if I start maundering on about venomous snakes, we'll never get to discussing the reason for your summons."

A subtle puzzlement infused St. Didier's features. "You're not exaggerating."

"I understate the matter, and only the English could believe such a land suitable for civilizing. You're in for a challenge, you lot, though I grant you, Governor Macquarie—a Scotsman, of course—has some worthy ideas and the determination to see them through." Macquarie would be toppled eventually by the contingent of prosperous settlers who saw the free labor of a penal colony as a greater benefit than a thriving, open society, but when that day came, Macquarie's radical ideas would not be recalled to England with him.

"One generally has the sense that the wonders of Terra Australis must be exaggerated," St. Didier said. "Here-there-be-dragons, but on land."

Somebody at the bar launched into a foul ditty about the queen's privy, and a lot of inebriated fools toasted the tavern maid's ankles.

Once upon a time, Graham had considered St. Didier a friend.

A warning was in order. "Do you ever miss your family seat, St. Didier? That grand, lovely estate, carefully tended for generations by your ancestors, now going to ruin in the hands of some royal tenant who'll bleed the place dry in a decade?"

"Of course I miss it."

"Now imagine," Graham went on, "that you're put on a ship that could well be your coffin and consigned literally to the other side of the earth. You are sent as far from your home as it's possible to go, this side of death. Throw in the spiders and serpents, the unending disdain of people who wouldn't dare look you in the eye back home, and add the even worse contempt from the honest criminals you were transported with. All the while, your home, your birthright, the land you were bred to cherish and protect, is in the hands of *solicitors*."

"Honest men, MacNeil. I made sure of it."

"*English lawyers* who know nothing about maintaining an estate in Perthshire. The court made sure of that. Thanks to that same court, I was banished for seven years on pain of death, but the court never counted on poor cousin John drowning, did they? Now I'm the earl. Such a pity."

St. Didier took a sip of his ale, the oldest dilatory tactic known to the adult male. "You're angry."

"I'm in the presence of a clairvoyant. Last time that happened, I was in India. One doesn't get over being convicted of murdering one's beloved granny, St. Didier. Innocent or guilty, the ordeal takes a toll."

"Not murder, involuntary manslaughter, and you pleaded guilty, MacNeil."

St. Didier, in his roundabout fashion, was asking a question that Graham was not prepared to answer directly.

"A trial would have killed my grandfather." As it happened, Grandpapa hadn't lasted out the year. "He saw me off." More to the point, the old earl had ensured that both comforts and necessities had accompanied Graham on the transport ship, along with tools, books, botanical specimens, and a few highly salable luxuries.

Grandpapa's generosity had been literally lifesaving. Even the Royal Navy's able seamen hesitated to steal cargo that was technically the property of an earl. Good old Highland height and heft had improved the odds too.

The rest had been sheer, unwavering contrariness, always an asset among the forcibly transported.

"You'll go to Perthshire, then?" St. Didier asked as the singer at the bar turned into a passable quartet, though the countertenor was flat.

Graham spoke more quietly rather than compete with the noise. "I did not come back to Merry Olde out of a sentimental attachment to Fat George. I've served my sentence, and now I'm the rubbishing earl. I've doubtless some traditional Scottish penury to enjoy. Worse yet, if I know my neighbors, at least three feuds will have all but lapsed for want of some reiving and drunken insults. One does one's duty, St. Didier, or hallowed traditions go entirely by the wayside."

St. Didier's expression became broodish, or reverted to its naturally thoughtful inscrutability. "That's a yes. You're heading north."

"I leave in the morning. I've met with the solicitors, obtained their final report and best wishes, albeit they refrained from shaking my hand. You'd be welcome to travel with me, though I appreciate that the notice is short."

Short enough that St. Didier could refuse politely, or demur until a later date that would never come around.

"Are you going by land or sea?" St. Didier asked.

"Overland. I've had a bellyful of the briny deep." To Rio by way of mind-shattering heat and doldrums—whoever clad British naval officers in wool had been in Lucifer's pay—then down to the Horn of Africa for some horrendous gales. The knife fights on the final push across the Roaring Forties had turned deadly and the drinking water brackish. Mountains of ice had floated by on the southern horizon, as forbidding as they were monotonous.

On the return journey, Cape Horn had been a nightmare wrapped in a hellscape tied up with banshee winds and bargains with the devil.

St. Didier finished his ale. "I can accompany you, if that is truly your wish."

"You *sought* to come with me. That's what this little *tête-à-tête chez L'Odeur de la Thames* is about. You're afraid I'll commit some premeditated manslaughter once I get back to Perth, aren't you? St. Didier, you are not my nanny."

"Will you?" St. Didier asked. "Commit manslaughter or homicide of any variety?"

"I would not know with whom to start. You can come along, St. Didier, but don't push your luck."

The ale was surprisingly good. Graham left half of it in the tankard for the gaunt lad trudging with his rag and bucket from table to table and put another coin under the tankard for the boy to slip into a pocket.

"Why?" St. Didier asked as he and Graham stepped out into the damp and chilly night. "Why bring me along?"

"I saved you asking to come along, of course."

"You intended to request that I travel with you. I'm slow, MacNeil, but I do get past the post eventually."

St. Didier wasn't slow, he was thorough. A different matter entirely. "I was convicted of killing my grandmother, whom I loved. I did not kill her, intentionally or otherwise."

"If you say so."

"I do say so, and if you question my word on that matter ever again, I will accidentally bash you into the next shire, St. Didier." The night air reeked of the sewage in the river, fish, tar, and piss.

"You're taller and stronger, I'm faster. That hasn't changed."

Yes, it had. "I was *wrongly accused* of Grandmama's death. You are along to ensure similar accusations do not befall me again. No telling whom I might be alleged to have tossed down the garderobe or heaved from the parapets."

"I'm your bodyguard?"

"You are my spare eyes and ears, laddie, and mind you fulfill that office with your usual attention to detail, faultless recall, and complete lack of humor."

The footsteps Graham detected were light, almost lost in the slap of the water against the wharves and the general raillery along any dockside street. Too light. Too furtive. Not another patron ready to sleep off some indulgence in a cozy bed.

Trouble, and so soon.

"You haven't asked about the ladies, MacNeil."

Technically, Graham was a lordship now. An accidental earl. St. Didier was doubtless being delicate by refraining from proper address.

The distance to the following footsteps closed to a few yards. "The ladies are thriving, I've no doubt. Peter would have told me otherwise. He's very fond of them."

Between the words *of* and *them,* Graham turned and withdrew a knife from his boot, threw, and shoved St. Didier into the nearest doorway. A satisfying oath sounded in the darkness, followed by an uneven tattoo of boots disappearing in the darkness.

"MacNeil, what in the name of...?" St. Didier cocked his head. "How did you know? I realized we were being followed only as you started blathering about extra eyes and ears. You meant to warn me with that reference, didn't you?"

"I meant to warn the poor sod who will have a very sore arm come morning—as well as possession of one of my cheaper knives. Move along, English. We don't want him coming back with his friends to return my blade."

St. Didier set a brisk pace toward more genteel surrounds. "I was wrong."

"I shall notify *The Times.* What were you wrong about?"

"You are faster. That shouldn't have been possible."

"And it should not have been possible that I found myself on that transport ship." No steps followed as the stench of the river faded and the lamplighters' diligence was more routinely in evidence.

"Nobody else calls me laddie," St. Didier muttered, "much less English. Your womenfolk worried about you, MacNeil."

Not half so much as I worried about them. "They are not my womenfolk. Morna and Lanie can inspect me to their hearts' delight when we reach Perth. You'll be ready at first light?"

"Of course."

"Then I will leave you to enjoy whatever passes for dreams in that hard head of yours, St. Didier. Expect to travel with more swiftness than comfort."

"We will travel with both."

"As long as we travel north. Good night." Graham sauntered off in the direction of his temporary abode and was calling it an adequately dignified exit at the end of a successful meeting when St. Didier's voice cut through the darkness.

"MacNeil!"

Graham turned to see the pride of the St. Didiers standing under a streetlamp, his attire that of a middling groom or stable boy.

"A man of your lordship's station cannot indulge in random rudeness." St. Didier extended a bare hand. "Good night, Dunhaven."

The proffered handshake was actually quite a presumption, from a commoner to a peer. Also a test.

Graham shook, touched a finger to his hat brim, and left his bodyguard, spare eyes and ears, and self-appointed finishing governess in the circle of dim light.

Bodyguard, governess, et cetera and so forth, and just possibly, maybe, after a fashion... but no. A convicted killer knew better than to attempt friendships, intentional, accidental, or otherwise.

"What did you miss the most?" St. Didier asked as the horses clip-clopped along the bank of the River Tay. Spring had yet to arrive, meaning the sunlight was more brilliant for being unbroken by foliage. Despite the brightness, the landscape yet held a bleak, forbidding quality. Bare trees, chill breeze, achingly empty, achingly blue skies.

"I missed everything," Graham replied, which was only half an evasion. "The air. You can breathe here. The light—just look about you. The sky is heavenly blue, the water blindingly bright. The quiet. No chattering monkeys—those were in India—or shrieking parrots, or deafening cicadas. This is the quiet, the sunlight, and the air that my soul understands."

Even the seasonal bleakness was familiar and thus almost dear.

"Scotland turns you up poetic," St. Didier said.

"Covering four hundred miles in little over a week turns me up glad to be on home soil." Glad, but also enduring a vague dread.

What seems too good to be true is too good to be true. The

Antipodes taught that lesson over and over, if British justice, months on a transport ship, and regular terror on the high seas failed to adequately make the point.

"The MacNeil castle has stood for centuries," St. Didier said. "By that reckoning, you merely stepped out for a cup of tea."

"I am not a castle." Graham turned his horse away from the river and onto the track that cut across MacNeil land. They'd been on the MacNeil stretch of the Tay for the past two miles, though the coaches would take a smoother, roundabout route to the castle.

"Why didn't you write?" St. Didier asked.

"I wrote to Peter. I wrote to you." Quarterly notes to Peter, like the dutiful epistles schoolboys send home. *Headmaster is quite stern, but I am making friends and getting good marks so you will be proud of me. I miss Cook's pudding very much.*

The headmasters had carried whips, the rations had been pathetic, the heat unrelenting and the bugs worse. Two years of that, though, and a conditional remission had come through, as it had for many convicts who avoided trouble and worked hard. Two years later, a land grant had followed.

"I've had longer letters delivered by pigeons," St. Didier said. "'Watch the trustees and keep an eye on Peter.'"

"My thanks for both."

"Peter is an adult now. Once he left university, he didn't need much minding."

"My baby brother is a MacNeil coming into his prime, St. Didier. Constant surveillance is warranted."

"Well, then, tell me, your lordship, just how—"

"Enough trying to distract me, English. The initial greetings will be awkward, the first few days and weeks a trial of another sort, but I'll muddle through. MacNeils are good at that." Some MacNeils were better at it than others.

St. Didier ceased trying to make conversation, which was fortunate for his old age. The next mile passed with reassuring familiarity.

At the sound of the horses' hoofbeats, old John MacIver came out of
the gamekeeper's cottage and stood by the lane. His face was more
lined, his eyes a more faded blue, but when Graham nodded,
MacIver nodded back.

"Welcome home, Laird." He pulled off his cap, revealing hair
gone snow white.

Graham drew the horse to a halt. "MacIver. Good to be back.
Any coneys left in yon woods?"

"Enough for a stew, no thanks to those damned MacHeath boys."

The MacHeath boys had gone for soldiers two generations ago,
but that wasn't the point. "A thankless task. Carry on as best you
can."

MacIver barely inclined his head, but when Graham half turned
his horse to open the next gate, MacIver was still standing by the lane,
cap in hand.

"What was that about?" St. Didier asked.

"Tradition. My grandfather ran riot with the MacHeath boys
before King George bribed them into taking his bloody shilling. They
could all supposedly catch rabbits with their bare hands, they were so
quiet and fleet. The current MacHeath scion served in Spain, and
I'm told he survived to take up his uncle's title."

No wild rabbits in Australia. The dread rose up again, worse than
before. MacIver had known to keep watch and had had some time to
decide whether and which honorific to use. *Laird* was better than
your lordship, and *my boy* would have been asking for too much.

MacNeils excelled at that too.

Inevitably, the castle loomed up on its prominence, pale gray
stone piled on pale gray stone, parapets and wings all drawing the eye
to the watchtower, which offered the best view of Perthshire known
to man. The MacHeath family seat was grander, but for sheer loveli-
ness, the MacNeil castle won all bets. Brick facing on the lower floors
added a hint of gentility and gave ambitious ivy a chance to subdue
medieval impregnability into graceful dignity.

Graham stopped his horse and beheld his home. No pennant

waving, because Grandpapa had died of grief, John had died of bad luck, and the present earl...

"Let's get this over with." Graham urged his steed forward.

The moat had long since been drained and the ditch filled in, but the approach still required crossing a plank bridge and riding beneath a portcullis. As a boy, Graham had never trusted that spiked portcullis to stay up. Grandpapa had showed him the heavy black chains wrapped around their massive capstan, but still the unease lingered.

Better to use the postern gate or enter the bailey through the gardens.

Nobody waited on the flagstone terrace. Nobody stood on the steps. No old-fashioned assembling of the household to welcome the new laird—thank God—and no eager faces peering from the windows either.

The courtyard was flooded with midday sun on hard, gray stone, the quiet complete.

Home, but the moment did not feel like a homecoming, nor even like much of a return. Somebody had planted daffodils that should have been geraniums in pots around the massive door to the great hall, and a pigeon landed on the curtain wall above the gate to the herb garden.

"Shall I whistle us up a groom?" St. Didier said.

"We'll take the horses around ourselves, unless you're too much of a town—"

"Graham!"

A tall, lithe figure in long skirts stood at the top of the half-dozen steps leading to the great hall doorway. Her hair was strawberry blond, a beacon in the sunshine. She'd come through the wicket door and left it open behind her.

"Graham!"

"She can't see you," St. Didier said. "Over here!"

The lady pelted down the steps and crossed the cobbled bailey at a dead run. At the last possible instant, Graham realized the significance of St. Didier's warning, took two steps to the left, and narrowly preserved his greeter from colliding with the horse's haunches.

"You're home. You're home at last." She squeezed him hard, hugged him harder, and then simply held on. "I knew you'd come back. Grandpapa promised me, and John said so too. Peter tries to be all manly and stoic, but I knew."

"Lanie." Lanie—Elaine Marie when she'd been naughty—all grown up and bearing a devilish, heart-stopping resemblance to her older sister. "Darling girl, you have become beautiful." Still coltish, still more elbows and angles than curves, and yet no longer a child.

Some of Graham's dread revealed itself to be grief. Lanie had grown up without him. Peter had finished growing up without him.

"I am an adult," Lanie said, giving him one more squeeze before stepping back and keeping a hand on his arm. "It can't be helped. Are you still handsome?"

St. Didier passed the horses to a puffing groom who'd emerged from around the side of the bailey.

"I am gorgeous," Graham said, "provided you like a bit of a nose on a man and don't mind that he's unfashionably tall and his face and hands are about the same color as old leather. My hair turned from auburn to gold on my travels, so I'm now much more *au courant*."

"Did it really?" Lanie ruffled her fingers through his hair.

"Of course not. I'm the same Graham, Lanie." Another half truth. "And I'm very glad to see you."

"Then come inside." She tugged him in the general direction of the door. "Peter said you would not want us to rush you all at once, and we must await you in the family parlor, but if I am patient and persistent, I will eventually convince Peter that he can't tell me what to do."

"Been at it a few years, have you?" Graham's voice came out steady, his tone light, but a knot had formed in his chest, and a lump the size of Stirling Castle was caught in his throat. She'd always been wee Lanie...

"I have been training Peter to respect my wishes since birth, so going on twenty years. He makes progress then slips back, and I am chattering. Are you well, Graham? You feel like stone."

I am not stone. "Muscles, my dear. Lots and lots of muscles. Those are unfashionable too. Steps, Lanie."

"I know. I can still see some about the edges when it's this bright. I have to turn my head like an owl and peer down my nose and such. Undignified business, trying to see. I'm hopeless indoors. I will be entirely in your thrall if you promise to read to me for two hours every night."

I am already entirely in your thrall. "Maybe I've forgotten how to read."

Lanie navigated the steps as easily as if she were fully sighted. "You surely forgot how to write, Graham MacNeil. Not well done of you. We worried."

"I wrote to Peter. He was remiss for not sharing my epistles with you. The wicket is open."

"I left it open. Saves me fumbling with the latch." She passed through the smaller opening cut into the massive oak double doors. "Graham is home!"

One could yell in a castle to greater effect than in some other venues. Footsteps echoed, a heavy, hurried walk.

"Graham!" Peter—also all grown up—stopped at the landing halfway down the staircase. "By God, you made it! Home at last." He trotted the remaining steps, hand extended, and then surpassed all bounds by pulling Graham into a hug and thumping him twice on the back.

"Peter. Good God, you've put on some muscle."

"But still not as tall as you, thank the heavenly intercessors. Turn me out in a kilt, and Edinburgh

falls at my feet. You have been in the sun."

"I am a testament to bad fashion. One longs for sunshine at sea but forgets that the results of fair weather linger in the complexion. I've brought St. Didier with me, as he was keen to dodge Mayfair during the Season."

"He went around to the stable," Lanie said.

How could she...?

"My ears are in fine working order, Graham, and my nose is the envy of every distiller this side of the River Tweed. For example, my nose detects a certain hint of rose in the air, and that tells me—"

"Lanie." Peter's tone held a note of warning. "We're all so pleased you're home, Graham, or do we refer to you as Dunhaven now?"

"You'd best not, if you know what's good for you."

Peter grinned and was doubtless preparing to deliver a pithy retort when a voice like a whipcrack sounded from the steps.

"I shall call you Dunhaven if I choose to. That is my lord's title, after all." The lady was another version of Lanie, taller, curvier, more self-possessed, and infinitely less happy to see him. Her dark copper hair was ruthlessly bound up in a coronet, and her demeanor was positively forbidding.

She completed her descent in no particular hurry and stood regarding him with the same sort of expression she might have turned on a pantry mouser presenting her with evidence of good hunting. One could not fault the beast for doing the expected, *and yet*.

"Morna." Graham bowed. "You may address me however you please." Assuming she condescended to address him at all.

Her scrutiny lasted another uncomfortable moment, long enough for Graham to realize that she still favored attar of roses.

"We'd best feed you," she said, "rather than argue over etiquette. A midday meal in the breakfast parlor awaits. Somebody find St. Didier and send him along. He'll not be winkling secrets from the stable boys when he should be doing justice to a good ham."

She whisked off down the passage that led to the breakfast parlor. Peter grinned, shrugged, and followed, and then Lanie seized Graham by the arm again.

"You have to be famished," she said, "but even if you aren't, we generally do as Morna tells us. More peaceful that way."

Once upon a time, Graham had delighted in arguing with Morna and she with him. More exciting that way. Then the whole business with Grandmama had arisen, and Morna's regard for him had waned considerably.

Graham allowed himself to be escorted down the dim passage by a woman who was all but blind. He who hoped things hadn't changed too much in his absence was sometimes given what he'd sought, and wasn't that just a damned fitting irony?

CHAPTER TWO

Morna did not label Graham MacNeil a killer per se, but rather, a man whose carelessness had nonetheless cost a precious life. In a just world, he would have returned home looking chastened and worn, a pale ghost of the robust young man who'd brought such sorrow and scandal to his family.

If he returned at all.

He did not deserve to be larger, more self-possessed, and, drat all the luck, more attractive because of it. He still looked a lady in the eye, still showed Lanie a subtle consideration that respected her pride, still had no use for pointless ceremony.

Morna stalked into the breakfast parlor and found Great-Uncle Brodie lifting the lids off the warming dishes.

"Uncle, the food will get cold. Graham has arrived." Dunhaven, rather. The earl. His lordship.

"Has he now? Lovely." Brodie set the lid back over the sliced ham. "Graham, there you are. Welcome home. A happy day, this, when the prodigal returns. We had snow on the hilltops the day before yesterday, but this morning all is awash in sunshine. We must conclude even the weather is conspiring to make your arrival joyous."

Brodie talked too much, in Morna's opinion. This fault was evident even before he started drinking and blatant thereafter. A gleam of mischief in his eye belied his friendly tone.

"Uncle, a pleasure to see you," Graham said, sounding as if he meant it. "I'm glad to be home."

While Graham used the basin and pitcher in the corner to wash his hands, Morna discreetly moved cutlery and linen. Uncle Brodie went on about the state of the roads, and how the parliamentary delegation claimed bad roads slowed invading English armies, but most of Wellington's troops had been Scottish or Irish, and those intrepid lads hadn't needed good roads to best the Corsican, had they?

By the time Brodie finished his diatribe, Morna had relaid a place setting at the head of the table and moved down to her usual seat at the middle across from Lanie. Peter occupied the place beside Lanie, and Uncle Brodie shuffled around to the chair at Morna's right.

"Shall we be seated?" she asked, though it wasn't a question. "Cook has gone to considerable effort."

"And I," Graham said, standing behind the chair at the head of the table, "have a considerable appetite, but might we wait for St. Didier?"

He'd put his query to Morna, and she wasn't sure if he was challenging her or deferring to her. The point became moot as the Englishman strode into the dining room.

"Sorry to be late. I was admiring your stables. Something smells delicious. Do I dare hope for a juicy ham?"

St. Didier could be charming, but on no account did Morna consider him trustworthy. He'd been on hand when Grandmama had died, a visitor Graham had collected on one of his jaunts to Edinburgh. St. Didier had seen the whole tragedy firsthand and by rights should have denied an association with MacNeils of any stripe.

Instead, he'd *dropped by*—hundreds of miles north of his London address—at least once a year and maintained a regular correspondence with Peter.

Up to something, no doubt. The English were invariably up to something.

"How is the lambing coming along?" Graham asked as the soup was served. He'd chosen his opening gambit well, because Peter was particularly keen on the flocks, though Brodie had opinions about sheep, wool, shepherds, shearers, and collie dogs.

"We need to improve our rams," Peter said, glowering across the table at Brodie. "Any nation that can grow grass can grow sheep, and the coarse wool the army bought in such quantity is no longer in demand."

Brodie countered with a prophecy of doom for the kelp industry, which was how half the crofters in the Western Isles kept body and soul together. Lanie observed that whisky would be the salvation of Scotland if the excisemen weren't so relentless.

In the midst of this predictable verbal affray, Morna paused between bites of buttered potatoes to find Graham smiling at her. Not the sort of boyish grin Peter indiscriminately aimed at half the world, but a slight, private, amused smile. A pleased smile.

She grabbed for the basket of rolls and busied herself applying butter that wasn't soft enough to bread that wasn't warm enough. When she looked up, Graham was in earnest conversation with Brodie about the challenges of growing barley in India.

India. He'd been so far away, and for so long. If John hadn't died...

"Tell me about the neighbors," Graham said when the sticky toffee pudding was disappearing apace. "How fares MacHeath?"

"He's going wife-hunting in London," Peter said. "But he ought to be going to Edinburgh. We don't need an English marchioness looking down her nose at us and ridiculing our plaids."

Sebastian MacHeath had been largely brought up among the English at his uncle's insistence. Know thy enemy, and all that. Morna approved of the philosophy. She did not approve of sending children far from home to be reared among strangers.

"MacHeath hasn't departed yet," she said. "Dunhaven should look in on him before the marquess is away to the south."

"Is that wise?" Uncle Brodie asked. "If MacHeath won't receive Graham, then nobody else will. Better to let the marquess disappear on his errand and dodge the issue altogether."

"MacNeils," said Graham softly, "do not *dodge issues*. Sebastian is the Marquess of Dunkeld now, and I owe him a neighborly call. Is there more of this most excellent sweet? I detect a wee drop of our own *uisge beatha* in the sauce, and that suggests a genius in the kitchen."

Point made, subject changed. Graham had had the same ability to steer conversation as a younger man. He was never loud, never rude, and never caught out in a falsehood, though he lied. He lied while looking a lady straight in the eyes.

"The genius isn't in the kitchen," Peter said, beaming at Lanie. "Our own Nose decided Cook should try fortifying the caramel sauce, and now it's Cook's signature sweet."

"I am honored by the menu," Graham said, "and hope my compliments reach Mrs. Gibson straightaway. A meal this good deserves a stroll and a nap."

Uncle's bald observation about Graham being unwelcome at the next castle up the hill hadn't produced the same awkward silence that the reference to Mrs. Gibson did. Not even St. Didier attempted to rescue the conversation.

"Mrs. Gibson quit," Lanie said. "Left after Grandmama died. We have Mrs. Anderson now. Much jollier, though the fare isn't as fancy. I actually prefer her menus."

Lanie was ignoring that Mrs. Gibson had quit amid pointed mutterings about men getting away with murder and old women being unsafe in their own beds.

"I see," Graham said, taking the last bite of his sweet. "Then my compliments to Mrs. Anderson and her staff. An excellent meal in fine company. I'm for a walk in the garden. Morna, might you join me?"

She ceased drawing rose patterns in her pudding sauce. Graham was neither smiling nor scowling. Was he issuing a summons or a polite invitation?

MacNeils do not dodge issues. Morna wasn't a MacNeil by blood, but years at the castle made her MacNeil-ish by association, and of necessity.

"Of course. I'll need my cloak."

The meal ended with Peter and Lanie squabbling over the preferred nationality for Sebastian MacHeath's bride, a common topic of local discord. Morna tolerated Graham's escort to the back hallway and even allowed him to hold her cloak for her.

"You aren't wearing a coat?" she asked when he would have held the door for her.

"Suppose I ought to wear something. I've been cold since leaving the Azores." He grabbed an old plaid cloak in the blue and green colors of the MacNeils of Barra. A pretty pattern. He would choose that one.

"That will be short on you, my lord."

"The wool is soft, and I like the colors. Let's get some fresh air, shall we?" He opened the door, and Morna made herself walk past him into the brilliant afternoon sunshine.

"Tell me about Lanie's eyesight," he said. "I will ask her directly, but one doesn't want to give offense."

Not where Morna had thought he'd begin. "Her eyes are failing, all but failed. She was losing ground before you... left, of course. The situation seemed to stabilize for a few years, but she tells me unless she's in strong sunlight, peering out of the very edge of her vision, she can see only a gray blur. She seems to detect movement, but I gather that's her acute hearing as much as her sight."

Graham did not offer his arm, which was a relief. "And her nose is keen?"

"The best in the shire. We don't tap a barrel unless she says it's time. She's a wizard with spices, and if I could interest her in flowers, she'd be a superb parfumier."

"What of Peter?" Graham descended into the lower part of the garden, where the walls provided protection from the wind and helped concentrate the sun's heat. "My dear brother seems at loose ends, which I suppose is to be expected. I used to be at loose ends myself."

Until your negligence cost a dear old woman her life. Time enough to hurl that accusation later. "Your grandfather extracted a promise that Peter would never join the military. Peter is not a scholar, and the church would be a poor fit. Loose ends, it is. Brodie has made a life's work of being at loose ends and seems to enjoy himself most of the time. Why?"

"I owe Peter a place to start, Morna. A place away from what happened here, away from an older brother who went from a fribble to a felon and now—through the parsimony of the crown and the grace of the Almighty—a peer."

"Parsimony?"

"St. Didier kept a close eye on the solicitors serving as trustees of the estate after Grandpapa's death. He insisted that they invest profits in improvements—on the crofts, in the herds, to the land itself. On paper, the earldom hasn't much cash as a result. We're barely solvent from one perspective."

Morna had suspected as much. "From another?"

"We're quite well fixed. Good acres, solid structures, enough personal coin to weather a bad harvest, and healthy livestock in every byre. To the crown, though, the earldom looked like another Scottish embarrassment, complete with crumbling castle and moldering grave-yard. Then too, the legalities didn't line up to George's advantage."

The garden wasn't warm exactly, but it was sheltered and quiet. The daffodils along both east- and west-facing walls were making a good effort, and some late crocuses were still blooming around the central sculpture of the stag. Did Graham see it as a refuge or a responsibility? Both? Neither?

"What does that mean?" Morna asked. "The legalities didn't line up?"

"St. Didier could explain this more clearly than I can," Graham said, gesturing to a bench. "I was already a convicted felon when John died. More to the point, I had served out my sentence and had my grants of clemency and land. I was not a peer when... when Grandmother died, so the House of Lords could not adjudge me attainted. They had no jurisdiction over me at the time. I wasn't even a courtesy lord. Now, they cannot modify the sentence of transportation retroactively so that I might be condemned to die and subject to attainder. That would be double jeopardy, or some such legal peculiarity. I am alive and legitimate; therefore, I am the titleholder."

"St. Didier excels at those legal peculiarities, doesn't he?"

"The College of Arms consults him and probably quizzed him at length on my situation. Fat George didn't want another drafty castle anyway, and attainder has a history of being trotted out to enrich rapacious monarchs. George wasn't keen on the penny press having another go at him, so here I am, an earl with a criminal past—Scottish of me, some would say—which brings us back to Peter."

"What to do with him?"

"Morna, I hardly know him. He was a mere stripling when I left, and now... He could be the next earl. He'd be justified in disowning me, but he hasn't."

Whatever she'd expected of Graham, it hadn't been humility, much less bewilderment. Shame perhaps, even arrogance, but not this puzzled concern for family.

"Ask him," she said, ignoring the sunny bench. "Peter is articulate and nobody's fool, though he can be foolish. I'd best make sure St. Didier's rooms are in order. You're in the earl's suite, unless you'd like your old rooms back."

"I bow to your superior judgment. The earl's suite will do for now."

For now? What did that mean? "Then I will wish you good day. Supper is at six, though you might be moving that later as the light lasts longer."

"Six will do. My thanks for everything."

"I do not want your thanks."

His lips quirked at one side, revealing a dimple Morna had tried and failed not to miss. "You've made that painfully clear. You have them anyway. St. Didier will want a bath, and the wagons should arrive well before dark."

Morna hadn't wanted to ask about either matter. "One assumed as much. Good day." She marched back toward the house at a smart pace, brisk but dignified, and left Graham—his lordship, rather—sitting on the bench beneath the stag, rubbing the lapel of the worn cloak against his cheek.

He should not have come home, and he'd figure that out for himself, eventually.

"You were busy spying in the stable," Graham said, passing St. Didier a wee dram, "so you missed the opening salvo at lunch."

"You already have a battle in progress?" St. Didier asked, nosing his drink. "I failed to notice anything in the way of real hostilities at either lunch or supper."

Graham lifted his glass to the portrait of the first earl hanging over the study's fireplace. "*Slàinte.*"

St. Didier did likewise. "*Slàinte mhath.* You resemble him around the eyes. Tell me about this war."

"Inherited my blue eyes from Auld Dingus, supposedly, though every MacNeil I ever met had blue eyes of one variety or another. Not a war, more of an opening skirmish in family antipathies. I am the earl now, so I should sit at the head of the table. No place was laid for me there at lunch. While I washed my hands, Morna addressed the oversight."

"Addressed it how?"

"She moved cutlery from a corner to the head of the table. Made no fuss about it. Saw it done. Didn't raise the topic in conversation when I gave her a private opportunity to do so."

"I cannot sample my whisky until you taste yours, Dunhaven, so drink up."

"Right. Any moment, I expect Grandpapa to march through the door, cursing in the Erse about taxes, foot rot, and Englishmen, in that order. I expect to find Cousin John shuffling along the corridors while reading a book about heraldry. Instead, I am *the host*. Bit of an adjustment."

Morna's animosity was the larger adjustment. Entirely expected, but still disconcerting.

"You are the host and the earl," St. Didier said, inspecting the bookcase along the inside wall. "An insulted earl, if the little drama at lunch is any indication. Maybe an aging footman simply grew confused about his directions."

"I'd rather think that than believe Brodie or Peter served me a first course of disrespect, though both of them are entitled to their pique." *Pique* being a polite term for resentment that might border on hatred. "I am prepared for more of same."

"If you knew you were walking into an ambush, why come home?"

St. Didier had yet to sample his drink. Graham took a sip, found the whisky as smooth as it had been aromatic. Only a whisper of smoke, plenty of honey and barley, with a hint of caramel and a finish that leaned subtly toward cinnamon. The whisky struck Graham as ladylike—all the complexities beneath the surface, the fire slow to manifest.

"I came home," Graham said, "because I do not like to live in fear of spider bites."

"I daresay your castle, civilized as it is, has a few spiders, Dunhaven. This is excellent potation. One expects a bonfire in a glass with most whiskies."

"We age ours, and apparently we have the best nose in the shire to oversee the whole process. If the spiders here limit themselves to shifting around forks and wineglasses, I will deal with them easily enough."

"Brodie was your grandmother's younger brother?"

"Seventeen years age difference, different mothers. Gran was protective of him. Left him a competence, as it happened, which was fortunate as the old boy hadn't a feather to fly with otherwise. Grandpapa tolerated Brodie as part of Gran's dowery. A superb angler with the gift of gab. As long as he doesn't get to wagering over the cards, Brodie is passable company." Uncle could also be a grouchy drunk, hardly the worst failing in a man, and he tended to tell the same stories over and over.

"Brodie certainly contributed to the conversations at lunch and supper. I've never been given the benefit of so many opinions on so many topics over an informal family meal. Somebody likes to read."

"We're a bookish lot by nature. Long winter nights can have that effect. Do you ever *not* spy?"

"I'm reconnoitering. You have a fine library, full of maps and plays and histories and collected letters, but you keep the fiction in here. Why?"

"Grandpapa's study is warmer than the library, much easier to heat." Then too, the MacNeil plaid was not on aggressive display here as it was in the library. Grandpapa's furniture was upholstered in butter-soft leather, the walls wainscoted in oak, the hearth sizable for the dimensions of the room.

A retreat rather than a ceremonial chamber. The only tartan in evidence was a pair of soft blankets in the MacNeil plaid folded over the backs of the wing chairs.

"A more comfortable place to read by the hour?" St. Didier suggested, taking a branch of candles from the mantel and peering more closely at the bookshelves. "I can't see you having much time for reading. Lambing, calving, foaling, visiting the local marquess, sorting out skirmishes... Will you miss the Antipodes in any regard?"

"No." A Scotsman did not dare grow fond of the land to which he'd been banished.

"Why did you come home, Dunhaven? The real reason."

"Unfinished business." Also duty, which might amount to the same thing when all was said and done.

"Enlighten me. Does that unfinished business have to do with the person truly responsible for your grandmother's death?"

St. Didier could not help himself. His very nature compelled him to poke and inspect and test. Even for him, though, the question was bold.

"I pleaded guilty to involuntary manslaughter, St. Didier. You were here. According to all concerned, I was careless with Gran's laudanum, and I should have known better. She was ailing, but nobody would have said she was dying. Justice demanded account-ability."

"The perishing fancy doctor demanded accountability, mostly to ensure he wasn't held responsible. What was his name?"

"Ramsey. Theophile Ramsey. Scottish doctors are among the best in the world, and Gran trusted him."

St. Didier set the candles back on the mantel in the precise spot they'd occupied previously. "Old ladies have been misguidedly trusting handsome young doctors since Hippocrates was in nappies. You seem to trust Morna."

Leave her out of it. "Why wouldn't I?"

"She was on hand all those years ago too. She was devoted to your grandmother, and her manner toward you isn't exactly warm."

"Her manner isn't warm toward anybody but her cats and her horse. Morna has always been shy." She hadn't always been so formidable. Eight years ago, she'd been observant, retiring, demure... Appallingly well-read and happy to keep the castle books to spare Grandpapa the trouble. "Grandmother's death devastated her."

Had devastated Graham, too, though he wasn't entitled to air that linen.

"And yet," St. Didier said, settling into a wing chair, "Miss Morna does not seem devastated now. Wellington would give her a wide berth when she gets a certain look in her eye."

St. Didier doubtless knew the great man. "She has kept Gran's cloak, all these years. It hangs in the back hallway and bears Morna's attar of roses scent. I put it on before I realized I was trespassing." And if Lanie's infallible nose was to be believed, Morna had watched for Graham's arrival from the Great Hall, but why do that?

"Your situation qualifies as ticklish," St. Didier said.

"I am weary of ticklish. Society in Sydney was very ticklish, what with the emancipists enjoying the governor's favor, the exclusives reeling with horror that a former convict could hold the office of surgeon, architect, or magistrate. The indigenous people simply wanted us to stop taking their land, while the army insisted on keeping its thumb on the scales of justice. Highland feuds were card parties by comparison."

"But you thrived in the Antipodes."

"Spices thrive there. Grandpapa sent me with healthy specimens of everything from basil to lavender to tarragon, and, particularly with the exclusives, the taste of home was valued."

"What's an exclusive?"

"Gentry, the settlers who did not arrive as convicts on transport ships. Snobs, a lot of them, though they sent their cooks around to my shop, and if they could not pay in coin, they paid in goods. A penal colony isn't supposed to be trading commercially. Don't tell Fat George, but smuggling is another custom from home that's been transplanted with astonishing ease."

"You should write your memoirs."

"I should go to bed." Bedtime meant a night spent in the earl's apartment. A perplexing prospect, at best.

"You should also watch Morna. I'm not saying she's your enemy, but she's not your ally."

"I would not mistake her for an ally, St. Didier. She will attend to her duties without fail, no matter how much she detests me." Her disdain should not hurt—the lady was nothing if not logical, and disdain for the instrument of Gran's demise made perfect sense—but hurt, it did. "She didn't engineer that little prank with the silverware at lunch, though."

"Has Peter's stamp on it. A bit sly, not quite mean, but the next ambush might be less benign. I would be of much more use to you, you know, if you'd simply tell me what you recall of your grandmother's death."

Graham had spent better than four hundred miles considering whether to take St. Didier fully into his confidence.

"One appreciates the offer, St. Didier, but right now, I am too tired to think. If you don't mind, I'll take my drink up to bed with me."

Graham bowed, resisted the urge to bow to the portrait, and made for the door. Before he'd escaped, the door opened, and Morna came to a halt, a green ledger book clutched to her chest.

"Gra—My lord." She curtseyed. "St. Didier. Excuse my informality."

Her informality was a dressing gown of brown merino wool that covered her from wrists to neck to ankles. The garment was doubtless warm and about as flattering as a wheat sack. And yet, with her hair braided over one shoulder and her feet in worn slippers, she was fetching. Not strictly pretty—Morna qualified more as striking than pretty—but subtly attractive for being unlaced and unpinned.

Laddie, give it up. "Morna." A slight bow. "I was on the point of retiring. Tomorrow promises to be busy, so I will bid you good night."

She edged into the room and left the door open, letting in a river of frigid air. "You'll call on MacHeath tomorrow?"

"You think I should?" The marquess was the ranking title for twenty miles in any direction. Graham had known him in boyhood, but that connection wasn't to be presumed upon.

"He won't turn you away," Morna said. "MacHeath was banished himself, as a boy. Then he went off to Spain, some say because he was unlucky in love. He's far from charming these days, but he'll receive you."

"Will you come with me?" The question was out in all its proud, hopeful, pointless stupidity. "You certainly don't have to, but I'd appreciate the company."

St. Didier, may he suffer boils on his backside, remained unhelp-fully silent.

"You want me to call on the marquess with you?"

"Aye, if it's no trouble."

She sidled past, put the ledger on the blotter, and considered Graham, then flicked a glance at St. Didier, who was standing beside the wing chair.

"I'll accompany you," she said, "this time." Then she was gone, closing the door with a soft click in her wake.

"Another skirmish," St. Didier said. "One doesn't envy you, Dunhaven. Sweet dreams."

What a notion. "Same to you." Graham collected his drink and eschewed a carrying candle. He knew the corridors blindfolded and drunk, but he did not know who had won that little exchange of fire with Morna. He'd not lost, though.

Perhaps nobody had.

CHAPTER THREE

"Sebastian doesn't speak of the war," Morna said, taking up Tempi's reins. "I gather he distinguished himself in various capacities, despite having bought his commission against his uncle's wishes. Thank you, Tavish." The groom touched a finger to his cap and stepped back from the ladies' mounting block.

Graham hadn't offered a leg up, which Morna would have found awkward in many regards.

"You call the marquess Sebastian?" Graham asked, swinging onto a sturdy bay gelding.

"I do. He blames the title for his banishment, and in that he's correct. Sebastian's uncle wanted him raised among the English, lest he be at a disadvantage should the title ever befall him. I've always called him Sebastian, and he saw no need for more formal address between old friends." *Friends* was stretching it a bit. More than a bit.

Graham nudged his horse forward. "We shouldn't be gone long, Tav. Two cups of tea, a bit of a chinwag, nothing more."

If Graham was worried that Sebastian would snub him, he gave no sign of it. If he thought calling a marquess by his first name too presuming, that wasn't obvious either.

I'm as blind as Lanie when it comes to the man who used to be my only real friend. That was a blessing, of course. "Tell me about Australia."

"Australia is beautiful, wilder than you can imagine, and not for the faint of heart."

The horses toddled down the path that led to the carriageway while Morna rummaged around for safe topics.

"Pretty day for a hack."

"Aye."

Hopeless. "The earl's suite was to your liking?"

"Aye."

Why had he asked her to accompany him on a call that amounted to a mere formality? "That's a handsome horse you're riding."

"True, short for Trueno. Means thunder in Spanish. Your mare has the look of some Clydesdale stock about her."

"On the dam side. Her name is Tempi." Short for Tempête, which in French could also mean... thunder. A lifetime ago, Morna had delighted in such coincidences with Graham. They were twinkling confirmation that two hearts had been meant to beat in happy synchrony forevermore.

Young people were so gullible.

The horses passed through the gates, and the situation struck Morna as both silly and sad. Once upon a summer, she and Graham had talked for hours. They'd argued, sung duets, gossiped, made up stupid limericks, and conversed on any topic they pleased. Nothing out of bounds, nothing too scandalous, though Graham's sense of privacy was as formidable as Morna's, or had been.

He was responsible for Grandmama's death, but made no apology for it. What friendship could bridge such a chasm?

"Will you be leaving?" Graham asked. "Now that I've come home?"

"Do you want me to leave?"

He turned his horse in the uphill direction. The ground was dry, the countryside washed in pale sunshine, and the air deceptively chilly. A Scottish spring day that would leave the teeth of any Englishman chattering. The road was also pocked with the usual crop of post-winter potholes and erosions and would make for hard going by coach.

"I want you to do as you please, Morna. The MacNeils will always look after Lanie, and the castle is your home, but I appreciate that my return might make life awkward for you."

"Your departure made life more than awkward, Graham."

"For me as well." Said with sadness and a bit of humor, but still no apology.

"You served out your sentence," Morna said slowly. "I thought the sight of you would inspire me to castigations and cursing, but much to my surprise, I can't seem to muster public displays of ire toward you."

"Private ire tends to be the more serious variety. You are entitled to be angry with me."

He sounded resigned. Weary almost, though a more vital specimen had never sat upon a horse. Graham had gone away a young man somewhat given to superficial pastimes and come back a mature fellow in his prime. No impulse would overcome his self-discipline, no foolishness escape his notice.

We all grow up. Grandmama had said that, then usually added, *Except for dear Brodie.*

"I am disappointed in you, Graham." Also angry, but the disappointment had been the most devastating.

"I am frequently disappointed in myself, but rather than expound on that gloomy topic, you never did answer my question. Will you still bide with us now that I'm home, or take your rightful place in proper society?"

What was he going on about? "I am on my way to call on a marquess of such longstanding acquaintance that he insists I use informal address with him. Exactly what proper society do you have in mind for me?"

The road wound upward, the gelding managing the incline as easily as Tempi did, despite carrying the heavier rider.

"Edinburgh boasts excellent entertainments come spring," Graham observed while appearing to take in the view of the greening countryside below. "For the truly dedicated, there's always a Mayfair Season."

This short hack to visit a neighbor was becoming daunting. "I spoke of a Mayfair Season when I was little more than a schoolgirl, Graham. The older version of wishing to be a fairy princess. You wanted to defeat the Corsican monster with your claymore in single combat, though nobody fights with a claymore these days."

He drew his horse to a halt. "Morna, will you be staying or going?"

She could read nothing, not one thing, from his countenance. He gave away neither impatience, nor dread, nor exasperation, and certainly not any hope. His eyes, the blue of the Scottish saltire, were merely steady and direct. His dark hair riffled in a frigid breeze.

Tempi plodded onward. "I have no plans to leave at present." Not for lack of speculating about same, a pointless pursuit when one had nowhere to go and nobody to go with.

"Good to know." His gelding caught up with Tempi in two strides. "You have my thanks for not haring off and for coming along on this call. MacHeath was always fair-minded to a fault, but even he might look askance at the neighborhood felon dropping by for tea."

"Sebastian killed people on purpose. Grandmama's death was the next thing to an accident. I have wondered if the Almighty so conveniently forgives the soldiers while condemning the accidental felon."

Eight years was a long time to ponder any subject. John had counseled Morna to summon patience and tolerance. Grandpapa had said little, but his actions—seeing Graham safely provisioned, seeing him personally on board the transport ship, organizing the earldom's affairs such that solicitors would oversee the lot...

Grandpapa, who'd grieved the loss of his wife sorely, had forgiven

Graham from the outset. He hadn't even believed in Graham's guilt, despite the evidence and a signed confession.

But then, Grandpapa had been old and bereaved.

"What else have you wondered, Morna MacKenzie? You look at me with the particular considering scowl that says you are engaged in deep cogitation."

"None of your business."

He emitted a short, rusty guffaw, and Morna urged her mare into a canter. Tempi obliged, and Graham was canny enough to allow several lengths' distance before he kept pace. The rest of the journey up to the MacHeath monstrosity—a true castle, complete with crenellations, walks, and dungeons—passed in silence, while Morna did indeed indulge in some cogitation.

She had loved Graham with the girlish devotion of the untried and hated him with the fervor of a woman betrayed. She faulted him for being careless with Grandmama's remedies, but that flaw, as serious as it was, could be considered an example of human imperfection in a tragic setting. Graham was subject to fatigue, preoccupation, lapses of concentration, the same as any other mortal being.

Or he had been as a younger man. He looked as if a Highland winter would barely cause him a chill now.

What had hurt Morna beyond bearing was his complete rejection of her from the moment the physician had demanded an official inquiry. That inexplicable breach of trust had fueled a bitter, flaming rage and a determination to verbally thrash the man responsible should the occasion ever arise.

The occasion had arisen, and all Morna felt was bewilderment.

Well, no. Beneath the bewilderment was also relief—she'd never wished Graham dead—and beneath even that, in the mental equivalent of her personal oubliette, she was glad to see him.

Damned glad.

"He saw us coming," Graham muttered. "That wretched tower of his. He could signal to Norway from that thing."

Sebastian MacHeath, looking serious, substantial, and undeniably Scottish in kilted attire, stood in the chilly air on the front steps of his castle. The edifice suited the man. Imposing dimensions cast in granite, no brick facing to soften the appearance or yield an inch to modern aesthetics. The present marquess was tall and broad-shouldered and eschewed the short hair fashionable in the south. Morna esteemed him, but was well aware that, like his castle, the interesting bits were kept behind curtain walls, drawbridge, and portcullis.

Safer that way.

"Dunkeld." Graham nodded from atop his horse. "Are you receiving?"

"Get off your damned horse, Dunhaven. Spain steals a man's tolerance for cold, and I've never been much of one for freezing my arse off for the sake of appearances."

Graham dismounted. Morna extricated herself from the saddle before either man could offer assistance.

"If you two intend to brawl," Morna said, "at least have somebody see to the horses first. My money would be on Graham."

She swept past them and let herself through the door, another great imposing oaken defense even more impressive than the MacNeils'. She turned around to see two men watching her carefully at the bottom of the terrace steps, though only one of them was also working on the beginnings of a smile.

Sebastian punched Graham on the arm. "Stop grinning. She pronounced you the better brawler, and you an earl. Did Australia cost you every pretension to gentlemanly deportment?"

Graham's smile muted to mere sweetness as he returned the blow. "No more than Spain cost you, my lord. We mustn't keep the lady waiting."

MacHeath let out a shrill whistle, a groom appeared, and Morna, oddly near tears, led the way to the MacHeath family parlor.

MacHeath had said that after the waiting, the first five minutes of any battle had been the worst. Beyond that, fighting instinct, orders, the enemy, and chance took over, and when the shooting stopped, if you were still alive, you considered that victory enough for one day.

Graham had wondered if those recollections had been offered by way of fortification: Get the first few social calls, the first few divine services, the first few company suppers over with, and the rest would sort itself out.

What a hope.

"MacHeath has changed since mustering out," Morna said from atop her mare. "He can put on manners a duke would envy, but the watchfulness never leaves him."

"He grew up among the philistines," Graham said. "The vigilance he developed being a Scottish boy among English heirs likely kept him alive in Spain." To say nothing of the quick fists that had doubtless been necessary in every schoolyard. MacHeath had the former soldier's half-hidden fatigue too. He likely slept poorly and kept knives in his boots and beneath his pillows.

Convicts and soldiers had much in common.

"He's still a sweet boy," Morna said. "Under the gruff and hearty performance. He welcomed us where any footman or chambermaid could see him being hospitable."

Riding downhill could be more uncomfortable than riding uphill, particularly when the road was rough and the wind directly in one's face.

"He was gracious," Graham said, wondering how many French soldiers that sweet boy had killed. "But then, as you noted, MacHeath knows all about being banished."

Morna adjusted her reins. "Is that why you started your social calls with him?"

"Partly." Mostly because Graham would have gone for a dip in the frigid waters of the Tay had Morna suggested it.

Graham wished he'd worn a scarf. Morna was braving the

elements with typical Scottish indifference, while Graham was hard put not to shiver. A scarf also hid most of her features.

"You knew Sebastian would be polite when I was on hand," Morna said. "I was your protection." She might have been offended to reach that conclusion. Instead, she sounded a bit smug.

"Or you would be the witness if MacHeath had thrown the first punch." Her word would be believed. Not even the local marquess would dare question her recounting of events. Assaulting a peer was yet another serious felony, even if the assaulting party was also a peer.

"When did you become a proponent of violence, Graham MacNeil?"

"I am not a proponent of violence, having been on the receiving end of a surfeit of same. A transport ship is a strange world, Morna, and for months, it was my world. If I learned to fight, you can thank the justice system for my tutelage."

"And in Australia?"

"We were mostly too tired to fight, and we'd sorted matters sufficiently on board ship that violence was no longer appealing. Does Lanie ride?"

"Not any longer. She refuses to be led about at the walk like a toddler on her first pony. I know she misses it."

Thank heavens for an effective change of topic. "Will she see the physicians? Consult them, I mean."

"No, and I've stopped asking. Perhaps you can change her mind. Do you plan to call on the parson next?"

"I'll wait a day or two for word to get around, then make my bow. I assume our tithes are current?"

"You assume correctly and then some. Why must churches always have new roofs and new organs and new pews?"

"Because we enjoy music, protection from the elements, and sitting down for our weekly scolding. Who is the vicar?" To have to ask that question was tiresome.

"Mr. Weatherby, nephew of old Mr. Weatherby, who now bides in Glasgow with his daughter. Young Mr. Weatherby is nigh on to fifty and not quite the firebrand his uncle was. What has put that scowl on your face, Graham MacNeil?"

"I'm not scowling, I'm thinking." Wishing he'd worn a scarf, more like. "The whole journey up from London has been an exercise in mental dislocation. The Great North Road follows the same route, but the coaches are lighter, the traffic thicker than ever. The vicar is still Mr. Weatherby, but not the same Mr. Weatherby. The wallpaper in the breakfast parlor has not changed, the sideboard is the same and the view unchanging, but Cook is now Mrs. Anderson. I'm sure the lochan lies at the bottom of the hill, but the last time I saw it, John was yet with us."

"The same but different," Morna murmured. "We buried him in the family plot."

"I know." Graham had begun the day paying respects to the departed, beginning with John, Grandmama, and Grandpapa, followed by the parents—his and Peter's, then John's, then Morna and Lanie's. The MacKenzies had been step-cousins, close enough to family.

Morna glanced over at him. "It's the same for us, Graham. You are the same but different. You never thought to be the earl, and we never thought to see you with the title."

Trust Morna to point out the neglected perspective. "Grandpapa warned me. Said John was too good a soul to bide long upon the earth and not inclined toward matrimony."

"Too fanciful, with his heraldry and Latin and manuscripts. The man should have been a monk."

He'd been a dreamer, a drunk, and a scholar of the sort who could stare off into the distance for hours, then come out with some prosaic observation about sheep that had all manner of symbolic depths and was also simply about sheep.

"How did he die, Morna? The solicitors were vague. Drowned in the lochan, presumed to have gone swimming at the end of a summer day. He wasn't, that I recall, an enthusiastic swimmer."

"We were spared an official inquiry," Morna said. "John liked to walk the perimeter of the lochan in the evening, and evenings in summer last forever. He was seen strolling along the banks—the midges weren't thick yet—and he was found the next morning in the water below the overlook. We presume he slipped and knocked his head, and of course, his flask was nearly empty."

Ah. Thank heavens for whoever had noted that telling detail. "An accident." John had been ever so fond of both the grape and the grain. Never notably reeling, but seldom far from libation either.

"John wasn't a commanding presence," Morna said, "but he could be sensible when pressed for a decision, and he wasn't prone to rages or sulks."

Morna might have been describing a horse for hire at a livery stable.

"We missed him terribly," she went on. "Much more than we thought we would."

"Too many losses in succession—Grandmama, Grandpapa, John..."

"You." Morna urged her mare to a faster walk. "For all we knew, you were gone forever too." The temper Morna controlled ruthlessly colored her words, and the sound of it was a relief.

"For all *I* knew, Morna MacKenzie, I was gone forever. I wasn't exactly on holiday. I had to watch Grandmama's funeral from the side of the hill. I parted from my grandfather knowing I'd never see him again, and by the time I got word that John was gone, he'd been dead for six rubbishing months."

She peered over at him. "You're angry."

"Ruddy furious, pardon my language. We were told to make a new start, to ignore the homesickness and rage and guilt. To get on with it and let hard work be our tonic of choice. As if the Scots don't already know how to bury their grief in exhaustion..."

The gateposts loomed, as did the temptation to turn around and gallop all the way to Glasgow. The thought of ever setting foot on another ship, though...

"Give it time," Morna said. "I wanted to shout at you to go back to your little spice farm on the other side of the world and leave us in peace. I'm not shouting. You want to curse the lochan and turn back time. You aren't quite cursing. Maybe you should consider that accomplishment enough for the present?"

That olive branch had clearly cost her, and she was right—as usual. "Victory for half the day," Graham said. "I'm supposed to meet with Abner MacIver this afternoon. Swearing might come into the discussion."

"He's a good steward. Well liked, knowledgeable without being overbearing. John trusted him."

St. Didier's warning came to mind, about Morna not being an ally. St. Didier was wrong, a rare occurrence, but it did happen. Morna might be carrying grudges—she was entitled to, after all—but she was still reliably honest and cared about the fate of the estate and the people on it.

The driveway curved gently, and Castle MacNeil, a tidy little edifice compared to its grand neighbor, came into view.

"Thank you, Morna."

"For?"

"For being honest with me. For being my protection, for warning me about the vicar." Graham studied the staid façade of his home, which looked like home but did not feel like home. No salvia where salvia should be.

She kept her mare moving forward. "You used to say I was honest to a fault."

"I said a lot of things." Blethered away like only a young fool in love could. "I missed you." Graham tacked that admission on as an exercise in futility, or self-flagellation, perhaps. A tremendous under-statement it was too.

"You missed me." Morna patted her mare. "Good." She gave the horse some invisible cue, and the beast lifted into a flowing canter, making short work of the last half mile of the drive.

"They are a beautiful picture," Graham said, which caused True to flick an ear. "She's proper angry with me." As True toddled along, Graham considered the nature of that anger. Morna wasn't angry at him *for coming home*. He was nearly certain of that much.

She'd called Grandmama's death the nearest thing to an accident, so perhaps the great crime of involuntary manslaughter wasn't the sole cause of her ire either.

But she was beyond peevish, for all she was playing fair regarding the neighbors and staff.

"'Give it time,' she says." Graham had had eight years apart from the lady, away from the life and family he loved. "Heard the same sermon often enough on the banks of Sydney Harbour. Wasn't much comfort there either."

True picked up his pace as a breeze brought the scent of the stable across the park.

MacHeath's words had been steadying: Survive the day, call it a victory. Survive another day, call that a victory. A recipe for enduring banishment, war, and maybe even a broken heart.

"She addressed me as Graham. I'll call that a victory too." On that marginally fortifying note, Graham rode into the stable yard and handed his horse off to Tavish.

St. Didier chose then to emerge from the gloom of the stable and fall in step beside Graham. "Your nose isn't bloody."

"Yours might soon be. The marquess was gracious. He's preparing to ride into the great battle for a bride and willing to charge all the way to Mayfair to do it. A reputation for brawling on the castle steps did not suit his purposes today."

"He would not offend Miss MacKenzie with such ill-bred behavior. Have you considered matrimony yourself?"

Why did St. Didier always bring such a sense of purpose to his toing and froing? "Are ye daft? I'm a convicted felon, and for reasons which you well understand, any cash associated with this estate has been kept well out of sight. My criminal history might be forgiven in light of the title—paid my debt and all that—but what Scottish papa will overlook a bachelor's poverty?"

Trust St. Didier to dispel any nascent sense of lightness the day might have acquired, or sense of not-as-grimness.

"You're an earl," St. Didier said, his pace increasing. "You could be a member of the Scottish parliamentary delegation. You've property in Glasgow, Edinburgh, London, and Paris. Any Scottish papa worth his porridge will know the difference between exercising discretion with your funds and lacking means altogether. You should consider marriage."

Marriage. At one time, Graham had assumed the institution was available to him for the asking. He'd had comfortable means thanks to Grandpapa and his own dear departed parents. He'd been healthy and claimed a good education. Charming Morna around to the notion had been the sole challenge remaining between dreams of bliss, passion, and laughter and the reality.

Graham stopped at the foot of the steps to the back terrace. "You're better off harassing Peter to propose to Lanie. The lad is sorely smitten, and I've no doubt the pair of them would do justice to the succession, if that's your concern."

"Noticed that, did you?"

"She can't see him. He doesn't guard his expression as carefully as he ought."

"No man in love does, MacNeil. Not even you." St. Didier stalked off, as if he'd say more, but the better part of prudence was to save the rest of the lecture for another time.

Smart choice. St. Didier had a fine nose. Be a shame to break it over the most foolish words an otherwise intelligent man had likely ever uttered.

CHAPTER FOUR

The remnants of Birnam Wood, made tragically famous by the Bard, lay not ten miles distant from the MacNeil family seat. "And how appropriate is that?" St. Didier muttered, letting himself into the library.

The room was cold and would be cold on a mild summer day. High ceilings, stone walls three feet thick, a single unlit fireplace in the center of a row of six tall windows... This had probably been the original castle's great hall centuries ago, and something of the fortress yet clung to the space.

Though Peter, swaddled in a MacNeil plaid shawl as he lounged at the reading table, was hardly the Highland warrior of old.

"Good afternoon," St. Didier said. "Sitting there, absorbed in your reading, you look much like your brother when he was younger."

"I meant to take this up to my sitting room," Peter said, rising and waving his pamphlet. "Fascinating stuff. Steam will usher in a new age of prosperity for all. We simply need to dig enough coal to create all that steam."

"And coal miners will live like kings? When has it ever worked that way, MacNeil?" St. Didier kept his tone light, but a debate on the topic of progress would sour what was left of his mood. "The coal burned in Wales to make all of our marvelous steel has so polluted the local skies, rivers, and land that even the farmers had to take to coal mining, because their acres became unfit to produce food. When mining is the only occupation to hand, the wages tend to be less than generous."

Peter took off his shawl and folded it over the back of a chair. "Clearances by any other name. I grasp your point, but still... Those same mines are already using steam power to move coal around, you know. If steam can move coal, it can move anything. The principle is really quite simple, and it all comes down to heat making air expand."

He spoke with the enthusiasm of the evangelist, and perhaps some evening over port, St. Didier would brace Peter on the costs of all that marvelous speed—ruined land, ruined air, starvation, slums, the best and brightest leaving home shores for even a chance at a decent life.

"Dunhaven's call upon the local marquess apparently went well," St. Didier said, rather than attempt a debate with a true believer. "The marquess was gracious."

"MacHeath's a good sort." Peter picked up two more pamphlets from the massive desk occupying a corner of the room. "A bit distant, but a substantial improvement over his uncle. The old marquess was a great one for tradition. Wanted a son to carry on the title, but even a lively young wife could not oblige him. The notion of a mere nephew inheriting sat ill with him."

"Was the younger MacHeath on hand when your grandmother died? I don't recall seeing him about at the time."

Peter eyed his pamphlets. "Sebastian was here. He sometimes was allowed to visit during summers. He'd have been at university by then, or on the way. Enough years lie between us that our paths didn't much cross, but I do recall him wandering about the country-side. Not exactly gregarious, but we made allowances because he'd been sent to dwell among the barbarians."

The insult was softened with a grin, and yet, St. Didier was annoyed. Raise the topic of a family tragedy, and people shied off the subject any way they could.

"Would you happen to recall who recommended the services of that physician to your grandmother? Theophile Ramsey was his name."

Peter ceased fussing with his precious pamphlets. "Does Graham know you're asking these questions?"

"Yes." A slight exaggeration. Graham would know soon. Graham, if he ever emerged from his present fog of besottedness, would ask similar questions himself. "I will be looking into your cousin John's demise as well."

"In God's name why?" The affable, harmless young fellow had become keenly focused and no longer affable. "This family has been all but cursed with misfortune. My parents, John's parents, carried off by the damned influenza in the same winter. Grandmama's death turned into an unnecessary tragedy, Grandpapa expiring of sorrow and shame, then John... What possible benefit could arise from dredging all those lochs of grief?"

If Graham hadn't accidentally killed the aging countess, somebody else had, perhaps on purpose. That somebody else might well perpetrate more tragedy to keep the truth submerged. The earnest proponent of galloping past inconvenient truths might eventually figure that out for himself—especially if he'd been responsible for the old woman's death.

"I ask these questions," St. Didier said, "because the truth itself is a benefit. Lead is poisonous. The Romans knew that, ignored it, and might still be ruling the Mediterranean had they faced the truth instead. My family's title was heading for escheat. I knew it, I planned accordingly and have independent means and security to show for my willingness to face facts."

"You sound like my grandfather."

"I'm flattered. A formidable gentleman." One unconvinced of Graham's guilt and sufficiently influential to ensure the verdict was transportation for a mere seven years rather than hanging or a longer sentence.

"John's death was an accident," Peter said, propping a hip on the desk. "I found him. Such a beautiful morning. Birds singing, the long, slow dawn turning the rising mist golden over the water. Two fawns had come down to drink with their mama, and I recall wishing that Graham was home to see it. He'd been gone for more years at that point, but those thoughts—missing my brother—still assailed me. The loch—lochan, more like—is a glorified farm pond. Graham and John used to race around it on foot."

While the younger cousin no doubt watched and wished he were older and *faster*. "Go on."

"The pond has plenty of trout, but fishing the Tay is better sport. I saw something dark bobbing in the shadows beneath the overlook, and at first I thought a grand old fish had met its reward. What I saw was John's hair and his shoulders. He'd taken his coat off and left it on the overlook—there's still a bench up there—and apparently got too close to the edge."

"He'd been in the water all night?"

Peter crossed his arms. "How would one tell?"

"From the appearance of the deceased. Water in the lungs?"

"No examination in that regard was performed. John was much given to rumination. He could sit for hours peering at books or old maps or the stars. When I found him, he had a great bump on his forehead." Peter touched his brow right below the hairline. "We assumed he'd been tippling and stargazing and tippling some more—he slept under the stars often enough—took a bad step, slipped, and fell to his doom. If he wasn't killed by the fall, he drowned shortly thereafter."

No nosy Edinburgh physician on hand to insist on an inquiry, much less an autopsy. How convenient if the cause of death had been a push rather than a tipsy misstep.

"How did you know he'd been tippling?"

"One does, when sitting and contemplating, and the sizable flask in his coat pocket had only a few drops left. John was not abstemious, though he could forget to eat sometimes."

A stray thought intruded on conjectures about lines of inheritance and impatient young men. "Did John have enemies?"

A portcullis of banked caution came down over Peter's usually genial features. "Why ask that?"

"Somebody should have considered that question. The solicitors were running the estate, but John was still wealthy and titled. The Scots are known to nurse grudges for generations."

Argue that, young man.

Peter pushed away from the desk. "John loved heraldry and the chivalric code, spoke medieval Latin, read law Latin like it was the Society pages. He was uniformly pleasant when in a mood to converse. He was *incapable* of offending anybody to the degree you suggest. Late for supper, invariably, if he showed up at all. Distracted, most of the time, but he no more possessed enemies than he did friends. He was happy, or at least content."

How many times had Peter told himself he was also content? "A steward turned off for chronic inebriation nearly killed my great-aunt and waited two years to do it."

Peter gathered up his pamphlets. "Perhaps the English have some capacity for treasuring their injured dignity. Who would have thought? How fortunate I am, to have plenty to do, family to love, and a long-lost brother returned from far away. My cup runneth over, and thus I need not ride roughshod over other people's woes merely to pass the time. Until supper, St. Didier, and please do feel free to explore the collection at your leisure."

Peter saluted with his clutch of pamphlets and made for the door. Not a fribble. Could look and flirt the part, but beneath the banter and humor lay a bone-deep shrewdness.

St. Didier had had the same thought about Graham MacNeil shortly after they'd met.

Peter paused at the door. "The pond is at the bottom of the hill, St. Didier. You take the path that runs north of the stable, and it will angle downhill after about fifty yards. Have a look. Make up your own mind." He departed, pamphlets in hand, no haste whatsoever.

"Steam engines can explode," St. Didier said to the cold, cavernous room. "One ignores that fact at one's peril."

"Is Sebastian well?" Lanie asked, knitting needles clicking.

Morna considered the question and the speed with which Lanie was knitting.

"The marquess's objective was to make us feel welcome," she replied, gaze on the view below the window. "He achieved his goal and did so in plain sight of the castle staff."

"Not what I asked, sister mine. Was he overly hearty? Was his congeniality the braw, bonnie laddie variety, or the real thing?"

"I haven't your nose, Lanie, or your ear. I would say Sebastian was genuinely glad to see Graham." Lanie could hear anxiety in a voice that to Morna sounded perfectly cheerful. The tread of Morna's foot on the steps, according to Lanie, could convey fatigue, ire, joy, or determination.

"We are all glad to see Graham," Lanie retorted. "What else did you notice about Sebastian?"

The countryside beyond the parlor window wasn't covered in snow, but winter yet held sway. The towering pines marching up the hill across the river looked grim rather than impressive, and the sheep in the pastures would need their dingy wool coats for months to come.

"Sebastian looked homesick to me," Morna said slowly. "As if he has already left Scotland in his mind and embarked on the business of missing it, yet again." Graham, by contrast, was not homesick. Whatever feelings he was keeping tucked out of sight, he wasn't pining for Australia.

Not even a little.

"Perhaps Sebastian misses England." Lanie started on a new row, her handling of the needles exquisitely competent. "He all but grew up there. He has to have friends among the English, perhaps even a lady friend."

Morna liked the marquess, and joining in the local parlor game of speculating about his marital prospects struck her as, firstly, a dull business and, secondly, disrespectful. "Leave the man his privacy, Lanie."

"One can have too much privacy. What is fascinating you outside the window, Morna?"

"You can see where I'm standing?"

"Something is blocking the light that should be coming through the window. I can hear Eustace purring on the hassock, so he's not sitting on the windowsill. You are the logical alternative, and you've been standing there since you joined me."

"Shall I ring for a tray?"

"The tray is on the sideboard, waiting for the footman to remove it."

Lanie had put it there, no doubt. When she was on familiar ground, lack of sight was little impairment for her.

"Graham is on the path to the lochan." Only as she spoke did Morna realize she'd been watching for him. He hadn't come in from the stable, and he wasn't enjoying a stroll in the garden. He'd apparently already been to the family cemetery, and now he'd make himself revisit the site of John's death.

"Why would he...? Oh. To say a farewell to John? Dreary undertaking."

Gossiping about the marquess was dreary. For Graham to make himself see the place where John had breathed his last was brutal and probably necessary.

"I'm going out," Morna said. "I'll see you at supper."

"Perhaps Graham needs privacy too, Morna."

He needed a friend more. Traitorous thought. "I've tried to keep my distance," Morna said. "He hasn't apologized, hasn't explained, hasn't shown any indication of remorse for his behavior, but he's not that man anymore." He was Graham and not-Graham. A dislocated version of the memory, to use his term.

"He's too serious," Lanie said. "The old Graham was merry. Not uproarious, but witty and sweet. This Graham doesn't smile in his voice."

"He doesn't smile much otherwise either." The sadness in him gave a woman pause. He was home at last, blessed with a title he'd never thought to hold, owner of a veritable fortune, and yet, the sadness had not left him.

"You don't smile much either, Morna, unless you're talking to Kenneth or Eustace, and a less worthy pair of reprobates never set paw upon carpet."

They'd been little more than kittens when Graham had been transported. They were venerable now and given to sleeping away their days. One orange, one black with white points. Huge and lazy, with stentorian purrs. Good friends to Morna while pretending complete indifference to each other.

Graham moved at a steady march, then disappeared into the forest. "Don't let Eustace slurp from the cream pot."

"I do believe you will already find it empty."

Morna stroked a hand over the cat's head. "Wretch. You encourage him, Lanie."

"The cream will curdle if it sits too long, right, Eustace?"

Morna left them to being mutual bad influences, grabbed Grandmama's cloak on the way out the door, and made straight for the path to the pond. She ought to leave Graham his privacy, and she ought not to trust him, and she had every reason to be angry with him.

But he'd arrived only *yesterday*, and he'd already been to the cemetery—alone. He'd been prepared to face MacHeath's rejection—alone. He'd made the journey to the Antipodes without an ally or friend in sight.

Now he was back, trying to reconcile himself to myriad losses and changes, and most of that miserable work he'd have to do on his own as well. Morna, by contrast, had endured the past eight years comforted by familiar surroundings and loving family, no *surfeit of violence* aimed her way.

She did not feel guilty, precisely, but rather... what? Worried? About Graham?

"I can spare him an hour's rambling around the pond." He was apparently in the habit of taking on all challenges as solo combat, and Morna well knew how difficult breaking that habit could be.

"Half an hour," she said, as the path turned downhill. "If he's so inclined."

She found him sitting on the bench at the overlook, staring across the water.

"Graham?"

He patted the place beside him. Morna took the seat gingerly, feeling halfway foolish and halfway relieved to have caught her quarry.

Graham produced a flask and offered it to her. She took a wee nip, feeling all the disorientation he'd described earlier. Same Graham, same bench, possibly even the same flask, though the whisky was much smoother than the brew he'd toted around years ago. She passed the flask back, and Graham held it up before them.

"To our John," he said.

Morna remained silent, though once again, for no reason, no reason *at all*, a lump filled her throat. Against all sense and determination to the contrary, she let her head rest against Graham's shoulder.

Three breaths later, Graham's arm came around her, lightly, half resting on the back of the bench. By invisible degrees, the nature of his touch changed, from tentative possibility to solid half hug. Morna allowed it, assayed her reactions, and found that foremost among them was simply comfort.

She had avoided this place for years. Avoided this pretty, peaceful view. Avoided the cemetery, avoided all the paths and rambles and fishing spots she and Graham had frequented.

Graham's affectionate nature had been one of his most attractive qualities. He had been a hugger, a kisser of cheeks, a patter of hands. Happy to dance with spinsters, beauties, or grannies. Morna hadn't seen the current Graham so much as pat his horse.

That he could still be affectionate was a relief, and also—what was wrong with her?—a quiet joy. They might have a rousing donny-brook at supper and remain at daggers drawn for decades thereafter, but for one moment, Morna allowed herself to rejoice that Graham was beside her.

Not the old Graham or the new Graham, but *her* Graham, the one she'd promised herself she never wanted to see again.

A danger unique to Australia about which nobody said much was the lack of women. The older transportees claimed that women had been all but harvested from London's more unsavory streets and trans-ported for any excuse or credible accusation—shoplifting a scrap of lace, public drunkenness, seditious utterings, and away they went for sentencing.

The unfortunate females had been packed off to the transport ships, where their best option often included a voyage-long liaison with a ship's officer.

Option being a towering euphemism. Graham had watched these transactions, sometimes literally, and felt nearly as great a sense of bewilderment as he'd had when first accused of Grandmama's death. The situation had been little better in the immediate surrounds of Sydney, but the business of enduring penal servitude, even the condi-tionally pardoned variety, had proved both exhausting and absorbing.

With Morna's head on his shoulder, and her warmth beside him, Graham untangled one of the puzzles of his past. He'd known all those other ladies hadn't been Morna, and that had been justification enough for keeping his hands to himself.

They didn't have her quiet smile, her surprisingly hearty laugh, her ferocious talent with a scold.

They also offered mere pleasure, the satisfaction of a physical urge. To undertake that satisfaction without any sense of shared joy—of true caring—had been beyond him. As a younger man, racketing about at university, wasting his days on what he'd thought of as adult pursuits, his perspective had been different.

What a swaggering ass he'd been.

Sitting on the bench beside Morna, Graham felt a touch of vindication and an easing of sorrow.

Morna beside him, breathing in synchrony with him and not even knowing she was doing it, was an occasion of both pleasure and joy, even as Graham told himself he was paying his belated respects to John.

"What's your best memory of him?" Morna asked.

Graham thought back over a childhood as happy as it could be for orphaned cousins. "John got me drunk when I was thirteen. Said it was his duty as the elder of us to explain to me the hazards of the bottle, though I knew only that I was being offered more than the occasional nip. I waited and waited for him to embark on some great diatribe—he was bookish even then, and we were fishing the Tay—but the sermon came in the morning and without a word. Never before or since has my head ached that badly. Temperance eludes my grasp, but moderation has ever been mine to claim, thanks to John. He could be painfully practical, when he chose to be."

Graham hadn't forgotten that memory—one did not forget misery or wisdom of that intensity—but he'd neglected it. "What about you?"

"He proposed to me. Waited until you'd been gone several years, by which time you would have had your conditional pardon. John offered marriage, said he'd long admired me, et cetera and so forth, another diatribe. The marriage he offered would have been, in his words, platonic. He'd already offered his heart to wisdom and to Athena, Goddess of Wisdom, and to her alone would he pledge his passion. I was nonetheless welcome to be his countess, his friend, his hostess, and chatelaine."

Graham nearly removed his arm from about Morna's shoulders, but caught himself. "You demurred?"

"Of course I demurred. The offer wasn't coming from a sober man, but rather, from a lonely one who was also in thrall to his flask. No woman wants to be taken to wife by half measures or out of pity."

Questions fluttered in Graham's mind like seagulls at a ship's taffrail.

Did Morna want to be taken to wife *at all*? By full measures? Who else had proposed to her?

Was a man rendered unfit as a husband simply because he was lonely?

Would she reject a similar offer from the present earl?

Steady, laddie. "John was lonely, you are right about that. His letters to me were positively gloomy at times, and yet, I read them until they fell to pieces."

"Because you could hear his voice in the words."

"Aye."

Chilly afternoon was sliding toward wintry evening, the shadows on the water becoming black on silver, and yet, Graham did not want to leave. John had died a dozen yards below, though on the old oak bench, something precious was being revived.

Hope, peace, trust... Graham wasn't certain what to call it, but he and Morna were having the sort of conversation they'd reveled in years ago. Confidences exchanged, life considered with the benefit of a friendly ear. Some friendly touches. Courage fortified.

"We should be getting back," Morna said, making no move to rise.

"Wait," Graham said. "We've company."

Morna lifted her head to peer across the pond at the stag delicately sipping in the shadows. Ripples fanned out from where he stood, two hooves in the water. When he'd had his fill, he lifted a magnificent head, his chin dripping.

"One does not hurry royalty," Morna said. "What a splendid creature. He'll be losing those antlers any day."

As she spoke, the great beast stepped out of the water, came about with majestic grace, and slipped back among the bracken and trees of the hillside.

"I wish Lanie could have seen him," Morna said.

"She has memories, I hope." Graham rose and offered Morna his hand. She took it, stood, and let go of him.

"Her memory is as faultless as her nose and her hearing. Some of that acumen is because of her poor eyesight, but she's also a little sister. I'm told they have powers that Wellington's spies would have envied."

"As do younger brothers."

The moment passed, as such moments did with Morna, and Graham knew better than to be greedy. He knew better than to ask why she'd followed him and whether John's proposal had tempted her. She'd have been a countess, wealthy, the ranking lady of the shire until MacHeath put his boot in Mayfair's marquess mousetrap.

The questions could all wait for another quiet moment. The joy remained, so wide, precious, and dear that Graham said not a word for the entire walk back to the castle.

CHAPTER FIVE

The hour before supper was the best and worst of Peter's day.

The best, because he could give himself up to anticipation. Without fail, Lanie would at some point join whoever had assembled in the family parlor, her presence illuminating a room she could not see. She resembled Morna—red hair, height, perfect complexion—but formed a more diminutive and graceful package. Morna was impressive, whereas Lanie... Lanie was special.

"Make yourself useful," Uncle Brodie said, closing the door behind him, "and pour an old fellow a wee nip to ward off the chill before the ladies arrive. They keep count, you know, bless their hearts."

No, they did not, but any fool could see whether the level of the decanter had fallen. Peter had learned that lesson by watching John, who'd had a prodigious capacity for drink.

"A wee nip," Peter said, passing over the requested libation. "I will wait until we have more company before I indulge, if you don't mind." Fitting Lanie's hand around her glass was just one of the delights the preprandial hour offered.

"Forcing me to drink alone," Brodie replied. "Bad form, young man, but needs must, and my fortitude is equal to the challenge despite my vast and advancing years. I'm like a fine whisky. I improve with time. We're in for more snow. I can feel it in m' bones. How are you adjusting to the prodigal's return?"

"'Prodigal' refers to wasting one's resources recklessly, similar to 'profligate.'" A man who gambled beyond his means qualified as prodigal, as Brodie ought to know. "I'd say Graham has been more errant than prodigal."

"Outlawed and banished, in the tradition of pigheaded Scots from time immemorial. This is good whisky, my boy. You are missing a treat."

Peter was missing Lanie. He'd been missing her since she'd risen from lunch and declared a need to catch up on her knitting. He'd nearly asked her to teach him how to knit, but the torment of her hands guiding his on the needles, her sitting beside him, her soft cinnamony scent stealing his wits...

Even the thought required fortitude.

"Tell me, Peter, have you forgiven Graham for killing your grand-mother?" Brodie asked with the same you-can-tell-your-old-uncle-anything air that Peter had found unappealing since childhood. Uncle never wanted to know about a boy's dreams or hopes. He wanted to know about naughty behavior, poor marks, and temp-tations.

"Graham did not kill Grandmama," Peter said. "Her death was an accident, and the rubbishing physician would not have it so."

Brodie's usually genial expression sobered. "I want to agree. I miss my sister sorely, even after all these years, though she was clearly suffering. Still, that doctor knew what he was about, and Graham should have been more careful." He drank to that—the whole not-so-wee nip.

Brodie was aging well, unlike his late half-sister. He was tallish, dapper, spry, and possessed of a head of luxurious white hair. His eyes were a faded blue compared to the typical MacNeil hue—he was not a MacNeil, let it be said—but he could be charming when he chose to be.

He apparently did not choose to be at that moment.

Because Graham had pleaded guilty to the charges, the official inquiry had been cursory, and thus no precise family tale explained Grandmother's demise. Too much laudanum was explanation enough, and Graham had admitted to measuring out the nightly dose. John had never offered details if he'd even known them, and Grandfather had declared the whole business a tragic disgrace.

Ancient history, and might the particulars please be permitted to rest in peace.

"Are you glad to have Graham back?" Peter asked.

"Of course, of course." Brodie refilled his glass at the sideboard. "The notion of a pack of English solicitors managing MacNeil properties was preposterous. Your dear grandfather must have been courting senility when he set up that arrangement."

Before Graham had left, he'd explained the why of it to Peter: John was not temperamentally suited to managing multiple properties and did not want the burden of same. With solicitors holding the reins, John would be safe from the perpetually importuning vicar and the charities with their worthy causes nobody had ever heard of.

Had the solicitors also kept John from Uncle Brodie's wheedling? Probably not, but the question was worth putting to Lanie. She was astonishingly astute, which made keeping feelings from her notice nearly impossible.

Peter was still smiling over his darling's general impressiveness when the lady herself walked through the door.

"Peter, Brodie, greetings. I vow I am famished. Knitting works up a prodigious appetite."

Brodie drained half his glass. "Fairest Lanie. Will ye have an aperitif with your old uncle?"

"Peter can pour me a drop, and I do mean a drop. If you'd add some peat to the fire, Uncle, my feet might possibly thaw out in an hour or so."

She made her way unerringly to the corner of the sofa closest to the fire, and Peter immediately set about fixing her drink, lest Morna, Graham, or the hopelessly English St. Didier take the place beside her. He wrapped her fingers around the glass and appropriated the coveted spot.

"Brodie says we're in for more snow." Not exactly a brilliant gambit, but Brodie was four feet away, trying to use the poker to spear a square of peat and deliver it to the fire. Uncle was more fastidious than any spinster auntie, but then, he hadn't the means to replace a jacket simply because it had a few stains about the cuffs.

"Snow never lasts this late in the season," Lanie replied. "Snow might slow down the curious, though. Graham's arrival will see us flooded with callers."

"With nosy neighbors," Brodie muttered, showering the hearth-stones with dirt as he lifted the peat over the fireplace screen. "Graham should not have called on MacHeath so soon. He should have waited a decent interval, got his bearings, been in no hurry. Popping up the hill posthaste like that lacked dignity."

Brodie's life lacked dignity. He was too cheap to live on his own means and too lazy to pursue any sort of purpose. He collected jeweled snuffboxes, though he didn't take snuff, and he read London newspapers, though he'd not seen London for years.

I will not be like him. Peter had made that vow frequently since the age of eight, when Brodie had introduced him to cigars. While Peter had coughed to the point of retching into the dirt, Brodie had stood around, chuckling and smiling as if the whole business had been hilarious.

St. Didier arrived punctually on the quarter hour and allowed Brodie to inveigle him into a drink and into a discussion of that most heinous of modern inventions, the Corn Laws.

"He can't help himself," Lanie muttered behind her glass.

"Uncle?"

"No, St. Didier. He's polite and patient to a fault, poor man. He and Graham have that in common."

"How did you know Uncle was already in the room?"

"The stink of cigars clings to him, Peter. Promise me you will never take up the habit."

"You have my solemn word."

"Be serious." She patted his knee. "Smoking is filthy, and it roughens the voice. Imagine what it does to the lungs."

Peter imagined what another pat to his knee might do to his composure. "Brodie asked if I was glad Graham was home. When I put the same question to Brodie, he said of course he was, but he also referred to Graham *killing* Grandmama. I wanted to hit him."

"I frequently want to kick him, but he's like an old dog. Malodorous, lazy, and frequently underfoot, but basically harmless."

"And helpless in a way. A cautionary tale. Are you pleased to have Graham home?"

Lanie sipped her drink, then held the glass out for Peter to place on the low table. "I'm not sure Graham is home, Peter. Some fellow who sounds like Graham and hugs like Graham has joined us, but even his walk has changed. He used to make a lot more noise. His steps would thump, he spoke and the whole room listened, and he laughed. I haven't heard this Graham laugh. He smells of heather now, when he used to favor cedar. He's not the same man."

"You fascinate me," Peter murmured, lest Uncle or St. Didier overhear. "You leap from impressions that I miss entirely to conclusions that would leave an oracle gaping." *Will you teach me to knit? Do you enjoy my preferred balsam scent?*

"I am not distracted by what can be seen. You look at Graham, and he's pretty much as he was the day he left. Older, of course, and with more muscles or maybe a scar or two, but the two images—who he was and who he is—bear a close resemblance. The scents, the footsteps, the silences... They have all become quite different. Morna and Graham went for a walk around the lochan together."

And what was the significance of that development? "No, they did not. I saw Graham take the path down the hill. He was alone."

"Morna saw him, too, and she followed, and neither one of them is here yet, are they?"

"They were friends, from what I recall."

"As we are friends?" Lanie said, gesturing for her drink.

What did a besotted fool say? What was the one thing he must not say? Brodie's back was to the sofa—holding forth about the free press and peasants never winning, but never behaving for long either—so Peter gave in to impulse and kissed Lanie's cheek.

"We are the best of friends, I hope." He took Lanie's hand and passed her the glass. "The very best."

Lanie was quiet for a moment as Graham joined the gathering, and to Peter's eye, his brother's expression was more relaxed. Not quite genial, not quite happy, but less fierce.

"How would you feel," Lanie said quietly, "if your very best friend admitted to the negligence that resulted in your grandmother's death, and he did so without making any apology or explanation to you? How would you feel if he cut you off without a word, banished himself from your life even as the days you had together evaporated one by one?"

"You are angry with Graham?" Peter certainly was—for being stupid enough to plead guilty to ridiculous charges, for being transported, for coming home as a grimly serious incarnation of a man who'd been a fine older brother.

"Morna is wroth with Graham and trying not to be. She has never asked me about that night, Peter, nobody has, and I was sitting with Grandmother for most of the evening."

Peter had known that—looking in on Grandmama had been a courtesy required of them all most evenings, and Peter had been designated to bring the countess her nightly posset. Graham had certainly been aware of Lanie's presence in Grandmama's bedroom, but nobody had mentioned it to the authorities. What would have been the point?

"Don't think about the past," Peter said. "Graham is back, he's the earl now, and life goes on. Shall I read to you tonight?" Graham's arrival had put the evening routine at sixes and sevens, but the two hours Peter spent reading to Lanie were the highlight of his day and not to be given up for anything.

"Please do read to me," Lanie said. "People assume a blind woman is stupid if she can't recount the Society pages or discuss the latest novels."

"So why do you insist on having me read from my pamphlets?"

"Because the Society pages are frivolous and novels often doubly so. I learn from your pamphlets, Peter."

Ask her now, you idiot. Please teach me how to knit. Six little words. "I learn things too. Fascinating stuff. I've also been reading Adam Smith. He takes a very dim view of government, you know, whether it's monarchy, empire, democracy, republic... Quite the grouch is Mr. Smith. Goes on and on about government existing to defend the rich against the poor. He gets quite fierce." *Not Adam Smith, you dolt. For heaven's sake, cease before you sound like Uncle.* "Morna has just arrived, and she and Graham are trying not to stare at each other."

"Her attar of roses gives her away. Offer to pour her a drink, Peter. She'll need the fortification."

"Graham's seeing to it."

"Ah. Well, then. They must have enjoyed their walk. I suppose that's a good thing." Lanie's tone suggested perhaps it wasn't a good thing at all.

"If they are putting the past behind them, Lanie, that's a consummation devoutly to be wished. It's all old business anyway. Tell me about your latest knitting project." *Come at the business sideways, and perhaps...*

"I refuse to bore you. Tell me about Mr. Smith."

Peter took the drink from her hand and drained the dregs. "I'll pour you another. We can read pamphlets tonight, all about steam engines and steam-powered sail. The packets to Calais won't have to wait on the wind or even the tides, and crossing the ocean will no longer take weeks."

"How exciting—assuming the ships don't blow up or catch fire, of course."

Peter wanted to kiss her cheek again, because she was smart and willing to poke a little fun at his enthusiasm and because she was Lanie and kissable. He instead took himself to the sideboard and measured out another scant portion of whisky. Lanie's objective had been to distract him while she eavesdropped on whatever Graham and Morna were saying to each other.

Lanie was worried about her sister, and about the past, and probably not the least bit interested in Adam Smith. Peter downed the drink and poured another and caught Uncle Brodie eyeing him with a damnably knowing expression.

Life in the Antipodes had been considerably easier if a man learned to tell himself some comforting half-truths.

Seven years isn't an eternity.

Australia can make a hardworking fellow wealthy.

The heat isn't that bad for much of the year.

Graham had leaned on all of those bouncers from time to time, but the falsehood he'd wrapped around himself most frequently—and with the least success—had been a bald-faced lie.

It wasn't love, not really. More of an infatuation. You were at that age, and so was Morna, and she's likely breaking half the hearts in Edinburgh by now.

As Brodie bored St. Didier witless with political maunderings, and Peter made sheep's eyes at Lanie, Graham watched Morna conferring with the head footman. Her smile would have charmed Cupid from his clouds, and the lilt of her voice carried under the other conversations like the murmur of the Tay on a pretty summer day.

Infatuations didn't last for half a man's life. They didn't send him around the world and back again. They didn't compel him to open a

Pandora's box of memories at bedtime every night. Morna on her mare, flying across the countryside like some happy Valkyrie. Morna fluffing Grandmama's pillows and fetching yet another extra blanket. Morna raging at the crown's extravagances while hardworking farmers barely survived...

Always Morna.

"You are pensive," St. Didier said, escaping Brodie's clutches when the old fellow excused himself, likely to heed nature's call.

"I went to the pond this afternoon—the lochan," Graham said. "I wanted to see the place, and I didn't want to see it ever again."

St. Didier swirled the whisky in his glass. "I made myself ride around the estate one last time after it had passed from my family's hands. Every couple of years, I go back and do a little trespassing in the name of self-torment."

For St. Didier, that amounted to an anguished confession. "Why?"

"For the same reason you went on that walk today. Because life took turns I railed against. Seeing the fences sagging and the orchard in need of pruning keeps me honest. I can grumble all I like, but the property does not belong to me and never will."

"I am the earl. I knew it, and..." Graham thought back to Morna's head on his shoulder, her warmth against his side. "I am also starting to believe it." More to the point, Graham knew he was in love with Morna MacKenzie and always had been. The most daunting realization, which had come over him gradually as they'd sat on the chilly bench in the deepening shadows, was that he always would be.

"You had to come back to Scotland to take up the title?" St. Didier asked.

"It's complicated." Graham had come back to Scotland to test one theory and explore others. "I hear you've been putting questions to my brother."

St. Didier let the maladroit change of topic pass unremarked, though as far as Graham was concerned, any and every topic eventually led back to Morna.

"You should be putting questions to your brother," St. Didier said. "What happened, MacNeil? All those years ago, a sequence of events transpired that resulted in your grandmother's death. Who orchestrated that sequence, if anybody? What sequence of events precipitated John's death?"

St. Didier would ask that question. "John tippled nigh constantly. He sat out under the stars contemplating weighty questions, eventually rose, took a wrong step on soft ground, dropped a good dozen yards onto rocky shallows, and expired. Leave his memory in peace, St. Didier."

St. Didier tidied up the decanters, which had already been sitting in a precise line. "Do you believe that?"

"Yes, and I also believe the inept footpad who tried to set upon us in London was merely coincidence. London is a cesspit of crime, as is known to all, and we spoke with more education than we dressed in that pub, and thus we made targets of ourselves."

That earned Graham a visual inspection. "I'd forgotten about the footpad."

"As well you should." As Graham should have, but in retrospect, he was half certain he'd been followed from his lodgings that night. A patient sort of footpad, to go to that much trouble.

"Who knew where you were staying?"

"You did, the solicitors, and thus Peter, of a certainty. Anybody who chanced on Peter's correspondence. The penny press might have spotted me. They certainly knew of my return."

"Did Miss MacKenzie?"

Miss MacKenzie sent the footman on his way with a pat to his arm. Graham didn't recognize him. The fellow was old enough to be her father and looked besotted enough to be her beau.

"St. Didier, your unfortunate experiences have warped your faith in human nature. Miss MacKenzie would never be so underhanded as to set minions upon an enemy in the dark. She'd trounce him properly in the churchyard and fight fair."

The butler appeared, another new face, or a face matured to the extent that Graham didn't recognize him.

"Think of it this way, MacNeil," St. Didier said. "Miss MacKenzie was among those in the household when the sheriff's man laid charges against you. She either believes your negligence caused the countess's death, or she knows for certain that your negligence had little to do with it. Either way, you should give her a wide berth."

St. Didier could be reckless. A revelation, that. "You insult a woman I esteem highly, St. Didier. Morna would never have mis-medicated Grandmama. Never."

"Somebody did. You should talk to Peter. He's hiding something."

"He thinks he's hiding his great love for Lanie when it nigh perfumes the very air. I wish them a fruitful union. The succession would benefit."

"Dinner is served." The butler's tone managed to be both gracious and magisterial.

Graham nodded to St. Didier and crossed the room to offer his arm to Morna. "Might I have the honor?"

She looked quietly splendid in blue velvet trimmed in MacNeil plaid. "We're to observe the formalities, my lord?" Her tone was teasing with a hint of challenge, a great improvement over her initial chilly good manners.

"We're to observe a few simple courtesies so that Peter escorting Lanie won't be such a departure from standard behavior."

Morna slipped her hand around his arm. "Lanie doesn't truly need an escort. She knows the whole castle, from cellars to parapets."

"Peter needs to escort her. One hopes his regard is reciprocated." Graham set a dignified pace for the dining room.

"I honestly can't tell," Morna said. "They like each other, and they have been friends for so long... For some, attraction arises like a sudden gust of wind. For others, it's more like a breeze that gathers force over time. Perhaps Peter is waiting for Lanie's breeze to blow his way?"

For others, the attraction was just there, like the air, the heavens, the habit of breathing in and out.

"Would you object to them marrying?" Graham asked quietly as Uncle Brodie came chattering along with St. Didier in tow.

"Would you?"

"Not at all." A half-truth, at best. "I'd like them to observe a decent interval of courtship, though." Long enough for Graham to either discover who had delivered Grandmama's fatal dose, or conclude that a definite answer to that question was impossible to discern.

"For some couples," Morna murmured, "a decent interval would be about twenty minutes. Leave them alone longer than that..."

She blushed. Graham seated her with as much punctilio as he was capable of. When he leaned down to give her chair one last little push, he let his hand rest on her shoulder. Straightening somehow involved his fingers gliding along the side of her neck.

"For shame, Miss MacKenzie," he murmured. "Every Scottish laddie knows that twenty minutes isn't nearly enough to properly express his most tender sentiments. Such an undertaking demands the whole of a long night and even into the next morning."

"Scottish lasses know utter balderdash when they hear it." Morna whisked her table napkin—more MacNeil plaid—across her lap. "Courtship doesn't stop at the altar. The genuine version lasts for years and is never complete."

"One doesn't argue with a lady, particularly a Scottish lady. That roast smells wonderful."

The venison was done to a turn, the potatoes swimming in butter, and the pear compote a superb finish to an excellent meal. As the conversation wandered from politics to local gossip to weather and the possibility of an excursion into Perth, Graham considered his exchange with Morna.

He loved her. His regard was not the half-invented prop of a homesick shopkeeper, nor the desperate fantasy of the transported felon. His feelings for Morna had roots in his youth and had only grown stronger for being separated from her.

Morna was at least viewing him in a friendly light, and he could work with that.

The difficulty he faced involved the need, the honor-bound *need*, to deal with her honestly, and that meant a frank and fraught discussion of the past.

Soon. Not yet, but soon.

CHAPTER SIX

"Why work in here?" Morna asked as Graham rose from behind the ornate library desk. "You'll catch your death, Graham MacNeil." She tossed him one of the plaid blankets draped over the chairs at the reading table.

Graham caught it one-handed, the other hand still holding a quill pen. "Burning candles at midday is a sacrilege. The light is abundant in here, whereas the study is..."

She saw in his eyes what he would not say. The study was dark and low-ceilinged, with thick midnight blue velvet drapes over the single window. Much like the hold of a ship. Compared to the library's chilly expanse, the study was oppressive and probably over-stuffed with memories too.

"The study needs airing," Morna said. "The next half-mild day, I'll see to it. I didn't know you wore spectacles." They gave him a scholarly air and made the blue of his eyes even more intense.

He set his quill pen in the tray. "A shopkeeper does nearly as much bookkeeping as a steward does, what with some customers buying on credit, others in cash, and some in kind. The ledgers become a court of last resort when disputes arise."

He came around the desk and draped the plaid about Morna's shoulders. The wool was warm from having hung before the fire and imbued with a hint of his heathery scent. Graham's hands brushing over her shoulders were... confusing.

"Do you still own that spice shop?" she asked.

"I do, and a bit of good acreage. Don't tell King George, but I also conduct some discreet trading beyond the shores of Australia." He stood close enough that she could see a smudge on the right lens of his glasses.

"Is that legal?"

"If the transportees and exclusives waited on England to send them out everything they needed, they'd never survive. The first lot nearly didn't. What we can't make for ourselves, we're learning to procure in a more timely fashion. The MacNeil plaid does become you, Morna MacKenzie."

She removed the spectacles from his nose and polished them on the wool draped over her arm. "I'm glad you kept a shop, glad you took to commercial trading. You have some charm and a head for numbers. Shopkeepers need both."

He watched her polishing his spectacles. "We all got on as best we could. I should probably sell my little business."

She passed his glasses back to him. "If you're making a profit, why on earth would you sell?"

"Because I am a rubbishing earl now." He tucked the spectacles into an inside pocket of his jacket and gestured to the sofa. "I read the solicitors' reports, as outdated as they were, and I'm reacquainting myself with the situation here, though not quickly enough. Grandpapa had me in mind as a general steward for John, and thus I'm somewhat acquainted with the basic running of the place—the places, rather, there being more than one property and dozens of tenancies—but other than that..."

Morna took a corner of the sofa. Graham settled into the nearest wing chair. A hassock was positioned such that had they been of a mind to, they could have shared it, as they'd shared many a hassock in youth.

"You aren't sure you can manage both the overseas business and the earldom?" Morna asked.

"I don't know if I can trust the people I've left in charge of the overseas holdings," Graham said. "They are good enough fellows, but the cat is definitely away, and mice will be mice. Life in the Antipodes hones one's practical tendencies."

"Then you plan on remaining in Scotland?" The question was out, unrehearsed, but much considered. Was home still home to Graham-the-Earl? A man who spoke of five thousand miles as a comfortable distance might be discontent rambling the few thousand acres of his family seat.

Graham rose and retrieved a stack of folded papers from the desk. "I should say that my plans are uncertain, that I've come back to see to my obligations, and then I'll reassess the situation. Many a transportee chose to remain in the Antipodes rather than return to Britain. Others wandered on to the Americas, and still others took a notion to see India."

"You saw India." She envied him that adventure, much to her surprise. "Everybody who speaks of the place says it's breathtaking."

"Parts of it are, and the mountains in the north will put the fear of the Almighty in you, if rounding the Horn hasn't already. Unimaginable heights, Morna. The Highlands aren't even foothills in comparison."

"Not good for sheep, then." Though Graham had clearly been fascinated.

He smiled. "Not good for anything but snow, ice, rocks, and awe." He considered the stack of papers in his hands and sorted through them. "You can read a description here."

She took the single sheet. "This is your handwriting."

He nodded and seemed abruptly absorbed with studying the portrait of the third countess, who held pride of place above the desk.

Morna examined the document he'd given her. *My dearest*

Morna, My travels have taken me, of all places, to India, which has to be the noisiest place on earth and also the most imbued with exotic scents...

"You wrote to me?"

He lifted the stack of papers. "Once a quarter, one page. If I'd permitted myself more, I would have used every sheet of paper in the shop."

Warmth bloomed that had nothing to do with the plaid around Morna's shoulders and everything to do with Graham gone suddenly shy.

"Why not send me the letters?" One a year would have been an annual highlight, a reason to rejoice and hope and *write back*. Two would have been endless delight, and four... Ire that had receded in recent days sent Morna pacing before the hearth. "Why waste the paper at all if you never meant to post the damned things?"

"I forgot that you swear," Graham said, which nearly earned him a smack on the back of the head.

"I can swear fluently in four languages and commend you to the devil in three more. I will soon demonstrate if you don't answer my question. Why not post the letters, Graham?"

He remained in his chair, which might have been an insult from St. Didier, but from Graham, it was reassuring proof of familiarity.

"For all I knew, Morna, you were taking Edinburgh by storm. I could not be writing to another man's intended, could I?"

"You could, you daft man. We've known each other since infancy. I worried about you so..." A proper tirade wanted to burst the banks of Morna's self-restraint, but another thought intruded. "Nobody let you know what I was about, did they?"

She sank back onto the sofa, considering Graham and the pile of letters he yet held.

He shook his head. "'The ladies are well.' Four words, and the solicitors sent them along rarely. St. Didier went so far as to inform me that you enjoyed good health, and that Lanie did, too, but for her eyes. His letters tended to arrive in December, and one year..."

"One year?"

Graham rose. "The ship carrying that mail went down, a not infrequent hazard, and how I survived until the solicitors' epistle arrived in March, I do not know. I cleared acres of ground and had blisters on my blisters that summer."

Summer in December, because the seasons were reversed in the southern hemisphere. Everything topsy-turvy.

"I was so angry with you," Morna said slowly, the words burdened with more sadness than rage. "For years, I told myself you deserved whatever fate held for you, but then Peter would have another one of your little notes, and I memorized each word."

"Angry with me." Graham nodded again, as if he was having trouble grasping the sense of the conversation. "Because of Grandmama. I understand."

"For pity's sake, Graham, not because of Grandmama. She was in torments, every joint aching, and her only relief was to be drugged into oblivion, and then she'd waken with a pounding headache to go with the dreadful rheumatism. She didn't want to abandon Grandpapa, but other than that, life was misery for her."

Graham stood before the fire, gazing into the flames. "She should not have died as she did, Morna. I realize you hold me responsible, and well you should."

Something about this discussion was off. Graham's remorse was sincere, but yet held a hollow note, a note of detachment or resignation where defensiveness should have been. Lanie would have been able to discern the subtleties. Morna could not.

She rose and joined him before the hearth. "Anybody could have measured out an extra spoonful of that medication or forgotten the precise hour of the previous dose. We were all in and out of Grandmama's bedroom of an evening, and she liked the company. Lanie loved her stories. Peter adored that Grandmama listened to him in a household where nobody else had time for a chatty boy. I told her my troubles, and you read to her by the hour. For all that she was nearly bedridden, her apartment was a busy place."

"You don't blame me for causing her death?"

"I did. I do, but you've served out your sentence, and after a few years, I had to admit that anybody could have made a similar mistake. John said so, often, but then, John was never very far from his flask and occasionally muddled. He would come down dressed for Sunday services on Saturday and look everywhere for the book sitting open on the sideboard."

"Right. John was easily distracted and frequently forgetful. I want to tell you something, Morna, and I want you to promise first that you'll consider what I say honestly, without bias or wishful thinking."

He was very serious about this disclosure, whatever it was. "I promise to try, Graham."

He stood straight and addressed the third countess. "I did not kill Grandmama."

Morna understood from his carefully neutral tone that he was testing her. That her next words mattered a great deal. And that he'd just taken a risk of some sort.

"Let's sit," she said, grabbing him by the wrist and steering him to the sofa.

"I tell you I was wrongly convicted, and you want to sit?" Despite the question, Graham took the place beside her on the sofa.

"If I believed you unassailably guilty," Morna said slowly, "I should have said, 'Don't lie to me,' or, 'You did kill her, and you confessed to the crime.' I did not say those things." She gathered her courage in the ensuing silence. "I did not even think them, Graham, but I am confused."

"As am I. I have gone over and over the events of that night. I reviewed the sequence with St. Didier at the time and questioned the staff until they nearly ran away at my approach. All I know is, I gave Grandmama but the one dose in her tea, at the usual hour. Nothing more, nothing less."

"Then why confess?"

"I did not strictly confess. I agreed that the sheriff could produce witnesses and evidence that would result in my conviction. The doctor's testimony alone would have convicted me. I was responsible for the evening dose, and Ramsey was desperate to avoid blame for the countess's death."

"I never liked him. He was kind to Grandmama and seemed to know his medicine, but he was too cold for such a young man. Too scientific. He and Uncle Brodie still correspond, though heaven knows what about."

"I suspect Ramsey was smitten with you, and sending me halfway around the world suited his plans nicely. Grandpapa thought my theory ridiculous."

"Grandpapa did not believe in your guilt. He muttered about needs must when the devil drives, but never anything more than that. Whom do you suspect?"

"The simplest explanation is that the physician was wrong. Grandmama did not die of an excessive dose of the poppy. She had a heart seizure or some sort of paroxysm and died in her sleep."

"John suggested that too. Said medicine is alchemy, even in these modern times, but Dr. Ramsey claimed the deceased bore no evidence of a heart seizure or paroxysm."

"He would say that, wouldn't he?"

Graham still held the stack of letters, and Morna kept the one he'd given her. The conversation was ranging very far afield from India and unsent mail, but then...

"You believe Ramsey was correct, don't you, Graham?"

"I believe Grandmama was essentially poisoned. The question is by whom, and was it intentional? We were all in and out of her apartment, you're right about that. Grandpapa also stopped by every evening to bid his countess good night, and when he did, they were usually alone together for at least a quarter hour. They conferred in the morning as well. Footmen and maids came in and out, and the housekeeper frequently brought a tea tray up."

"Why didn't the sheriff's man look into all of that?"

"He could have, but would John, Peter, or Grandpapa have survived transportation?"

Graham put the question to her quietly, and the answer was plain enough: No, of course not. John hadn't been frail, exactly, but he'd been partly fey and partly tipsy. Grandpapa hadn't lasted another six months amid all the comforts of the castle, and Peter had been a stripling with more pride than sense.

"St. Didier was on hand that summer too," Morna said. "Do you suspect him?"

"I do not, for the simple reason that he'd have no motive whatsoever. My job was to prove my own innocence, but proving innocence is impossible—how do you prove you *did not* commit an act when you have no alibi? If somebody had to be transported, I was the most fit candidate."

"And that," Morna said, brandishing his letter at him, "is why I am furious with you."

"You're furious with me?" He had the sense to be cautious rather than amused. "Might you explain?"

Morna rose before he could take her hand or she could seize his. "You've known me your whole life, Graham MacNeil. I've stood beside you in the graveyard and suffered through your attempts to learn polite dancing. When you had a lung fever, I read to you until I was hoarse, and when I beat you in horse races, I never bragged about it before others. You closed the door to friendship in my face when all this trouble erupted, and for that, I have not yet forgiven you."

Graham stood and looked down at her as if he were translating that tirade from a complicated foreign language.

"I kept my distance," he said, once again remote and severe. "Damned right I did."

When Morna would have made an exit in high dudgeon, Graham took her wrist and stuffed the rest of his letters into her hand.

"I apologize for keeping my distance, Morna. If I had it to do over,

I'd do the same again. Be angry if you must, but believe that my intentions were honorable."

Morna was too near tears to come up with a pithy retort. Sticking out her tongue would not do, and throwing his letters into the fire would cause her lifelong regret.

"Honor makes a cold bedfellow, *my lord*. I wish you the joy of the company you chose. I'll see you at supper."

"That could have gone better." St. Didier emerged from between the shelves of biographies and foreign translations. "Not a complete disaster, but hardly a victory for Scottish manhood." The man made not a sound on a wooden parquet floor that routinely creaked and groaned.

"Shut your gob," Graham said. "Morna will calm down."

"If so, she will be the first woman scorned in the history of womanhood to do so. You hadn't planned on giving her those letters, had you?"

"I planned to burn them. Hadn't got 'round to it yet." Graham had been considering burning them, for perhaps the hundredth time or so. They were a connection to Morna and a record of a heart struggling with banishment.

"Would a wee dram settle your manly nerves?" St. Didier asked, crossing to the sideboard.

St. Didier's needling was doubtless offered as an attempt to restore Graham's composure, though the tactic wanted subtlety.

"Feel free to indulge. I have ledgers to see to. One wants a clear head when tending to the accounts."

"Your head is so muddled at the moment, Dunhaven, that one plus one equals fifteen."

Not my head, my heart. Graham hadn't been expecting Morna to confront him so soon, hadn't grasped the nature of her complaint against him. He certainly hadn't meant to put her in possession of all those damned letters.

Unsent letters. "Morna is canny. She'll sort out motivations and reach her own conclusions. She didn't want me to be the guilty party." Some consolation.

A lot of consolation, actually.

"She didn't care if you were guilty or innocent," St. Didier said, pouring himself a tot from a decanter on the sideboard. "To her, the death was accidental. You've introduced the notion that it might have been intentional."

How delicately St. Didier avoided the word *murder*. "She'll get to the next part: The death was very probably accidental, but allowing me to be transported for a fatal accident I did not cause was an intentional act. Somebody should be nervous that the innocent earl has returned to the scene."

St. Didier nosed his drink. "Whisky always tastes better in Scotland. Has more character and less bite."

"We've been making it longer than you have in the south. Ale is better in England. I could leave."

St. Didier stared at his drink for a moment. "If you blow retreat, you have accomplished nothing."

A rousing altercation with Morna wasn't nothing. "You assume the guilty party knows they precipitated Grandmama's death and knows I had nothing to do with it. Another possibility suggests itself." After years of pondering. "The guilty party might not know they're guilty. Grandmama would ask anybody to pour her a spot of tea, simply to give her caller something to do. If that caller had been Grandpapa or Peter, Grandmama might have also asked them to top up the cup with a tot of the poppy."

"Because her medicines made her forgetful and muzzy-headed? Would a tot or two extra have killed her?"

"I don't know. She was old, she was in constant pain, she ate little. I believe a call on Dr. Ramsey is in order."

St. Didier set his drink on the sideboard. "I'll leave for Edinburgh in the morning. My mother's decline was long, painful, and slow. I quickly learned how to wring answers from the physicians." A rare touch of ire infused St. Didier's resolve.

"Peter and I will take the ladies shopping. You are welcome to join us, or you can bide here—guarding the fort—among one of the finest collections of Scottish medieval manuscripts in the whole of Britain. You like all that heraldry folderol, and John would be pleased to know somebody was appreciating his treasures."

"Shopping."

"Aye. Ribbons and bonnets and fabric and boots. MacNeil plaid is all well and good, but a lady also likes some variety in her attire."

"Bonnets." St. Didier made a face such as a boy might aim at cold, unsalted neeps.

The door opened, and Morna strode in. She held a volume bound with the green leather typically used for ledgers.

"Read this," she said, thrusting the book at Graham. She nodded coolly to St. Didier.

"What is it?" Graham asked.

"The contents speak for themselves. Nothing urgent."

Whatever the book was, the handwriting was Morna's. "I'll be traveling into Edinburgh next week," Graham said, setting the book on the desk. "I was wondering if you and Lanie might like to join me and Peter in the excursion."

Ah. He'd surprised her. Perfect auburn brows drew down. "An excursion."

"A raid on the shops, a passing skirmish with the solicitors, a call upon a certain Dr. Theophile Ramsey."

The russet brows rose. "You were wondering...?"

St. Didier sauntered forth from the sideboard. "Dunhaven was *hoping*. The word he sought was 'hoping'—hoping you would accompany him, and he's willing to put up with Peter and Lanie as well for the sake of appearances."

The wretched man was trying to be helpful and perhaps succeeding. Morna looked amused.

"Lanie would enjoy the outing," she said, "and I'm not about to let her go without me. She'll buy every scrap of yellow silk in Edinburgh because the texture is so pleasing, without a thought to the horrid color."

Morna retreated as abruptly as she'd arrived.

St. Didier raised his glass. "To Scottish manhood, in victory and defeat."

"To blazes with you." Graham collected the green journal and left at a dignified stroll.

CHAPTER SEVEN

"The earl is a gifted correspondent," St. Didier said.

Morna set aside the ninth letter and allowed herself a moment to adjust to the notion that Graham was the earl. Not Grandpapa, not John, *Graham*. The present Earl of Dunhaven had earned his keep in Sydney as a stable boy and been happy to have the "lighter" work. He'd gained further notice because he'd been capable of training horses, and horses were as necessary to the success of New South Wales as free penal labor.

All the while, Graham had somehow kept his spices thriving.

"I didn't hear you knock, St. Didier."

"No doubt because Dunhaven's epistles are so absorbing. He asked after you in every missive he sent me. 'I trust the ladies are well.' When he was particularly worried, he trusted you were 'thriving.'"

St. Didier struck Morna as a man who seldom lacked a purpose. What was the purpose behind this intrusion?

"Are you ready for tomorrow's journey?" she asked, gesturing to the chair opposite Grandpapa's desk.

"I am to remain behind, immersed in ancient manuscripts, learned tomes, and excellent whisky."

He was handsome in a dark-haired, dark-eyed, watchful way, and his manners were faultless. He nonetheless made Morna uneasy.

"Why are you here, St. Didier? The truth, if you please."

"To guard Dunhaven's back."

"Why does his back need guarding?" Morna had worked at that puzzle, but could not be sure of her conclusions.

"The earl hopes that his grandmother's death was an accident and that her demise was occasioned by nothing more than one chambermaid fixing the countess a cup of doctored tea, followed by a footman performing the same courtesy thirty minutes later, and then the old earl offering yet a third medicated cup thirty minutes after that. No malicious intent, none of the guilty parties even aware of their culpability."

Possible. "Go on."

"I am concerned with a different hypothesis," St. Didier said in the same detached, even tones. "Somebody deliberately sent the countess to her reward, knew Dunhaven—or some other party—would be blamed and further knew Dunhaven would accept responsibility rather than implicate anybody else."

"Somebody killed the countess to get at Graham?" A horrible notion, one Morna had shied away from even in the bravest corners of her imagination.

"This possibility haunts Dunhaven, though he hasn't quite admitted as much to me."

St. Didier shot his cuffs, which were fastened with discreet gold sleeve buttons. *Such* an Englishman, and yet, Morna had seen him carry off full Highland kit convincingly too.

What was the point of this little tête-à-tête? St. Didier was trying to pose an argument without being contentious.

What theory justified...? "Graham kept his distance from me," Morna said slowly, "because if he confided in me, if he recruited me to defend his innocence, I might have been in danger from whoever set him up. He let me believe him to be guilty because I was safer that way." The wretched, damned, stubborn fool. "He could not trust me to grasp the complications and do a bit of playacting accordingly."

The pile of letters in nigh pristine condition sat on the old leather blotter. Graham had carried them halfway around the world after somehow preserving them for years in a climate inhospitable to paper, prisoners, and banished peers.

Stubborn, wretched, impossible man.

"The situation," St. Didier said, "wants facts. The explanation might be as simple as I described initially, with all relevant parties long since off the premises."

"Or we might have a murderer in our midst, ready to do Graham a fatal injury if he should ask too many questions."

"In your shoes, I'd lock up all the medicinals for a start," St. Didier said. "I've been keeping an eye on the staff, watching the comings and goings, looking for the malcontents or anybody living above their means."

What had that to do with anything? "The wages we pay are generous."

"Dunhaven assigned these tasks to me, and they make sense. If the countess was dosed by means of a tea tray, then somebody in the kitchen might have seen that tray being prepared, or noticed a patent remedy sitting on the worktable where it ought not to have been. A scullery maid in possession of that information is in a position to bribe the cook, isn't she?"

"The cook left. Now you have me wondering why." The stated reason had been that old women were not safe in their beds at Castle MacNeil.

"Good. The more questions we ask, the more answers we'll uncover, until Dunhaven knows where he stands."

"But Graham himself cannot be seen asking the questions."

St. Didier's smile was mostly in his eyes. Lanie might have heard it in his voice. "He's just returned after being away for years. He can ask a lot of questions, and he's asking them. You mentioned playacting, and Dunhaven is doing a very credible impression of a peer new to his honors and not quite sure what the job entails."

Graham arrived at meals looking tired and distracted, though he was usually out on the property by the time Morna came down to breakfast, and he missed lunch frequently. His first appearance at divine services had caused a minor riot, quelled only by the news that the earl would be journeying to Edinburgh and would be happy to entertain callers upon his return.

"He's contending with a lot," Morna said. Had Graham found time to read her journal? "And he may never know what caused the countess's death."

"Somebody knows," St. Didier said, rising.

"Graham wants to question Dr. Ramsey." Morna stood as well, making a note to put a new cushion on Grandpapa's old chair. "I will suggest that we meet the physician someplace out of the way, where we are unlikely to be disturbed."

"*We?*"

"You have just implied that Graham MacNeil went to hell and back at least in part *to protect me*, St. Didier. The very least he can do, the least he must do, is allow me to do my best to protect him."

"Your decision is not up for debate?"

Even Morna could hear the genuine curiosity in St. Didier's question. "Is not now up for debate and never has been. Graham told me that his reasons for ignoring me during the worst summer of his life were honorable, and apparently they were, also blindingly wrong."

"I'm sure you will persuade him of his error."

"At length, in detail, and I will also explain to his lordship that the path to forgiveness lies in never making the same mistake with me again." None of which was St. Didier's perishing business.

"I'm off to lurk in the library," St. Didier said, bowing. "Enjoy the letters."

He closed the door silently in his wake, and Morna sank into the more comfortable embrace of a wing chair next to the hearth.

St. Didier's purpose had been to explain to her why Graham had distanced himself from her all those years ago. Graham himself should have offered the explanation, but hadn't. Why not? He could prose on for half a page about parrots and orchids, but he hadn't found a way to say, *I was trying to keep you safe.*

Morna reread the first letter, the one that began, *You might never read this...* and ended with *All my love...* Every letter ended that way, which was nearly enough to make Morna cry, if she were inclined to allow herself that degree of foolishness.

"You did take Edinburgh by storm." Graham tried to make his words a neutral statement of fact, neither accusation nor inquiry. The reality, though—that Morna had braved the high seas of polite society without him *and managed easily*—was both reassuring and daunting.

Morna went right on perusing the titles in the biographical section of the bookshop. The proprietor offered both bound and unbound versions, in keeping with the eclectic nature of Edinburgh society. The average Edinburgh brewer tended to be astute on the topic of universal suffrage, just as the city's aspiring physicians might be knowledgeable about the impact of excise taxes on Lowland agriculture. Debate was a public pastime, and ideas were offered up for intellectual delectation from pub to ballroom to coffee shop, all perspectives welcome to join the affray.

The Athens of the North took marketplace discourse very much to heart.

"I did the pretty," Morna said, choosing a volume bound in red leather. "Lady Dunkeld would not relent. She claimed that the old marquess expected her to turn a medieval castle into a fashionable country house, and such a miracle required serious shopping. I went along with her, thinking to help her choose fabrics and lampshades. The next thing I knew, I was taking tea with some French countess who wrote treatises on ancient Roman winemaking."

That Morna had had the opportunity to inspect Edinburgh's polite society at close range was... wonderful. Lovely. Nothing less than her right.

"I wish I'd seen you standing up with all the lordlings and poets."

Morna shoved the book back between other volumes. "I wish you had too. At least you eventually learned to dance. I thought the waltz would be the death of my toes."

"I'm not familiar with the waltz," Graham said. "Came along after I departed."

"After you confessed to a crime you did not commit. When are we meeting with Dr. Ramsey?"

Morna had been adamant that she be present at that interview, and Graham had been pleased with her insistence, also a little puzzled by it. His default state of mind lately seemed to be bewilderment and fatigue leavened by dashes of hope, much like life in a penal colony.

"We meet with Ramsey tomorrow morning. He suggested a quiet tea shop in the Grassmarket." Graham had not consulted Brodie regarding the doctor's whereabouts, but had instead relied on the good offices of an underfootman at the MacNeil town house. Brodie would have asked questions and, worse, delivered lectures, admonitions, and tiresome exhortations.

"I've been thinking." Morna moved along the shelves until she halted before the bound volumes of poetry. Burns, of course, everywhere and always Burns, but also Ramsay and Fergusson, along with a few of the more popular English talents, the rare American, and some French verse.

"One suspected you were ruminating." Graham manfully ignored how her gloved finger caressed the spine of the book. They were shopping, for pity's sake, and having a substantive discussion of the difficult matters.

"St. Didier suggested that Grandmama might have died as the result of several well-meaning individuals topping up her tea, one after the other, none of them aware that she was being repeatedly medicated."

Morna chose another volume of poetry and opened it to a random page. The curve of her neck, echoing in the line of her cheek and brow, begged for the attentions of a gifted portraitist.

"Successive, well-meant errors is one possibility," Graham said. "One benign possibility."

"No,"—Morna snapped the volume closed—"it is not." She shoved the poems at Graham's chest. "The teapot used for her medicinal tea was blue jasperware. We didn't use it for anything else, and we always prepared it for her evening dose. The whole kitchen knew those rules, and they were enforced without exception."

Graham thought back to the many nights he'd fetched the tray from the kitchen and taken it up to Grandmama's apartment.

"I knew that," he said slowly. "I always knew to take the tray with the blue pot, if several were in readiness. Black tea, but on the weak side. Enough flavor to hide the poppy when taken with some honey and cream."

"Precisely. You added a tablespoon of medication to the cup of tea. Dosing the whole pot would have been wasteful and uncertain, but a green tea or a tisane would not have done. You took the blue pot every time."

"The lady's maid or footman might still have fixed a second doctored cup of tea."

Morna shook her head. "Graham, they knew how fussy Dr. Ramsey was about the patent remedies. Peter brought up the nightly posset. You were responsible for the evening dose of medication, I was responsible for the afternoon, and Grandpapa was on hand for the morning. If I was out of an afternoon, I might have asked you or Peter to substitute for me, but the staff was forbidden to dispense medication."

Morna would know this. She'd been all but running the castle since the day she'd put up her hair, and Grandmama had been grateful for the assistance.

"The accidental theory becomes less and less credible," Graham said. "Am I to buy this volume of poetry for you?" *Scottish Verses of Love and Courting*.

"Buy them for Peter to read to Lanie."

I could read them to you. Graham leaned close to whisper that suggestion just as Morna strode off to the next set of floor-to-ceiling shelves.

"Were these selections popular when you and the marchioness were gracing Edinburgh Society?" Graham asked, thumbing through the pages. *An' I'll kiss thee o'er again; An' I'll kiss thee yet, yet...*

"Very likely. Burns never goes out of style. How much longer do we let Peter and Lanie linger among the novels?"

"Morna, tell me about Edinburgh Society and swanning around with the Marchioness of Dunkeld. Did you enjoy yourself?" *Were you tempted? Did you give your heart away?*

She regarded him with a cross expression. "I went through the whole nonsense for Lanie's sake. One has to know the terrain, you see. If some fool thought to court me, the marchioness would have let me plead a retiring nature or domestic responsibilities, but if her ladyship got it into her head that she must launch Lanie, then I wanted to know what I was up against."

"You scouted the terrain?"

"I learned to waltz, and I trotted out my French and laughed at all the witty gentlemen, some of whom were genuinely amusing. It's all in the journal, Graham."

Well, no. The journal had been sparse going there for a few months. References to sore feet, fatigue, the occasional aching head, and missing home had filled most of the pages. Those months were in contrast to the section where Morna had described old John MacIver bidding farewell to his only daughter on the occasion of her taking ship with her husband and children for Nova Scotia.

Every detail of the scene had been minutely described, right down to the tears MacIver had refused to wipe away. *Mind you write to me, Pa. I'll worry.*

Graham had wanted to say the same thing to Grandpapa and to Morna, but hadn't been able to form the words for fear he'd lose his composure.

"I don't see Peter or Lanie," Morna said. "They were here a minute ago."

A cursory search of the shop revealed no sign of either the young lady or her escort.

"Graham, we must find them." Morna, typically so composed, was clutching his sleeve. "Lanie thinks her nose and her ears are compensation enough for her poor sight, but this is *Edinburgh*. The smells and sounds are all too much and too unfamiliar."

"She's with Peter," Graham said, taking Morna by the hand. "Peter would lay down his life for her, and we're not three streets from the town house. They can't have gone far."

"Find her," Morna said. "Please, Graham, just find her. I can't lose her too."

A hint of panic infused those words. "I'll take you back to the town house and rouse the staff. Lanie is distinctively pretty, and Peter knows his way around the city."

"No," Morna said, giving his hand a fierce jerk. "You will not deposit me in some wing chair at home to stitch a rubbishing sampler while my sister is unaccounted for. You will not leave me behind again."

"I didn't leave you behind. *I was transported.*"

Morna dropped his hand. "I would have gone with you, but you never gave me the chance, did you?"

She glowered at him, then exited the shop without a backward glance. Graham followed, barely remembering to leave the volume of poetry with the clerk before pushing through the door.

I would have gone with you.

No, she would not. She would not have left Lanie and Grandpapa to travel as the wife of a disgraced man to a foreign and ferocious land. That wasn't the point.

The point was: *He hadn't asked her to.* Hadn't asked for her insights or assistance when charged with a crime he hadn't commit-ted. Hadn't asked her to accompany him on the transport ship. Hadn't asked her if she'd teach him to waltz now that he'd be expected to know how.

He could remedy one of those oversights, just as soon as he found Peter and Lanie and lectured them for all eternity on the foolishness of ever again disappearing without notice.

"What was I to do?" Peter asked, sounding to Morna a bit like Uncle Brodie in a peevish mood. "I mentioned that a yarn shop stood directly opposite the bookshop, and the next thing I knew, Lanie was pulling me bodily through the door. Was I to leave her *to cross the street alone* while I went to ask permission of you and Morna?"

"Not to ask our permission," Graham said patiently. "To let us know your plans had changed, as in future, we will let you know if a similar circumstance arises."

Morning light caught Peter in profile, showing Morna his resem-blance to both Graham and John. Peter was the in-between model, not as tall or broad-shouldered as Graham, but more muscular and robust than John. Some would say Peter was the ideal, but to Morna's eye, Graham was the more attractive specimen.

He was tall enough for her, which ought to be a detail, but wasn't. Dancing with a man who addressed one's chin looked and felt ridicu-lous. Graham was also...

Morna cast about for the right word as she topped up her tea. Graham was the earl now. When Lanie and Peter had gone missing yesterday afternoon, and Morna had been nigh levitating with worry, Graham had made the logical suggestion: look in the nearest dozen shops, starting with the sweet shop—Peter would have been drawn there—and the yarn shop, an irresistible lure to Lanie. Five minutes later, they'd found Lanie exclaiming over a skein of wool spun from goat hair.

Nothing had been said to Lanie at the time, but supper last night had been somewhat wanting in conviviality. Lanie had taken a tray for breakfast.

Over eggs and toast, Graham had gently suggested to Peter that yesterday's detour to the yarn shop had given him a bad turn. Morna had been ready to... She did not know what. Stand in the middle of the street shouting like a madwoman.

The same way she'd felt when Graham and Grandpapa had ridden through the castle gates bound for Glasgow all those years ago. Furious, but also bereft, panicked, helpless. The same way she'd felt when the countess had died, and then Grandpapa had expired soon after. The same way she'd felt when her own parents had succumbed to influenza.

Shrieking mad and unable to utter a sound.

Peter slathered raspberry jam on his toast. "Then you won't mind telling me where you and Morna are off to this morning."

"As an attempt to change the topic," Graham replied, "I commend your tactics. Morna and I are doing more shopping. Uncle Brodie must not run out of cigars, and I have been personally charged with replenishing his inventory."

Peter made a face. "Damned smelly habit. He claims it's his sole vice, but then one watches him at the brandy and the whisky as he polishes those dozens of snuffboxes. He scares me."

That observation had Morna looking up from her tea. "Brodie? He's the next thing to a potted fern, if you can ignore his blather." Seldom left the estate except to attend services and blessed with only infrequent letters from his old cronies in London or Edinburgh.

Peter put the cork lid back on the jam pot with a decisive thump of his fist. "I could be him in twenty years, and well I know it. If Graham hadn't come home, I'd have done right by the castle as the de facto steward or tenant or whatever, but Graham is here now." He set the jam pot in the center of the table. "Sorry. I was at the brandy last night after I read to Lanie. I'm a bit sore-headed."

"At your age," Graham said, requisitioning the jam pot, "Brodie was a sot, worse than he is now. He had engaged in three duels that Grandpapa was willing to tell me about. Brodie's worst offense was gambling beyond his means, which he did frequently. When some lordling or Honorable came around to collect his vowels, Brodie would retreat behind his sister's skirts in Perthshire and expect Grandpapa to settle the matter.

"When Brodie got some lady's maid with child," Graham went on, "Grandpapa delivered an ultimatum: bide at the castle with a modicum of self-restraint or take ship on remittance. To Brodie's credit, he developed some self-restraint. In later years, he could be trusted to jaunt into Glasgow or Edinburgh without supervision, but as a younger man, he was a walking scandal."

Peter frankly stared at his brother. "Brodie has a child?"

"The poor mite didn't survive past thirty days. Grandmama had her planted in the family plot. Her grave is the little stone nearest the corner."

"Wee Mary," Peter said. "I did wonder."

"Cease tormenting yourself," Graham said, prying loose the cork lid. "You could never be like Brodie, and if you want the stewardship of the castle, it's yours. You are my heir, though. Stewarding is a bit beneath your station."

"No," Peter said, brandishing his toast, "it's not. We have the wrong sort of sheep, Graham. Did you hear Lanie rhapsodizing about goat hair? You can make an even finer wool from rabbit fur, if you have the right sort of rabbits, and we do have them. Every other schoolgirl in polite society has an Angora bunny, and the little beasts shed the most luxurious fur imaginable."

Graham applied an even layer of jam to his toast. "First, you're on about steam. Now, it's furry rabbits. Grandpapa had your sort of mind. Passionately interested in everything all the time. Wears a lowly convict out. Think about which direction you'd like to go, Peter. Settle on two or three ventures that will hold your interest for the next five years, and I will support the undertakings any way I can."

Peter stared at his empty plate. "Do you mean that?"

Graham smacked him on the arm. "You have been the de facto steward at the castle since finishing up at university. Uncompensated, too, I might add, which is not exactly fair to you. St. Didier speaks highly of you. The tenants trust you and like you—I've been hearing your praises incessantly for the past week. 'Such a fine young man,' 'not afraid of hard work,' 'a good head on his shoulders,' 'a credit to the castle.' Monotonous, all those compliments from people who are supposed to be dour and critical."

Peter was blinking at nothing. "I was the only one left."

"Aye," Graham said. "Grandpapa gone, me sent to perdition, Brodie worthless, and John in a fog between Robert the Bruce and inebriation. You have been the last man standing, and you've done well. Your sentence is served, your banishment over. You are free now, and God pity the person who attempts to come between you and your dreams."

Morna was blinking too. Before her eyes, Peter shed the last vestiges of adolescent uncertainty, sat taller, and picked up his tea cup in a different, more assured grip.

"Wool," he said. "Lanie knows wool like old MacIver knows the game in the woods. She loves everything about it—the smell, the feel, the softness, the durability, the warmth. Wool keeps you warm even when it's wet. Few other fabrics can do that. Whatever ventures I choose next, wool will be part of them."

"Very Scottish," Graham said, munching his toast. "Plaid is all the rage in Mayfair these days, and those people spend obscene amounts of money on fashion. Mad, the lot of them."

"Excuse me," Peter said, rising so quickly he nearly knocked his chair over. "Enjoy your shopping." He sketched a bow to Morna and plucked another sweet bun from the sideboard before leaving the breakfast parlor at a lope.

Graham rose and closed the door. "Would you be offended if I indulged at such an early hour?"

"Of course not."

He produced a flask, tipped it up, and sipped. "I just found him, Morna. My baby brother, all grown up, a braw, bonnie laddie with a good head on his shoulders. I just found him again, and..."

"...and he's not afraid of hard work, a credit to the castle."

"A fine young man." Graham saluted with his flask and tucked it away. "And he is all of that, but if Peter emigrates to Nova Scotia, Morna, I will lose my damned wits."

And yet, Graham had opened that door and invited Peter to consider stepping through it, to follow his dreams, as young people ought, *as Graham never had.*

Morna rose, crossed the room, and wrapped her arms around Graham's waist. "If he takes Lanie with him, I'll lose mine too."

Graham draped his arms around her shoulders and gave her a squeeze. "He'll not leave without her. She'll be reluctant to leave you. Perhaps we won't lose them after all."

I love you. Morna had never given him the words. They would have been true for most of her life, but they were true in a different way now. She loved him because he'd left in disgrace to protect the people he cared for, because he'd come through loss and hardship without bitterness, because he was honorable to his bones, even to sending his only sibling adventuring out into the big, exciting, dangerous world.

The last man standing. Peter had nearly collapsed under the weight of Graham's praise and understanding.

She kissed Graham's cheek. "We'd best move on if we're to be punctual to our meeting with Dr. Ramsey. Peter and Lanie will be here when we get back, or they will leave us word where to find them."

Graham gave her another squeeze, this one gentler. "Peter should be the earl. He can't see that."

"You are a fine earl," Morna said, stepping back. "I'll meet you out front in ten minutes."

He managed a crooked, bashful smile. "I'll lose him to a lot of damned hopping rabbits and stinking steam engines. Grandpapa would be proud of him."

"You are proud of him, and now he knows it, so he can be proud of himself. Don't keep me waiting, Dunhaven. Dr. Ramsey has answers, and I have questions."

"Ten minutes." Graham bowed. "And, Morna?"

"Your lordship?"

"Thank you."

"Don't be ridiculous." She left to fetch her cloak, to settle her nerves—a hopeless undertaking when Graham was being so noble—and to pause outside Lanie's door. Peter was already holding forth within, where he ought not to be and where he absolutely belonged.

Morna belonged in Graham's embrace. He'd taken her in his arms as naturally as breathing, and everything, from the muscular fit of his body to the heathery scent he wore, to the warmth he exuded, had felt exquisitely right. Like coming home and being set free and a pardon for all transgressions past, present, and future.

She gave herself two minutes at the top of the steps to savor that wonder, then descended to find Graham waiting for her, precisely ten minutes after she'd left him in the breakfast parlor, and there it was again—the conviction that she was coming home just because she was once again coming to him.

CHAPTER EIGHT

"I would have handled matters differently now," Dr. Ramsey said, regarding Graham impassively. "Your lordship."

The form of address still jarred, though Ramsey's use of the honorific came off as belated rather than disdainful.

He wore his dark hair brushed straight back and a trifle long, the same as he had when Graham had known him previously. He was still trim, handsome in a severe way, and kitted out as the perfect gentleman-about-town. He'd half risen at their arrival and offered a stiff semblance of a bow, then returned to his seat. At his brusque gesture, the tea shop serving maid brought over a laden tray.

Ramsey was a good-looking devil, and he now enjoyed that phase of adulthood between dashing young manhood and distinguished middle age. Graham's senior by only a few years, in fact, which came as something of a shock.

Ramsey had been quite young when he'd attended Grandmama —about Peter's present age, would be Graham's guess. Graham came to that conclusion as he assisted Morna into a chair and took one himself. The hard little seats begged for cushions that would encourage patrons to linger over a second pot.

"You would have handled matters differently." Morna pulled off her gloves and laid them in her lap. "Is that a confession or an apology?" The civility in her tone would have frozen the North Sea.

"An apology, certainly," Ramsey replied. "I was newly fledged as a physician, full of the latest medical advances and full of myself. I had landed the plum job of personal physician to a titled family, and then the countess expired on my watch."

"You pointed fingers as loudly and convincingly as you could," Graham said, pouring out for Morna and adding honey to her tea. When Ramsey made no effort to see to his own serving, Graham poured him a cup as well.

"I wanted justice for her ladyship." Ramsey took a delicate sip from the fussy little cup. The table was near the back of the shop, a quiet location, though at this midmorning hour, the establishment hadn't much custom.

An old fellow sat up front, reading a newspaper at the windows. A tidy young lady of apparent African extraction moved from table to table, placing a single daisy in a plain vase of green glass on each one. Her long apron sported embroidered daisies on the bodice, and the teapots all bore the same flower.

This very shop would have thrived madly in Sydney.

"You wanted justice for her ladyship," Morna said, stirring her tea in a fashion Graham could have called ominous. "Do you delude yourself that justice was achieved?"

Ramsey set down his tea cup and gave Graham a slow perusal. "I had and have my doubts."

"Did you share those doubts with the sheriff's man?" Graham asked.

"I might have mentioned that the cause of death did not implicate anybody in particular."

"Balderdash," Morna spat. "The countess died in her sleep, and Dunhaven was the last person responsible for handling her medication every evening. The circumstances alone convicted him, and you did nothing to prevent that."

"Somebody sent her ladyship to her reward, Miss MacKenzie. To you, the countess was likely ancient and frail, but you were a robust girl without much experience of illness in the elderly. I tell you, her ladyship had a strong heart. Her pipes were in good order. Her mind was alert when she wasn't dosed to manage the pain. Rheumatism is a cruel disease in that it debilitates the joints and senses, while leaving the rest of the patient well enough to endure great suffering for years."

When Ramsey was agitated, the impenetrable phonetic thicket of the Aberdeen dialect bordered the edges of his diction.

"You're from a large family?" Graham asked.

Morna looked at him as if he'd just volunteered for a return voyage to the Antipodes.

"One of ten," Ramsey said. "Ten living. Four others failed to thrive."

And those four others had likely sparked Ramsey's interest in medicine. "How many siblings are you supporting?" Graham offered Morna the plate of sweets, which included two French chocolates along with shortbread in flower shapes and an assortment of brown and pink macarons.

She waved the plate away.

Ramsey was a good physician but a poor thespian. He clearly considered personal questions rude. "I've put two of my brothers through medical training. The third is making good progress with his studies. My older sisters are married. The younger two bide with me."

The weight of the world had been on young Dr. Ramsey's shoulders. Of course he'd pointed fingers. His family's survival had likely depended upon it. Oh, the irony.

"Tell us what you can recall about the specifics of her ladyship's circumstances," Graham said. "We know it was a long time ago, and you've treated many patients since, but I assure you, I did not knowingly poison the woman who'd been like a mother to me."

"Nobody thought you had," Ramsey replied. "Her husband was

vocal on that point. You'd made a mistake, been forgetful or careless, but your actions were by way of an accident."

Morna's eyes took on a particular gleam. Graham passed her a chocolate macaron. She took it and put it on her plate.

"Grandpapa would still say the same if he were sitting at this table," Graham said. "The charge was involuntary manslaughter."

"Why plead guilty if you did not commit the crime?" Ramsey asked. "When I doubted your culpability, I found that guilty plea all the evidence necessary to quiet my uncertainty."

As had the sheriff's man. "I assumed," Graham replied, "that whoever was responsible had also intended no harm, and of all the possible suspects, I was the one best suited to surviving transportation. Of that, *I* am certain." Grandpapa had been, too, albeit reluctantly.

"But you aren't sure who you were protecting," Ramsey said, starting to reach for the plate of sweets, then apparently thinking better of it.

"The situation is worse than that." Morna spoke quietly. "Dunhaven looks to assure himself that the death was, in fact, accidental. Otherwise, you, Dr. Ramsey, have enabled a murderer to roam free while an innocent man took on a fate that has killed many a hardened criminal."

"Surely, you don't suspect me." Indignation, or possibly worry, had again shaken his polished diction from his grasp. As a young physician, he'd likely been terrified the titled family would throw him to the wolves of justice.

"I do not suspect you," Graham said. "Grandmama liked you, and Grandpapa respected you. You were conscientious regarding her care and confident of your medical knowledge. You had no motive for putting an end to such a post and every reason to hope her ladyship struggled along for many years."

"As we all did," Morna added. "But you insisted that the countess had been killed."

"She was," Ramsey said. "We're taught to keep thorough notes, and I've reviewed her ladyship's case often. I examined the remains carefully at the time. Her mouth was bone-dry, lips and fingernails had a bluish tinge, pallor of the face was marked, and the younger Miss MacKenzie, who often sat up with the countess, claimed her ladyship had been snoring, which was unusual. Miss Lanie had lost most of her eyesight, and I would trust the hearing of the nearly blind over the vision of the sighted any day."

"You think Miss Lanie heard a death rattle rather than snoring?" Graham asked. Did Lanie realize what she'd heard?

"Possibly. The poppy can ease us away from pain, but it also slows respiration. In cases of an overdose, the breathing becomes too slow to adequately exchange the air in the lungs or clear the throat. Taken with the other symptoms and the fact that I had witnessed her ladyship sleeping quietly on many occasions—no snoring—I concluded that an excess of the poppy ended her days. I've seen an appalling number of similar cases since and am confident of the cause of death."

When holding forth medically, Ramsey's accent was all genteel education and drawing-room tweed. He fell silent as the daisy-bearing maid placed a flower in the vase at the center of the table, then moved off.

"I cannot tell you more than that," Ramsey said when the serving maid had departed. "An overdose resulted in the countess's death. You've suggested two possibilities—murder and negligence. I must remind you of a third."

"Suicide," Morna said, suggesting the theory had occurred to her previously. "Which would require that the countess exhibit a degree of selfishness foreign to her nature. She was too fond of her family, even of her reprobate brother, to do that to us, and if she had, she'd have penned a note to ensure no nonsense ensued of the exact variety that did follow."

"She could not pen a note," Graham said. "Grandmama could no longer hold a pen." Which begged the question: How could Grandmama have uncorked a bottle of patent remedy, poured herself a large dose, replaced the cork back on the bottle...?

"Her ladyship's death was no suicide," Morna said more firmly. "She loved us, and we kept her comfortable. We relied upon her, all of us. The old earl was lost without her, Lanie inconsolable, and John... Before he lost his grandparents, he was better. Not as untethered. After that..."

After the earl and countess died and I left. "Ramsey, we thank you for your time. You've mostly confirmed what we already knew. Is there anything else you believe relevant to the situation?"

Ramsey took his hat from an adjacent chair, a fine beaver with an exquisitely curled brim. "Miss MacKenzie, I understand your protestations. You loved the countess, and she was very fond of her family, as you note. She loved you all enough to come to meals, though holding a fork or spoon was most uncomfortable for her. She had you trooping through her apartment like some Edinburgh at-home that lasted from noon until night every day.

"The young man," he went on, "Peter, did much of his schoolwork by reading and reciting to her, and the old earl discussed every facet of his holdings with her morning and night. He wrote me a character at her insistence. She'd demanded that of him after I'd been treating her for only a few weeks. She was a woman of formidable character whose generosity of spirit meant much to me and my family."

"We wanted her to be included," Morna said. "She was the heart of the castle, and we all knew it."

"Of course." Ramsey tapped his hat onto his head. "What you cannot know, what I pray you never learn, is how vile the course of a rheumatic illness is. The pain never relents. With each passing season, it finds new joints and tendons to afflict. Vision and hearing can be affected. Memory becomes unreliable. The spirits sink. Winter intensifies the suffering, year by year."

He took up a walking stick of plain polished oak with a contoured silver grip. "The poppy dulls the pain, but nothing truly eliminates it. The disease has no cure and little relief, and when it has stolen mobility and independence, it does not stop until it has also taken every bit of dignity and hope. The countess's case was progressing. I made certain the earl knew what to expect, and he asked me to keep that information to myself. I'd already told the countess what awaited her, because that good woman asked me directly and deserved to know the truth."

He rose slowly. "I saw the same monstrous ailment in my own mother. I can assure you, after a certain point, she would have ended her own suffering by any available means, had she been capable. You would not wish such an affliction on Lucifer himself."

He bowed to Morna, leaning heavily on his cane, nodded to Graham, and departed with a slow, uneven gait. A painful, arthritic gait.

"The poor devil," Graham muttered, pouring himself a cup of tea. "He's not an old man."

Morna bit into the chocolate macaron. "His family will care for him. They'll know how if anybody would."

"We knew how," Graham said, mentally reviewing the conversation and finding nothing of note in the whole exchange. "No cure, he said, and he's an expert." *Physician, heal thyself—if you can.*

"No hope," Morna added, "and Grandpapa had been apprised worse was to follow. He loved her, and she might have put him up to it, Graham. Grandpapa was fading too."

Graham drank the tea plain, mostly because tea should not go to waste. He could not bring himself to sample the sweets.

"What we're contemplating feels beyond wrong, Morna. They loved each other. They'd weathered decades and tragedies together, lost grown children—plural. We needed them. Not a reliable adult among us, and I include Brodie in that assessment."

Morna patted Graham's hand, stirred a skein of honey into his tea, and chose another chocolate macaron.

What occurred to Graham as he sampled a treat he didn't want was that he needed Morna. She'd put the fear of belated repercussions into Ramsey and pried from him a disclosure he had doubtless never intended to share. She'd insisted on coming on this outing, then comported herself like Graham's devoted henchman, prepared to guard him from even conversational menaces.

He recalled her wrapping her arms around him at breakfast, when he'd been nigh incapable of standing. Morna understood how the prospect of Peter and Lanie emigrating could loom like a worst nightmare, and a real possibility.

She was still his heart's desire and his ally, a gift that consoled and amazed in equal measures.

"Ramsey's mother," Graham said, brushing crumbs from his fingers. "If Ramsey's mother's situation had been made known to the sheriff's man, the whole matter might have gone very differently. Ramsey has a family to support, but he's also a healer by calling, and he was young and from humble means. If suspicion had fallen on him, I might have won a Scottish verdict."

Insufficient evidence to convict. Not the same as an acquittal, but for the accused, the result was still liberty.

"Grandpapa would not have left that stone unturned," Morna said. "If he'd seen any way to keep you home, he would have moved heaven and earth to make it so."

Graham drained the tea cup, abruptly ready to be quit of the cozy little shop with its forced daisies and fancy French sweets.

"Grandpapa would not have invented evidence against Ramsey."

Morna dunked her sweet in her tea. "Would you have wanted him to?"

"No." Well, probably not. "I thought Ramsey was a bit rude, making me pour his tea for him. He probably can't trust himself even to hold a full pot."

Morna munched her macaron, gaze on the old man reading his newspaper by the window. "Did we learn anything, Graham?"

"We learned, once and for all, that Grandmama's death was not an accident. We learned that Ramsey entertained the possibility of her committing suicide, but told no one when that theory might have kept me from transportation or exposed him to suspicion. We learned that his position was more precarious than we'd known, because he watched the same disease kill his mother. I learned, not for the first time, that you are very fierce and very dear."

Morna dusted her palms together. "One could say the same about you, were the surrounds not so public. Where is this cigar shop, and will I scandalize all of Edinburgh by visiting it with you?"

So fierce and dear, *and shy*. That hadn't changed, and the knowledge warmed Graham from the heart out.

"You will scandalize all of Scotland, so let's be about it, shall we?"

She beamed at him and even let him tie the ribbons of her bonnet, which was so much foolishness Graham nearly forgot his hat. Morna further gilded his morning by taking his arm when they joined the throng on the walkway.

The tobacconist's establishment was only a short distance away, but the going was slowed by more wheeled conveyances filling the street and more shoppers on the walkway. On the corner, some of Graham's joy drained away. Ramsey, across the intersection and only two dozen yards ahead, made slow, bobbing progress, one hand on his cane, the other within balancing distance of the buildings to his left. The physician kept his head down, as if the oncoming pedestrians were so many winter gales buffeting him and not mere foot traffic.

"Do you think he told us the truth?" Graham asked.

Morna followed his gaze. "Yes, but not the whole truth. He's protecting his family, and having had some experience with the type, he'll choose family over the truth any day."

The very same conclusion Graham had come to. The doctor had held back but had not precisely lied. "Are you scolding me, Morna?"

"More like admiring you." She stepped off the walkway and half dragged Graham with her. He did not recall much about the transaction in the tobacconist's shop, but he left the place having arranged for delivery of the specified merchandise to the MacNeil town house by the end of the day.

Perhaps by then he might have worked out just where and how to commence his courtship of Miss Morna MacKenzie, for nothing less than courtship would serve now, come fire, flood, or flaming arrows of misfortune.

~

"Greater devotion hath no swain than he who will go bonnet shopping with his lady," Morna murmured, meaning every word. The bonnet shop was middling busy, though every patron other than Peter and Graham was female, and all of them had sent Morna envious glances.

Graham scowled. "Peter wore the same besotted expression when Lanie was choosing yarn, for pity's sake. The lad has no dignity."

Morna held a length of plaid ribbon against the fabric of Graham's jacket. "I wasn't referring to Peter."

That ferocious MacNeil scowl became a grin. "You haggled with the tobacconist this morning, Morna MacKenzie. Stood right beside me and informed half the Grassmarket that Edinburgh has taken to condoning thievery within sight of the castle itself. I was touched, I tell you."

And Graham had left the shopkeeper to defend himself, then paid the agreed-upon sum, winked at Morna before the gawping clerks and smirking male customers, and escorted her down the lane. A sweet moment.

"You think Peter is being devoted," Graham said, bending near enough that Morna caught his heathery scent. "He's stealing a march."

Morna wound up the ribbon and chose another patterned in blue and green plaid. "He's escorting her in plain sight, my lord. Nobody's stealing anything."

"Watch. He will tie the bonnet ribbons for her, adjust the curl behind her ear, smooth the lapel of her cloak. Half the patrons are in love with him, the shameless lout."

The half that wasn't already smitten with Graham, perhaps.

Morna did watch, and Graham was right. "Peter can't court Lanie by making sheep's eyes at her. They will likely never dance in a crowded ballroom, and they can't race over hill and dale on horseback. This is how Lanie can be wooed, with small touches that delight her, and soft words, and time spent doing the things she cannot do alone."

"Then you were wooing me in the tobacco shop, Miss MacKenzie?"

Graham's mind had always worked like this—inside out and upside down, with unexpected insights. He was capable of humor so droll as to be almost imperceptible.

"Nearly plighting my troth, of course. When we attend a horse auction together, you will know yourself to be in anticipation of a formal engagement."

"My heart throbs with hope. That is the MacKenzie tartan, if I'm not mistaken. Hard to tell with just a ribbon to judge by."

Morna peered more closely at the length of satin in her hand. "I hardly recognize it."

"We must remedy the oversight. The lighter colors flatter you, and one grows tired of the MacNeil's darker pattern. If Peter doesn't cease his—ah. A decision at last."

Lanie had chosen a simple straw hat with a wide, slightly drooping brim. The various trimmings—ribbons, silk flowers, what looked to be a necklace of green glass beads—accompanied the millinery to the side of the shop, where a clerk ceremoniously boxed the lot.

"For the love of God and Scotland," Graham muttered, "might we call the expedition a success and return to the town house?"

"You don't fancy another sortie to a tea shop or gallery or glove-maker or—"

Graham passed Morna her parasol. "If you mention the jewelry store three doors down, Peter will faint with rapture. Let's save that delight for the next fine day, shall we?"

Peter made the arrangements to have the booty delivered directly to the town house, and before Morna could ask how Graham knew the precise location of the nearest jewelry store, the party was once again on the walkway.

"I vow I am exhausted," Lanie declared. "Peter, take me home. I am so peckish I could even walk past a new yarn shop."

"Our Lanie is propounding a falsehood," Graham said, offering Morna his arm and setting a course down the street. "She could no more ignore fine wool than I could ignore the scent of saffron."

"Bakeries defeat me," Peter said, bringing up the rear with Lanie. "Anything that combines fruit, pastry, and cream. Raspberries especially. What of you, Lanie? Have you a favorite treat?"

Morna listened while an earnest dialogue transpired about the merits of peaches versus raspberries and cherries. Graham smiled down at her and shook his head while they waited for the next intersection to clear.

Young love was sweet and a bit silly. What Morna felt for Graham was sweet and serious, but also warm and...

"Onward," Graham muttered, stepping off the curb.

Because Morna was looking up at him, she saw the menace he had yet to perceive. "Graham!" She hauled him back just as a shabby coach and pair went racketing by at a hard canter. The horses' hooves clattered on the cobbles as the vehicle nearly careened onto its side at the next corner.

"Damnation!" Peter yelled. "Graham, are you hurt?"

"Unhurt," Graham said. "In future, I will make a greater effort to watch where I am going."

"Distracted by the scenery," Peter said. "Best be more careful, though. Wretched fool coachman was likely drunk in broad daylight."

Graham appeared unruffled, but Morna nonetheless noted him looking over his shoulder more than once on the way home. She climbed the steps to the town house front door with a sense of relief out of all proportion to a simple accident—a simple near accident.

"Graham wasn't careless." Lanie spoke firmly as Peter helped her remove her cloak in the foyer.

"Not careless, perhaps, but a bit unaware," Peter said.

"He wasn't unaware either."

Graham hung Morna's parasol on a hook. "What do you mean, Lanie?"

"Edinburgh is like a symphony," Lanie said. "So many sounds, and the tall buildings over in the Old Town mean the sounds bounce around from all directions. When we are out and about, I have to listen intently to keep my bearings. Half the sounds don't make sense to me. Others I can figure out."

Morna passed Graham her bonnet. "What exactly did you hear?"

"The cobbled streets are noisy," Lanie said. "I like that. I can hear a vehicle coming and going. Horseshoes on cobbles make quite a racket. Wooden wheels have one sound, metal-rimmed wheels another. I could probably pick our town coach out of a herd of coaches if they all traveled along the same stretch of street."

"Let's step into the parlor," Graham said, opening the nearest interior door.

The parlor was heated, also private. Peter led Lanie to the sofa, and Graham handed Morna into a wing chair and then tossed another square of peat onto the fire.

"You heard that runaway coach coming?" Graham asked, remaining on his feet.

Lanie nodded. "You muttered the word 'onward,' Graham, then a whip cracked. Horses that had been trotting charged into the canter—the change of gait is unmistakable—and you and Morna were nearly run down. I felt the breeze of the coach passing that close to us."

Morna asked the obvious question. "You're sure you heard the crack of a whip?"

"Yes. The streets on the Old Town side of the loch are narrow and hilly, and cracking a whip in such surrounds makes little sense. Here in the New Town, where the streets are broad and flat, perhaps, but not outside the bonnet shop. I can safely say that is the first use of a horsewhip I've heard since we arrived."

"I heard it too," Graham said slowly. "I wasn't paying attention. My thoughts were elsewhere."

Peter casually laid an arm along the back of the sofa and very nearly around Lanie's shoulders. "An accident," he said. "Edinburgh is dangerous. We all know that, but Morna's reflexes were sufficient unto the day. Would anybody like a wee dram to ward off the chill?"

Peter was shaken, as was Morna. Graham seemed merely preoccupied.

"I am famished," Lanie said. "Peter, let's raid the kitchen and get ourselves in trouble with the cook." She found his hand, rose, and tugged him toward the door.

"Your willing accomplice," Peter said, "particularly if biscuits, cheese, and cider are involved."

Graham closed the door and took the other wing chair. "Lanie's ears don't lie."

"Dr. Ramsey said he'd trust her hearing over the visual evidence from a sighted person. Who would want to run you down, Graham?"

"Run *us* down, though St. Didier and I experienced a similar incident in London." He recounted a tale that could have been mere dockside mischief or an attempt on his purse—and life.

"I don't like this," Morna said. "People are killed by footpads and runaway coaches."

Graham closed his eyes and leaned his head back against the cushions. "More often, they are merely injured and frightened. I find my reaction includes a goodly dose of rage."

And yet, his tone was deceptively calm. "Rage?"

"You were put at risk of death or injury, too, Morna, and that I cannot have. We will wrap up this jaunt to the shops sooner rather than later."

A younger Graham who'd not literally traveled around the world would never have taken such a firm tone. "I want to argue with you."

Graham patted her wrist without opening his eyes. "Have at it. I'm rusty, but still up to your weight, I hope."

Rusty. Bah. "We just got here, and Lanie and Peter are blossoming. I haven't bought half the books I want to add to the castle's collection. Then too, John MacIver will disown me if I don't bring him a fresh supply of fiddle strings and a new collection of airs."

And yet, that coach had *charged* at Graham. He'd been on Morna's right, positioned to take the impact if the carriage had struck them.

"Vicar will expect some fancy brandy from me," Graham said, opening his eyes, "and I did want to visit the local spice shops. How much can you accomplish in a day, Morna?"

"One day? How will you explain this to Peter and Lanie?" They were so happy, so pleased to be away from the castle and indulging in the fashionable outings a couple enjoyed when courting.

Though she would never admit it to a soul, Morna had been enjoying the same pleasures with Graham.

"I've concluded my necessary business," Graham said. "Our interview with Ramsey yielded little new information, and that was my primary motive for this excursion."

So brisk. So sensible. "You could explain to Peter that a similar mishap occurred in London, and you are concerned that somebody resents your return."

Graham pinched the bridge of his nose. "The situation is complicated."

The welter of frustration and upset plaguing Morna coalesced into disbelief. "You cannot suspect Peter of wishing you harm."

"I can't, you're right, but neither can I blithely confide in him. He will discuss every possibility and outlandish theory with Lanie, and they are so absorbed with each other that anybody could eavesdrop on them."

Morna had eavesdropped on them, nigh daily. "I hate this."

"I'm far from enchanted with the situation myself. Let's plan on leaving the day after tomorrow. In the alternative, you could stay behind with Peter and Lanie, and I'll return to the castle, but I object to that proposal even as I make it."

"Certainly not. If you think I'll leave you to make a journey alone on horseback along roads where any number of mischiefs could befall you, you are much mistaken."

"I can hire a carriage, Morna. I don't want to be the reason MacIver goes into a pout."

"Heed me, Graham MacNeil. We travel together or not at all."

He kissed her knuckles, then stroked the back of her hand. "I do so adore your scolds. We'll travel together the day after tomorrow, then. Let's tell the infantry at supper. They can raid every bakery in Edinburgh in the morning, but they'll take two footmen with them wherever they go."

Morna knew wheedling when she heard it. "As will you."

"As will *we*."

CHAPTER NINE

To St. Didier's astute eye, the trip to Edinburgh had brought changes in Graham, Earl of Dunhaven. His lordship's imposing physique had acquired not quite a swagger, but a greater freedom of movement. The earl's burr had become slightly more pronounced, the r's more inclined to roll, the vowels to subtle rumbling. He'd climbed out of the traveling coach wearing a cloak of finest black merino wool trimmed in the MacNeil plaid, and on him the garment had appeared dashing.

The smile he'd offered Morna MacKenzie when handing her down had been pure charm with a leavening of awe. And—St. Didier prided himself on his honesty—the lady had beamed right back at him. The primary salubrious influence had not been the smoky air of Edinburgh, apparently, but rather, the affectionate regard of a formidable female.

Peter and Miss Lanie had exhibited a similar state of romantic inebriation, though they were less discreet about it.

"What did Dr. Ramsey have to say?" St. Didier asked, returning *The Lay of the Last Minstrel* to its place of honor on the study's top bookshelf.

Dunhaven settled into a wing chair with a sigh. "Help yourself to the decanters. Ramsey apologized for his zeal and explained that he was the sole support of half a dozen siblings, give or take. He also informed us that he had very personal experience with the course of rheumatic illness. His mother was sorely afflicted, as he is now himself. He said nothing to the sheriff's man about his family's history with the malady, of course."

"His first post might have been his last if he'd been blamed for the countess's death. Very well, he's convicted of excessive self-interest, but absolved of murder. Are Peter and Lanie engaged?" Why was romance so easy for so many?

"Stop prowling and pour yourself a brandy, St. Didier. Peter and Lanie are not engaged that I know of, and you are not to meddle."

But meddling is what I do best. "Have you proposed to Miss MacKenzie?"

"No, I haven't, and you won't be proposing to her either."

"She's not in love with me. What would be the point?" St. Didier made free with an excellent French brandy. "You're not indulging?"

Dunhaven shook his head. "Sit. Please sit. After I'd served out an interminable penance escorting Morna to the milliner's, some fool tried to run me down with his coach and pair. The general consensus is, harm was intended."

St. Didier took a seat, set aside his brandy, and prepared to listen. "Details, Dunhaven. As many as you can recall."

The earl explained about Miss Lanie's aural recollections, about Miss MacKenzie having been at his side—fortunately so for his lordship—and about the hasty return to the MacNeil castle.

"I vow, St. Didier, I spent the longest forty-five miles known to the Scottish roads expecting highwaymen, kidnappers, and bandits to stop the coach around every turn, and there are hundreds of turns between here and Auld Reekie."

"You believe somebody tried to run you down in broad daylight on a busy Old Town street?"

"I must take the possibility seriously."

St. Didier sipped his brandy and chose his words carefully. "I'm not so sure. The walkways are narrow and often crowded. If the driver had misjudged, he could easily have injured half a dozen passersby, which would have set up a hue and cry. You say this happened at midday, meaning witnesses would have had a clear view of the vehicle, the horses, and the driver."

"The team was a pair of bays, no white markings. Plain bays, St. Didier, the most ubiquitous equines ever to be put in harness."

Bays were easily matched for that reason. Dark coat, black mane and tail. Not flashy, but tidy and handsome if well groomed.

Easily matched and easily forgotten. "The driver?"

"Peter says he wasn't in livery. Top hat, black greatcoat, skinny—that's about all Peter saw. Could have been some swell driving his own cattle, but in the usual course, a swell rides his fancy horse. He doesn't drive an empty coach and pair along a busy street and whip up the horses for no reason."

"I grant you the circumstances are ambiguous, but some of them weigh against intentional mischief—the crowded walkway, the full daylight, the failure of the incident to effect any real harm."

"Morna hauled me back by my arm, St. Didier. If she hadn't, I might well be sporting a shroud. It's a ruddy, rubbishing irony that I felt safer surrounded by felons in Sydney than I did strolling home from the milliner's in Edinburgh."

"I can think of one encouraging aspect to the situation: Peter was with you, as was Miss Lanie."

"Standing right behind us. Not two feet back. Believe me, I've lost sleep over that. Bad enough Morna was at my side, but Peter and Lanie... Lanie heard the coach coming, heard the crack of the whip. But she would not have let go of Peter's arm. She'd have fallen with him, just as Morna could have been knocked top over tail with me."

The earl had tormented himself with conjectures, and from what St. Didier had observed, they were accurate conjectures. Miss Lanie would have Peter by the figurative arm for all the rest of his days.

"Peter might well wish you to perdition," St. Didier said, "but he would not have put Miss Lanie within thirty miles of harm's way. I admit this with some reluctance, having a fondness for simple explanations over more arcane theories."

"Peter does not wish me harm," Dunhaven said tiredly. "He yearns to build steamships. I never want to set foot on another ship for as long as I live."

Which might not be very long. The words hung in the air like the stink of Brodie's cigars.

"Then, by all means, stay on land," St. Didier said. "I am a firm believer that beyond the dictates of honor, one should live as one pleases. Fate throws us into enough unpleasant situations without our adding to the total out of some misplaced sense of martyrdom."

A ghost of a smile touched Dunhaven's eyes. "You sound like Morna. Stubbornness parading around as common sense. Did Brodie behave in our absence?"

The topic of the runaway carriage was tabled, though St. Didier would consider particulars at length when he had the privacy to do so.

"Brodie was a gracious host, acquainting me with more MacNeil history, and more of Brodie's dashing exploits as a younger man, than Sir Walter could convey in a dozen stirring poems. I gather Brodie fancies himself something of a raconteur."

"Perhaps that's the fate of the failed fortune hunter. Brodie never made a Grand Tour—the Continent was already a dicey proposition thirty years ago—but he was allowed to sport about London for a few Seasons. He was too fond of the outlandish wager and too obviously in need of coin. Got his face slapped more than once and still has a few acquaintances from those halcyon days of stupidity, sex, and song."

"You don't like your uncle very much, do you?"

Dunhaven's brows rose. "I do like him, in small doses. Brodie has been a fixture at the castle for my entire life."

"He would have been the logical guardian for Peter and the estate following your grandfather's death, if John wasn't to be relied upon."

The earl yawned behind his hand and took the plaid blanket from the back of his chair. "John would have resented that. I always found it odd that both John and Brodie were overly fond of their wee drams, but they were not drinking companions."

"Perhaps the difference in age accounts for that, or a competing need for best-storyteller honors. What will you do now?"

"About runaway carriages and London footpads?" Dunhaven wrapped the blanket about his shoulders.

"One does wonder. Third time's the charm and all that."

"Then you have abandoned the unfortunate-accident theory of my anticipated demise?"

The earl looked to be settling in for a nap. Time for plain speaking. "Unfortunate accidents have brought this family to grief on at least one previous occasion, so no, I cannot entirely abandon that theory. I add to it the possibility that somebody is trying to frighten you off, Dunhaven, to send you back to parts distant rather than hasten you to your eternal reward."

"I cannot go anywhere just yet. I might want to speak with Ramsey again." He closed his eyes and moved about on the cushions. "Ramsey's mother suffered years of agonies due to her afflictions. Ramsey knew what lay in store for Grandmama and assured us that her death was at least in part a mercy."

"A mercy... provided by her loving husband? A devoted grandson? *Her own physician?*" The situation was taking on the complexities of a Shakespeare tragedy.

"Ramsey didn't want the sheriff's man speculating in that direction. More pertinent to present troubles, Ramsey did not appear surprised to learn that I was in Edinburgh. Morna noted that Ramsey still occasionally corresponds with Brodie—perhaps they share a fondness for ornate snuffboxes. On the other hand, my arrival on Albion's shores was remarked by the penny press, which is read by half the realm. 'Poisoning Peer Returns'—that sort of thing. Perhaps Ramsey has the same penchant for reading London gossip that Uncle has."

That sort of thing would have destroyed a lesser man. "Do you suspect Ramsey?"

"I suspect him of lying, but not of murder." Dunhaven toed off his boots and put largish feet clad in thick wool stockings up on the hassock. "He is abidingly loyal to his family and sensible by nature. He wasn't about to commit murder, however merciful, to end his patient's suffering. The longer he kept the countess alive and cheerful, the more certain his own successful career became."

"Which leaves the question previously posed: What will you do now?"

"Send you to Edinburgh to retrieve a package I could not entrust to the mail."

Now was not the time for the earl's designated spare eyes and ears to be sent on foolish errands. "You began your day in Edinburgh. Did you forget something?"

"The item will not be ready until the end of the week, and you are to keep the nature of your journey in confidence. I will have more detailed orders for you once I've had a chance to recover from my travels."

Meaning the earl had schemes to refine. "Upon whom am I spying?"

"Nobody. You are retrieving a small package from a jewelry shop in the Old Town. Now please leave me in peace. Morna will want to review the latest developments with you, but we're not apprising Peter or Lanie of any suppositions or theories at the moment. One doesn't want young love tainted by old suspicions or new threats."

The earl crossed his feet in a manner that signaled the commencement of a long overdue forty winks.

"You trust Miss MacKenzie with information you haven't confided in your own brother."

"I'm not buying rings for my brother either. I can't exactly propose to the woman when she was nearly run down standing next to me. If, however, our situation should grow more encouraging—I am counting on you, St. Didier, to support the arrival of that happy day—then one must be ready with the appropriate tokens."

St. Didier withdrew in silence, though it was clear the Earl of Dunhaven had been utterly flattened by a force greater than the heaviest coach and four in full gallop. Miss Morna MacKenzie's patience was to be rewarded, as was Graham MacNeil's.

St. Didier was happy for them both. Beyond happy—also beyond worried.

When Graham had gone periodically missing as a youth, Morna had known exactly where to find him, and that, at least, hadn't changed.

"What's his breeding?" Peter asked from within the shadowed depths of the stable.

"Clyde draft on the dam side," Graham replied. "Supposedly a first-rate steeplechaser for a sire. Pass me the soft brush, will you?"

Morna remained in the shadow of the stable's overhang, reluctant to interrupt, more reluctant to return to the castle without having confronted Graham.

"Mr. Bell is already running a steamship service on the River Clyde," Peter said. "*The Comet* can travel as fast as a trotting horse on steam power alone and, with a following wind, even faster."

"Are you wooing Lanie with talk of steamships, then, Peter?"

A slight pause ensued. "We talk about other things."

"Such as?"

"Wool, sheep, goats, rabbits. Lanie loves animals, and she loves wool too."

"Seems your interests overlap in the area of steam-powered looms. Design her a loom that will make satin from fancy wool. She might like that."

She might adore Peter for even thinking of such a creation. Virgin merino might serve. Lanie would know.

"Lanie says satin is pleasant to wear because of the graceful drape, but hard to clean. It's also beyond dear, when it's woven from silk."

Silk and steamships. Was a courtship ever based on such an unlikely foundation?

"Take Lanie up before you in the saddle," Graham said. "I'll trade you the brush for the hoof-pick."

"Up before me?"

"Use my saddle—it's roomy—and take True, here. He can manage the weight, provided you don't gallop or have him out too long. Lanie loved to ride before the damned measles befell her. She went everywhere on her pony, tagging after Morna and me."

"She did?"

The distinctive sound of metal scraping against the hard sole of a horse's hoof interrupted the conversation.

"Lanie was nine when she fell ill," Graham said. "Of course she loved her pony. You loved yours too."

And yet, Morna mused, Lanie never talked about that pony, nor had she gone to visit him as she recovered. He was enjoying a long, lazy retirement for want of other children to ride him.

"You think she'd like to ride double with me?"

The scraping sound came again. "I think if you offer, and she realizes that she will be all but sitting in your lap, your arms nearly around her, she will develop an impossible longing to return to the saddle—provided you're doing the steering."

"We'd have to walk everywhere."

"At first. True has a lovely canter, and his trot floats. Steam and speed are not the solution to every challenge, laddie. Give Lanie the chance to feel the wind in her hair and the power of the horse beneath her. Save the steamships for later."

"I've ridden on *The Comet*," Peter said. "All that power and not a horse in sight."

"All the noise, the dirt, the thought of the men, women, and children toiling away for a pittance in the mines so the steam engine can befoul the air for miles around with its coal smoke. Very romantic."

Graham leavened the observation with humor, but to Morna's mind, he'd made a telling point.

"Lanie doesn't like the noise or stink either." A reluctant admission on Peter's part. "Are you taking True out now?"

"I am not. I needed to do some thinking, and his company calms the mind."

"Might I try a hack on him?"

"Please do. He's had more than a week to laze about while we were doing the pretty in Edinburgh. When you've tried his paces, invite Lanie to climb aboard."

"She doesn't have a riding habit."

How had Peter come across that fact?

"Then tell her to wear breeches. Many ladies do, under their habits, but challenge her to get back on the horse, Peter. Life can't be an endless knitting project, no matter how luxurious the wool."

"I've told her that. I've said almost those exact words, and she gets very persnickety, and what-would-you-have-me-do, and then I feel like an idiot. She is so capable that I don't realize how little vision she has left."

"In the dark, vision doesn't count for much, does it? I'll gather up True's saddle and bridle. You find Lanie some breeches and make sure they're freshly laundered. She'll smell the dirt a mile off."

"Right. I might have an old pair. Morna never throws anything away. Drives Brodie daft to have his socks darned when he'd rather have new."

"Brodie would grumble about his morning porridge being served with too much butter and honey. Away with you."

"I might tell Lanie that other part, about vision not counting for much in the dark."

Naughty, naughty, naughty, but Peter was no longer a schoolboy, and Lanie wasn't a schoolgirl. How had that happened?

"Tell her anything you like," Graham said, "but you won't be *showing* her until she's wearing your ring, or you will have any number of reasons for wishing me and my fists back to the Antipodes."

"You're old and slow," Peter said, his bootheels rapping on the cobbles. "You'll never—blast!"

"If you treat Lanie with anything less than utmost honor, I will do much more than trip you as you strut along. Do I make myself clear, Peter MacNeil?"

"Are you *showing* Morna utmost honor?"

Morna was touched that Peter would ask and that his tone had been serious rather than teasing.

"Of course, and if my judgment should lapse in that regard, St. Didier—emphasis on the Saint—will sort me out before you can lay a hand on me, and that's assuming Morna herself won't mercilessly explain to me the error of my ways, which she is perfectly capable of doing."

Oh, Graham.

"They're formidable, aren't they, the MacKenzie sisters?"

"Veritable steamships in skirts. Silk-furred bunnies in bonnets. Be off with you."

Peter marched forth from the barn without looking back and without noticing Morna lurking beneath the overhang. His goal was clearly to entice Lanie into an outing on horseback, and Peter was a fellow with a prodigious ability to pursue a goal.

"Morna MacKenzie," Graham called, "you'd best show yourself. True and I both know you're out there."

She stepped into the barn aisle. "How did you know?"

"True probably heard you breathing—his ears flicked back in your direction—but in the middle of a stable, the scent of attar of roses does stand out. In a good way, of course. How much did you hear?"

Graham stood beside his great dark horse, stroking the beast's neck and looking delectable in worn riding attire and scuffed boots.

"You meant to go for a hack, didn't you?" A youthful Graham had claimed to do his best thinking in the saddle.

"True has other business on his agenda for the morning. Are you preparing to scold me, Morna? Peter's intentions are honorable. I simply meant to remind him that his behavior must measure up to the same standard."

"I know you." She marched up to him, took the horse's lead rope from him, and returned True to his loose box.

"To my eternal delight, you do know me," Graham said, watching her remove the horse's halter and lead rope. "I count our association among my dearest blessings."

"You are pondering that business in Edinburgh, with the coach. You've discussed it with St. Didier. He's wishing it was just an accident, but wishful thinking is not his forte."

"He should spend some years in a penal colony. His wishful-thinking skills will blossom like heather in high summer."

"You are concerned," Morna said, leaving the stall and securely latching the half door, "that somebody wishes you dead and doesn't much care if I'm hurt in the process. You are telling yourself that you should keep your distance from me."

Graham took the halter from her and hung it on the hook by the stall door. "Am I, now?"

"Working up to it. You were nearly silent at supper last night, and you missed breakfast this morning. I know the look you get when you're worrying a problem. I don't want to wake up on Monday to learn that you've left for London, Graham."

Had she not been glowering at him, Morna might have missed the flash of guilt that passed through his eyes.

"Not London," he said, "but I did think to look in on the properties in Glasgow, Peebles, and Inverness. I can wait until summer to visit Mull, and we've just made the rounds in Edinburgh."

"Keep moving, and the enemy can't track you so easily?" Morna wanted to smack him, and hug him, and decimate his foes. She instead opened the door to the saddle room, a tidy, oak-paneled space that held saddles, bridles, brushes, blankets, and all manner of horse gear.

The scent was mostly leather and horse, with an undertone of the lanolin used to keep the leather supple. No grooms were lounging about on a midmorning break, which was fortunate.

Graham joined her in the saddle room while she located the bridle designated for his horse.

"Morna, I honestly don't know what to make of that mishap in Edinburgh. If somebody hadn't feebly attempted to waylay me on the London docks, I might be able to ignore the carriage incident. Had not somebody given Grandmama an excessive dose of the poppy and let me take the blame, I might be able to ignore both the London and Edinburgh episodes, but I cannot. St. Didier was beside me in London, and you were at my side in Edinburgh."

Morna dodged around him, closed the saddle room door, and wheeled to face him. "Precisely. I was *beside you*. I spotted the danger and pulled you from harm's way. You are *safer* with me on hand, so we'll not be having any more talk of you making a *target* of yourself by parading around half of Scotland *on your own*. Do you hear me, Graham MacNeil?"

"Your logic wants work, but I'm sure they can hear you in Glasgow."

"Good, and my logic is sound. You ran off to Australia, taking the blame for what you still hope is an accident, trying to protect me, or Peter, or Grandpapa, or John. Very noble of you, but have you ever stopped to think that had you allowed us to fight for you, you might not have needed to go away?"

"I was transported." Said very softly, about three inches from Morna's nose. "I did not *run off*, and yes, Morna, I had years to consider every possibility, including the possibility that I'd left a cold-blooded killer behind, not some innocent family member, and me half a world away when my kith and kin needed me most."

He'd not merely considered that possibility, he'd clearly been tormented by it. Morna poked him in the chest, which was like poking the castle walls.

"Then don't"—poke—"hare off"—poke—"alone." She smoothed

her palm over the spot she'd poked. "Safety in numbers, Graham. We don't even know for a fact that you're in danger."

He drew a forefinger down her nose. "I am well aware of the uncertainties, and that alone has kept me from parading around, as you put it, on my own. I seized upon the notion of pleading guilty to Grandmama's death, and it seemed like a solution to several problems. I could not be talked out of it. Grandpapa tried. I wanted desperately for the family to put the whole sorry tragedy behind us. I want these incidents and episodes to stop too. I am lecturing myself about not leaping to conclusions, but the conclusions leap at me, Morna."

"No mishaps have befallen you here at the castle. Stay here, watch and wait. I'll watch and wait with you."

The blasted, wretched, blighted man apparently intended to think about Morna's offer, which would not do at all.

She sank her fingers into his hair, looked him straight in his blue, blue eyes—fair warning—then kissed him like the long-lost lover he very nearly was.

CHAPTER TEN

Kissing Morna was coming home and rejoicing and all the wondrous emotions rolled into a sense of lightness that spread out from Graham's middle to engulf his whole being. His mind was so much sparkling jubilation, his heart sang paeans, while his wits danced clear to John O'Groats and back.

And his body knew damned well what sort of dance should come next.

For long moments, Graham simply marveled. He and Morna had kissed a few times years before, clumsily, sweetly, and without guile. Morna had been working on her strategy since then, ambushing him with a hand around his waist pulling him closer, then sliding that hand down over his bum.

She tucked in, leaving nothing to the imagination, and all the while, she plundered with lips and sighs and—ye gods—her tongue.

"Mercy," Graham whispered, easing his mouth away. "Cease fire, Morna, please, or I'll be begging for what I haven't earned."

She muttered something, which gave Graham an excuse to whisper against her temple. "Didn't catch that. My ears are buzzing." No exaggeration.

"I said you would not have to beg."

"Wheedle?"

She shook her head, and Graham gathered her close and put his chin on her crown.

One moment, they'd been arguing about safety and runaway coaches. The next... "Morna, you have resorted to unfair tactics."

"Then I am done and through fighting fair with you, you wretched bounder."

Never had the term been so laden with affection. "At this rate, I will soon be done and through with thinking straight. We must be sensible." Nothing sensible was happening behind the falls of Graham's riding breeches. He took a step back and led Morna by the hand to an old chest topped with a folded Stewart plaid blanket. The red was faded, but the wool was still thick and soft...

Down, laddie. The intensity of Graham's desire baffled him. He'd learned years ago to control himself, to think of menacing icebergs the size of Edinburgh Castle, of hard labor and exhaustion that went on for years. Dull, sad, boring realities that doused a conflagration of physical yearning down to a flickering notion.

With Morna, he was eyeing the lock on the door and entertaining disrespectful thoughts toward the royal tartan.

She took a seat on the chest and tugged Graham to the place beside her. "I've missed you, sir. Here." She tapped her heart. "I told myself I was infatuated and I'd outgrow such nonsense. I told myself my feelings were unreciprocated, because no other theory explained how easily or thoroughly you set me aside that long-ago summer."

"If I reciprocated your feelings any more intensely, your skirts would be around your waist, and St. Didier would have to thrash me into next week."

"No, he wouldn't. You told Peter I was more than capable of sorting you out, Graham. If you persist with your plan to once again abandon the castle, this time to draw enemy fire, I will decamp for Edinburgh and become a fashionable poet."

She'd do it too. Morna was a talented writer, and she did not issue idle threats.

Graham kissed her knuckles, earning himself a whiff of roses. "I cannot keep you safe in Edinburgh and also manage matters here at the castle, Morna."

"Such a pity. I cannot keep you safe if you are determined to martyr yourself once more in the Clan MacNeil tradition. I will not lose you again, Graham, most especially not to your muddleheaded notions of honor. We fight together, or you can go back to selling your spices and complaining about parrots."

The whole time she lectured him, she stroked her fingers over his hand.

"You are so brave, Morna MacKenzie." So damnably, relentlessly brave. She would banish him from her heart and take up poetry. In a week flat, Sir Walter would find himself with daunting competition.

Or so Morna would have Graham believe. The cherishing caress of her fingers suggested the plan might cost her a few regrets.

"If I'm brave," Morna said, "then I must get my courage from the local whisky, because the same shortcoming afflicts you sorely, sir."

She proposed a shift in tactics—from Graham protecting his family, to Graham and Morna protecting their future and their family.

Which left no choice, really, given the alternative. So simple and so terrifying. "You ask a lot, Morna. I can't lose you either."

She slipped an arm around his waist and laid her head on his shoulder. "Are we agreed, then? You are not to go off on the high road alone, taking unnecessary risks, plotting and scheming without consulting me?"

Not so fast, Miss MacKenzie. "We are agreed that *neither of us* will go off alone, taking unnecessary risks, plotting and scheming without prior mutual consultation, correct?"

She made him wait, but that was as it should be. "We are agreed."

The moment was right for more kissing, sweet, slow kisses that both soothed and aroused. Graham took the initiative, which apparently surprised Morna, but she was soon into the spirit of the undertaking, imperiling Graham's sanity and making him so very glad to be alive.

He was mentally exploring the notion of hefting Morna into his lap when an unwelcome thought intruded.

"Saddle," he muttered against her lips.

She wiggled closer. "Kiss me."

"Morna, darling, Peter and Lanie will soon be back and expecting..."

Morna kissed him, and Graham's command of basic English went flying. He retaliated with a glancing caress to her breast, which inspired her to panting.

"We must stop," Graham said, single-syllable words being barely within his grasp. "Peter and Lanie will come."

Morna nodded. "Right. Blast and botheration."

They stayed like that, breathing together, frustrated, pleased, and yearning, until Graham rose and drew Morna to her feet.

"I'm sending St. Didier to Edinburgh," Graham said. "The nature of his errand of record is sentimental and has nothing to do with old business or accidents."

Morna dropped his hand and brushed at her skirts. "He told me. He's to retrieve some item from the shops that you did not want to entrust to the mail. I don't mean to trample your privacy, Graham. Lanie and I will still whisper in corners, and Brodie and I have a limerick competition going. He's better at it, also very naughty. I inspire him to greatness, or so he claims."

I love you. The words popped into Graham's head, courtesy of a heart that dealt in eternal verities and courage, even when some sense was wanted. Morna was putting aside a moment limned in glory, rolling up her sleeves, and planting both boots firmly on the ground. Her tone of voice was the usual brisk, pragmatic flow of words Graham associated with her, but a softness lingered in her eyes, and that hand brushing at her skirts hinted of shyness.

Bless this contradictory, dear, unstoppable woman. Graham kissed her cheek. "You grab the bridle and saddle pad. I'll take the saddle. The horse is already groomed."

She took down the bridle, fetched a clean saddle pad, and paused at the door as Graham hefted the saddle over his arm.

"You mean it, then?" she asked, all careful diffidence. "You won't disappear on me again?"

"I mean it, Morna. I won't disappear." The promise made him uneasy, but the prospect of Morna larking about Edinburgh's narrow, busy streets on her own... Not to be contemplated.

Morna's hand was on the door latch when the door opened from the other side.

"Oh." Peter looked from Morna to Graham. "Getting the gear together. Right. Lanie will be down to the stable directly. She's mad keen to try riding double. She went to find a pair of Morna's riding boots."

"Let's saddle up True," Graham said, carefully avoiding Morna's eye. "You can try his paces while we wait for Lanie."

He sidled past Morna through the door, forcing Peter to move along ahead of him. Graham nearly dropped the saddle, though, as Morna delivered a discreet pat to his bum before exiting the saddle room herself. She passed Peter the bridle and saddle pad, then went sashaying on her way.

"Are you and Morna arguing?" Peter asked, watching her go.

"Working out some agreements," Graham said. "Morna is a talented negotiator."

Peter snorted. "Next, you'll be trying to woo her with talk of icebergs and spiders. Take her out on a hack when we get a mild afternoon."

"Excellent advice, assuming my horse is free to accommodate me."

Peter smacked his arm, and Graham went about saddling True. All was far from right with the world, but Graham was right with Morna, and that mattered a very great deal.

❦

"D'ye fancy Auld Reekie?" Uncle Brodie asked, interrupting St. Didier's reading for the third time.

St. Didier had sought the light in the library, and Uncle Brodie had come prowling along about a quarter hour later, just as the MacNeil clan history of the wars for Scottish independence was getting interesting.

Kidnappings, midnight raids, spies, and mad gallops, all with a dash of sleeping with the enemy and disappearing to France in the face of gale-force winds. Heady stuff.

Brodie, by contrast, seemed to be a common variety of busybody bachelor. "I do enjoy Edinburgh," St. Didier said. "The city doesn't sprawl quite the way London does, and the company is varied."

"We don't put on airs, ye mean. The man with initiative and some sound ideas can earn the respect of all, while the strutting peacock wins universal contempt, despite his fancy dress and lofty manners."

Which did not explain why the likes of Sir Walter Scott himself showed slavish adoration of the Regent, the biggest peacock of them all, though His Majesty's gait was more of a waddle than a strut.

"Agreed." St. Didier turned a page in hopes of appealing to Brodie's manners. "Edinburgh Society is a refreshing change from some of the company farther to the south."

"I spent many a fine hour in that company," Brodie said, taking up the cast-iron poker from the hearth stand and attacking the fire. "Many a fine hour. Of course, we didn't insist on ceremony to such a ridiculous degree as you young people do in these modern times. A handsome lad whose sister was married to an earl was welcome everywhere. Now, the London hostesses want to count his teeth and see his ledger books before they'll admit him as a guest."

Balding, white-haired Brodie hadn't seen the inside of a Mayfair drawing room for at least twenty years, but he spoke as an expert observer. He finished making a racket with the poker and replaced it on the hearth stand.

"Do you miss London?" St. Didier asked, running a finger down the page of his book as if trying to recall the spot where he'd been most recently interrupted.

"Indeed, I do. Always so much to do, so much to see. My loyal correspondents keep me informed, though. London has a Philharmonic Society now, made up of the best musicians, and I'm told the performances are sublime. The Royal Academy exhibitions are unparalleled displays of artistic talent, and one finds more wit in the London Society pages than in all of Edinburgh's dreary poets and philosophers combined."

The London slums were also unparalleled, the stench of the Thames far from sublime, and the London skies nigh perpetually dreary with coal smoke.

"Shall you journey back south with me?" St. Didier asked, though he was being a bit unkind, baiting the former great man of the world, bachelor-beyond-compare, and international authority on everything fashionable.

"One is tempted," Brodie said, opening each drawer of the library desk and banging it closed in succession. "One is sorely tempted. When might you be departing?"

"My itinerary is uncertain. Scotland in springtime is not to be missed, but the lure of the London Season is strong too." Dunhaven's habit of semi-prevarication was apparently contagious.

"I might consider a jaunt south, but for the fact that Graham has so recently returned. One doesn't want to appear disloyal, nipping off to the blandishments of civilization just as the family scandal takes his place as the earl. Whatever else is true, Graham has served his penance for killing my sister, and he is owed the appearance of deference, if not actual respect."

"You think he administered an excess of medication to his grandmother?" Graham himself was very certain he had not.

"What other conclusion can one draw when the lad confessed at the first opportunity, and the old earl—as stubborn a curmudgeon as ever wore plaid—permitted the boy to be sentenced? I had my differences with the previous earl—vociferous, entrenched differences—but he allowed the law to take its course, and in that decision, I must support him in memory."

St. Didier gave up on MacNeil family history, added a square of peat to the fire, and watched the flames blaze up.

"You don't think John, for instance, might have offered the countess an extra cup of tea and added a dose of patent remedy in a semi-inebriated fog? Might Miss Morna MacKenzie—a prodigiously busy woman—have failed to measure a dose accurately? Could Graham have been protecting another party by pleading guilty?"

Brodie went to one of the tall library windows and struck a contemplative pose, hands behind his back, gaze on the park rolling away from the formal gardens.

"You don't understand the nature of the Scot, Mr. St. Didier. We are honest to a fault. If Graham said he was responsible, he was responsible. We take our honor seriously here, unlike some other places I could name, where chivalrous words fall from every pair of masculine lips while a determined blind eye is turned on the lame soldiers begging in every church doorway."

Brodie apparently read more than the Society pages of the London penny press. "I can assure you, no beggars darken the door of Mayfair's houses of worship." Perhaps the ultimate irony, that the most prosperous, when displaying their piety, were spared the sight of those who'd sacrificed limbs and eyes to safeguard that wealth.

"And I can assure you, Mr. St. Didier, that if Graham confessed to a misdeed—let's not call it a crime—then Graham himself was responsible. I grant you, my sister's sickroom would have made the Royal Mile look deserted by comparison, but Graham stepped forward out of honor, not guile."

Hardly dishonorable to protect the weak from a perhaps fatal dose of judicial excess. "Do you recall the physician coming under suspicion? I, for one, cannot, but inquiries in that direction should have been made."

Brodie rocked up on his toes, then settled back. "Dr. Ramsey was young, and in a physician, that is a fortunate characteristic because his education is right up to the moment. He was not some doddering old relic spouting Galen and Hippocrates. Had Ramsey been guilty of malpractice, he would have said the countess simply expired in her sleep. No scandal, no accusations. Her death would have been sad, but not entirely unexpected. Thus no suspicion should have been cast on the young physician. You were here at the time. You saw the tragedy unfold firsthand. Why pry into the past like this, St. Didier?"

Because you won't let me read in peace, you old fusspot. And yet, only when the topic of the countess's death had arisen had Brodie stopped making noise and behaving as the neighborhood's most spoiled child. The topic mattered to him, perhaps because Graham's supposed guilt sat ill with him too.

"I have no family worth the name," St. Didier said, joining Brodie at the window. "I was fascinated by the sense that the MacNeils were loyal to their own, no matter the specifics of pedigree or provenance. Graham brought me home with him in part because I'd nowhere else to go that summer, and then to see tragedy descend from out of nowhere... I will not soon forget my first visit to the castle."

The truth was, St. Didier would never shirk a sense of somehow being responsible for the whole sorry situation. If he'd been more observant, if he'd paid closer attention to the ailing countess, if he'd spent less time with his nose in books and more time watching the staff, the countess's death might have been prevented.

Or Dunhaven's transportation averted.

"Blessed Saint Andrew, that boy is daft." Brodie was peering intently across the garden at the greening expanse of parkland. "They're going to break their fool heads if they aren't careful, and that is Graham's horse they're larking about on."

A couple rode double across the park on a big, sturdy bay gelding, whose smooth, rhythmic canter would have done a rocking horse proud.

"They look to be enjoying themselves." Miss Lanie was astride before Peter, her feet in the stirrups, her hands buried in thick, dark mane. Peter held the reins, his arms necessarily on either side of Miss Lanie's waist.

"We all fret about our Lanie," Brodie said. "Measles is a cruel disease, but it spared her hearing and some of her vision. She never complains. She missed the countess most, you know, being the youngest. The girl was lost for months after her ladyship's death."

Peter brought the gelding from a canter to a walk and turned the horse back in the direction of the stable. Lanie beamed, the horse plodded along like an oversized lamb, and Peter found it necessary to put the reins in one hand, the better to keep his free arm around Miss Lanie's waist.

Such concern for the lady, and at a meek little toddle. "Peter is being a bit bold, don't you think?" Of course, he was on home territory, and Miss Lanie was encouraging him.

"MacNeil men tend to boldness," Brodie said, "and perhaps that appeals to Lanie. As a child, she was a fixture in the countess's sitting room, curled in a chair much too large for her, or napping in a corner of the sofa. We always knew where to find her, and when the girl was so ill, the countess would read to her. Lanie became the devoted little nurse when her ladyship's ailments worsened. Quite touching, really, and all a very long time ago."

Lanie relaxed back against Peter's chest, and St. Didier knew a pang of sympathy for the gallant cavalier having to deal with that temptation while on horseback. Boldness could extract a toll on a young fellow's dignity.

"Miss Lanie was with the countess the night her ladyship died, wasn't she?" St. Didier asked, collecting his book from the reading table.

"She might well have been, but you're not to ask her, St. Didier. I forbid it in the name of gentlemanly discretion. Lanie was a child, and you must not upset her now, when she's finding some happiness in life."

Brodie had no authority to forbid anybody anything, and his uncharacteristic vehemence convinced St. Didier of one thing: Even Brodie wasn't certain of Graham's guilt.

"You assure me Graham would not have pleaded guilty to protect Morna, Peter, John, or even the old earl," St. Didier said, "but are you confident he would not have pleaded guilty to protect a young girl recently rendered blind and trying to be the countess's best companion and supporter?"

Brodie shook his head. "Don't be daft. Don't be a foolish, arrogant, meddling Englishman. Lanie was and is all but blind. She would never have presumed to have handled her ladyship's medications. Never." He left the library, still shaking his head and muttering.

St. Didier tried to resume reading, but the medieval battles of Clan MacNeil had lost some of their luster compared to the family's present struggles and recent past. Brodie vehemently protested the possibility of Lanie's involvement in the countess's death, but was he protesting too much, and if so, whom was *he* protecting?

Lanie's yarn and knitting needles lay in her lap, and Eustace, in all his fat, black, feline glory, sat on the arm of her chair, purring loudly. To Morna's eye, they made a picture of domestic contentment by the hearth in the family parlor—a deceptive picture.

"Peter says St. Didier is leaving for Edinburgh next week." Lanie stroked the cat, who head-butted her hand shamelessly. "We were just in Edinburgh. If St. Didier had a burning need to see the sights, why not go with us?"

Since Lanie had slid off True's back into Peter's waiting arms two hours ago, *Peter says* had become the beginning of every other sentence from her mouth, up from the usual every fourth sentence of recent days.

"You and Peter must have spent your whole ride in discussion."

"Hard not to, when one is sitting on the same horse. I'd forgotten, Morna, how glorious it is to be in the saddle. You tell a horse to go, and he goes. You tell him to go faster, and he flies. Peter says we can hack out as often as I like, and he'll find us a big, draft-cross mount like True."

Such longing infused those words. "Peter putting you in the saddle has made you think, hasn't it?" Morna knotted off her blue thread and sorted through her workbasket for the white. "You are wondering what else you've left behind that you might revisit, despite your blindness."

"I'm not truly, completely blind. When I play the pianoforte, I can see my hands. I could see True's mane and Peter's hands on the reins. He has lovely hands."

More longing, more wistfulness. "Peter is a lovely man." Not as lovely as Graham, not as fierce or substantial, but for Lanie, Peter would suit wonderfully. "If he's waiting for me to be married off before he proposes to you, tell him he needn't."

"Proposes to me?" The yearning turned to caution. "No man wants a blind woman for the mother of his children, Morna. Peter is sweet and dear, and we're friends—wonderful friends—but orange blossoms aren't part of the bouquet."

"Lanie, listen to Peter's voice when he talks to me or Graham or Brodie, then listen to his voice when he talks to you. He is in awe of you, as we all are, but Peter holds you in very special regard."

"What are you working on?" Lanie tried to cease petting the cat and got a lapful of feline in response. The beast settled right on top of the knitting and began kneading away.

"Graham reminded me that I haven't done much work with the MacKenzie plaid. MacNeil colors are everywhere, but not so, our own. I'm trying to embroider the MacKenzie motto on a handkerchief as a practice project."

"'I shine, not burn,'" Lanie said. "Strange motto. I do like our stag's head, though."

The coat of arms belonged personally to the clan chief, whom Morna had never met. "Lanie, you mustn't be afraid to dream. Peter loves you as a man loves the woman he wants to marry. At first, I thought he was merely infatuated. But his affection for you hasn't waned or wavered, and if you could see how he looks at you..."

"And there you have it: I cannot see—how he looks at me or much of anything. I tell myself that's simply my lot, and if I could see, then Peter would not read to me by the hour, but I don't want his pity, Morna. I don't want him taking care of me when I can't take care of him."

This conversation was long, long overdue and also well timed. "To whom does Peter confide his dreams, Lanie?"

"To me, by the hour. Steam and electricity and gas lighting and rail travel... Peter is nothing if not imaginative."

"To whom does Peter confide his troubles?"

Lanie scratched the cat's chin. "He can't very well rely on Brodie to hear him out, can he? Brodie isn't quite mean-spirited, but his favorite topic of conversation is his own mythically marvelous past, his latest shrewdly bargained snuffbox purchase, and his own expert, completely uninformed opinions."

"Peter could rely on me, on old John MacIver, on the vicar's oldest daughter, on—"

"She fancies him," Lanie said, hand going still. "Vera does. She told me as much. Said younger sons had to marry the daughters of gentlemen, and a vicar is a gentleman."

"Vera Conroy has no more chance of marrying an earl's heir than she does of becoming famous for her Italian arias." The poor thing could not, as it was said, carry a tune in a bucket. "The point is, Peter turns to you for counsel, support, and inspiration. You know his favorite dishes and what foods he won't touch even to be polite."

"Can't stand pickled herring," Lanie said, shifting to the cat's shoulders. "Tried it once and went howling from the kitchen. The old cook thought it was funny. I don't miss her."

What a memory Lanie had—for all things Peter. "I'd like you to consider a theory, Elaine Marie Margaret MacKenzie."

"I'm listening."

"Peter esteems you greatly, but he's concerned that you regard him as a mere friend. He's concerned that he hasn't much to offer you and that you don't need him."

Morna waited for an explosion of disbelief.

Lanie's hand went still on the cat. "Peter has means. I know he does. The old earl saw to it, and so did the countess. Graham has personal means too, Morna. Means other than the earldom."

"The issue isn't means, Lanie, it's pride, tenderheartedness, and the certain knowledge that if a friendship is all you'll grant him, then he'd rather have that than a bungled proposal and awkwardness."

The cat switched his tail. Lanie ignored him. "You and Graham have discussed this?"

Luceo... I shine, or perhaps the sense was *I am luminous*. "More or less."

"Morna?"

Morna set aside her embroidery. "Graham foiled an attack on the London docks, Lanie, and he's concerned that the runaway coach was another attempt on his life."

"Those horses did not run away, Morna. I know what I heard."

The cat glowered at his negligent human, though Lanie of course could not see the creature's displeasure.

"In London, Graham was with St. Didier, and we accompanied him in Edinburgh. Being Graham..."

"He'll worry for everybody but himself. Will he banish himself again, Morna? Before, when Grandmama died, nobody explained to me what was going on. Then she was gone, and everybody was whispering, but nobody was *talking*. The next thing I knew, Graham was gone too."

"I hated him for that," Morna said, "but he was doing what he thought best."

The cat dug his claws into the knitting and got summarily deposited on the carpet. "Being honorable. Why is it honorable when men do it but featherbrained when anybody else does?"

"Does what?"

"Make dunderheaded decisions all on their own? Women are headstrong or stubborn or unruly when they write their own pamphlets, run their own shops, or refuse the first offer of marriage to come along, but men are determined and persistent and independent."

What would Graham say about that logic? The cat cast Morna a winsome look, which she ignored.

"Do you and Peter discuss men's stubbornness?"

Lanie took up her needles and pushed the yarn around. "We talk about almost everything. I want to kiss him, Morna, but I don't want to *discuss it*. I want to do it."

"Then you simply tell him, 'I would like to kiss you,' and give him a moment to decide whether he wants to be kissed. Then suit your actions to your words."

"What if I miss? I can't see him when we're that close." Lanie wasn't blushing. She was sorting tactics.

"I haven't taken a survey, but I believe most people kiss with their eyes closed. Frame his handsome face in your hands, get your bearings, and trust Peter to lend a hand." Or a pair of lips to go along with his heart, soul, mind, and strength.

"You make it sound simple."

"Simple, yes, and sweet, too, I hope." Not necessarily dignified, but that was part of the magic.

"I must think." Lanie began knitting, finished six stitches, then stopped. "You know, there's one topic Peter does not wish to discuss, ever."

Money? Intimacies? His amatory forays at school? "Only one?"

"The night Grandmama died. I have some idea what happened,

Morna, or what was supposed to have happened. I was with her at the time. But the details are fuzzy, and I keep thinking they matter. Peter says to set it all aside, that we must put it behind us. He says something like that at the merest mention of Grandmama's death."

Morna had not thought to discuss masculine pride, much less kissing strategy with Lanie, and had most assuredly not intended to bring up Grandmama's death.

"What do you recall, Lanie?"

Lanie's hands resumed moving with the steady competence of the seasoned knitter. "Grandmama's room was always warm. I loved her, but I also loved that her apartment was the one place in the whole castle that was always warm. I could not read anymore, but I could listen to her tell me stories, and she loved to tell them. I often fell asleep in the wing chair while she regaled me with tales of how she and Grandpapa courted. She'd tell me about our own mama and papa and about when John and Graham were small."

What a treasure trove. "I heard some of those stories. Grandmama knew how to spin a narrative."

"I wanted to take care of her, as she had taken care of me, but all I could really offer her was my company."

What would Graham have given for some company during his years of exile? What would Morna have given for an hour here or there with him, even if all they did was read to each other?

"Go on, Lanie."

"The night she died, the tea tray came up, the same as usual. The blue pot, which I always thought was too plain. I had half a cup—tea usually keeps me awake, and I didn't want to overindulge —and Grandmama had at least two. We left the final cup for her medicinal serving. Peter came by with her posset and some biscuits, but I don't recall him leaving. I don't recall much of anything, because I soon fell asleep. The next thing I knew, I could hear Grandmama snoring—she never snored—and all the candles had been put out."

Lanie could perceive light. That hadn't changed.

"You want to ask Peter if Grandmama was well when he left? Ask Graham if she had that last cup of tea?"

"I don't recall Graham coming by, Morna, and he was nothing if not conscientious about serving Grandmama her medicine. She called it her nightcap."

Getting liquid nourishment into Grandmama had been simpler than asking her to hold utensils. She'd started and ended her days with possets, mostly honey and cream with a dash of cordial and spices. Even holding sandwiches and biscuits had challenged her dexterity toward the end, and utensils had become all but impossible for her.

"Peter might not know anything relevant, Lanie. He might have tucked you in and gone on his way."

"Nobody tucked me in. The chair was half turned toward the hearth for warmth, and I certainly didn't need any candles to read by, did I? I was cold when I woke up, though, cold and uncomfortable."

And Peter had told her repeatedly to leave the discomfort undiscussed. "Uncomfortable how?"

"I ached, and I wasn't sure where I was—the fire had burned down to coals—and even the air felt wrong. Then I heard Grandmama and realized we'd both fallen asleep. I wandered across the corridor to my bed. Grandmama would not let me spend the night in her apartment, I think because she wanted to waken without me pestering her."

"Grandpapa looked in on her every morning. She might well have wanted some privacy with him."

"I woke the next day to Grandpapa shouting at the physician. Grandpapa never shouted unless he was displeased with King George or the nitwits in Parliament. I grabbed my dressing gown, thinking to tell him to lower his voice lest he wake Grandmama. He told me to go back to my room, and I knew then something was very wrong. His voice was so sad, Morna. Despairing. I hope I never hear such a voice again in my life."

"Dr. Ramsey was certain Grandmama's death was a result of too much medication, but you're telling me you were fast asleep when Graham came by?"

Lanie finished her row and switched her needles. "*If* he came by."

"You should discuss this with Graham, Lanie."

"Why? Peter says it's all in the past, and he's not wrong."

Morna tried to resume her embroidery, but the needle had developed a mind of its own. If Lanie had been fast asleep when Grandmama had been served her fatal dose, then the investigating authorities would have been unable to convict Graham of the crime. No witness could place him at the scene or support the notion that he'd administered the last dose of medication.

He'd confessed and been transported for *nothing*. Whoever had sent Grandmama to her reward and Graham to the Antipodes had to know that.

CHAPTER ELEVEN

"Dunhaven, good morning." Sebastian, Marquess of Dunkeld, nodded at Graham from atop a horse nearly as big and dark as True. "We heard you were back from Edinburgh. Not much of a trip to town, was it?"

Graham turned True to fall in step with the marquess's gelding. "A bit of Auld Reekie goes a long way. Why aren't you in London yet?"

The morning was brisk rather than bitingly cold. Spring was creeping up, with earlier sunrises and later sunsets and a subtle softening in the air.

Dunkeld glanced off to the south, beyond the glistening ribbon of the River Tay, past the forested hillside on the opposite bank. "When you'd served your sentence and were free to come back, did you leap upon the first passing ship?"

"I wanted to."

"And yet, you didn't. You dithered, you made excuses, you tidied up affairs that were already in order."

His lordship was in a mood. "If I deliberated, Dunkeld, I did so for a procession of instants. I did not dither. I gather you have been deliberating?"

The horses ambled along beneath stately pines, the carpet of needles making their passing nearly silent. A slight breeze whispered above. To the immediate left of the track, the hillside fell away down to the river. To the right, the slope rose sharply toward the magnificent edifice Dunkeld should have called home. A gorgeous parcel of earth on a day that promised to be gorgeous as well.

"I am told I should marry," Dunkeld said in the same tones he might have announced a determination to subsist on cod liver oil. "My aunties are nigh incapable of discoursing on any other topic."

Those aunties, Hibernia and Maighread, were local institutions. They'd been sweet little old ladies for as long as Graham could remember, also prodigiously well informed and not above putting vicars, marquesses, or any other variety of wayward fellow in his place.

"They want to see you settled," Graham said, feeling some sympathy. "The war is over, time to find a bride."

"Something like that, but finding a bride isn't like picking out an afternoon horse from the newest lot on offer at Tatts."

To some, finding a marital partner was exactly like that. "You don't mind the prospect of a wife and family so much as you dread the ballrooms of Mayfair. A daunting proposition indeed."

Dunkeld directed his horse around a fallen branch. "I wasn't good enough for them when I was merely the old man's heir. He had a young wife, and any season, she was expected to announce that she was with child. I was the backward Scottish boy, then the difficult officer, and now..."

"You are in the habit of following orders and doing your duty, but what is the use of having the ruddy title and the castle and the whole lot if you can't ignore the occasional order too?"

Dunkeld sent him a brooding glance. "I'm the marquess now, and the blighted penny press has already started speculating about when I'll leave my 'spectacular Highland aerie and swoop down upon

London's loveliest,' delighting hostesses and gracing Almack's with my dashing presence."

"Don't, then. Deliberate. Go build a castle that's actually in the Highlands. You have the blunt."

"Castles are bitterly hard to heat, as we both well know."

This discussion was not about castles. Something drew the marquess to the Mayfair whirl, and something else made him reluctant to involve himself. Reluctant to stay, hesitant to go. Graham could understand the reluctance. Mayfair did not deserve Dunkeld's attention, given how he'd been treated by polite society earlier in life.

Rubbing the hostesses's noses in their hypocrisy was beneath Dunkeld's dignity. He would not care an empty whisky bottle for their opinion of him now.

What if Morna disdains even my friendship? That question had kept Graham deliberating for months, even as he'd made his way homeward.

"This involves a woman," Graham said slowly. "A woman you esteem but who did not return your regard. You dread to think she'll consider you now, because if she does, you won't consider her." And yet, Dunkeld was torn and tempted. What a coil.

Dunkeld kneed his horse around a huge fallen pine. "Something like that. The lady and I were cordial previously, but it was a long time ago, and we grew apart, though we were never... That is, we didn't..."

"You behaved yourself rather than get shown the door. Always the prudent course. My younger brother is taking the prudent course with young Lanie, and it's nigh killing him, poor sod."

"The aunties predict a wedding for those two by midsummer." The buried thread of envy in the marquess's observation might have passed unnoticed, but Graham had been listening to Peter extol Lanie's virtues by the hour. Repressed longing was arriving along with spring itself.

Graham had also been listening to Morna's silences, savoring her smiles, exchanging pleased glances with her down the length of the supper table. When had life ever been so sweet and so complicated?

"Well, you'd best go to London and get it over with, Dunkeld. If nothing else, you can assure yourself that you're immune to the lady's charms now. Let her watch as half the heiresses at Almack's swarm you each week."

Dunkeld made a face. "She's not the Almack's type."

"You haven't seen her for years. You don't know what type she is now." Graham was guessing, but if the marquess had crossed paths with his previous interest in the autumn, he'd hardly be dithering now.

"I'm friends with her brother. She's faring well enough."

"Right. Brothers are always impartial and thoroughly well informed. Just ask mine what day of the week it is. If you want the most accurate, up-to-the-minute report on a lady, always ask her brother."

"Go back to Australia."

That idea had no appeal, but neither did it terrify him, provided Morna made the journey as well. "When you're ready, you'll go south," Graham said. "I deliberated until I was doing little else but watching the horizon, Dunkeld. I eventually decided it was better to know than to torment myself with speculation. I could not concentrate to read what books the ship possessed. I did not pass the time with the other passengers. I was short-tempered and forgetful, and—"

"And if you'd had aunties on hand, they would have nodded knowingly every time you misplaced your spectacles or nearly sat upon one of their damned cats napping in your favorite reading chair."

Kenneth no longer assumed he had napping privileges in the study's wing chairs. "Trust that your dignity and your honor will be equal to the challenge and get it over with, man." Easy to say, now that Morna had kissed Graham witless, declared her allegiance, and threatened the unthinkable should Graham thwart her decrees.

"Dignity and honor are lousy bedfellows."

"No, they are not, not when compared to taking some passing bit of distraction to bed, not when the alternative is to marry just to keep your aunties from plaguing you."

Dunkeld's dark brows drew down. "You have a point." They rode on in silence until they came to another path crossing the track. Dunkeld halted his horse.

"What made you come home, Dunhaven? The best that can be said is you were treated badly here, but the MacNeils were managing in your absence."

"Treated badly, despite killing my own grandmother?"

"Nobody thought you'd intentionally done her harm. The aunties are very clear on that. You might discuss it with them when you look in on them in my absence."

"I might. First, I'll ask my own family what they recall. Do I conclude you are resigned to traveling south?"

Dunkeld turned his horse through half a walk pirouette. "I suppose I am. You are glad you came home, aren't you?"

I am now. "Yes. I haven't answered all the relevant questions yet, but the most important matters are falling into place." Soon, if all went well, falling into bed with Morna might figure among those important matters. She was very clear on her decisions, was Morna MacKenzie.

"Morna has forgiven you?" Dunkeld asked, fussing with his horse's mane.

Graham tossed the marquess's words back at him. "Something like that."

"Your smile could not be more satisfied, Dunhaven. You'll have the aunties betting against your bachelorhood."

"Let them. They are a delightful pair, and we MacNeils hold them in great affection."

Dunkeld finished turning his horse onto the uphill path. "I considered courting Miss MacKenzie, you know. She's a profoundly impressive lady, and I flatter myself she thinks well of me."

Such was the magnanimity of Graham's present mood that he felt mostly pity for Dunkeld. A bachelor afflicted with a bad case of the deliberations was seldom thinking clearly.

"She holds you in high regard," Graham said, which was the simple truth.

"She was too sensible to settle for a cordial match when she'd long since given her heart to another. If you break her heart again, I will personally thrash you to flinders, Dunkeld."

"You'll have to argue order of precedence for that undertaking with Peter and St. Didier, should the occasion arise, which it will not." *Ever.* To be certain of Morna's regard was the greatest blessing to come Graham's way, well worth sailing halfway around the world for.

Dunkeld gathered up his reins. "I'm off to make travel arrangements, then. You will look in on the aunties?"

"Regularly, and if you leave them your direction, I will pen the appropriate dispatches."

Dunkeld nodded, then sent his horse ambling up the track, a man in no hurry whatsoever.

Graham guided True back the direction they'd come and, when the path leveled out, gave his horse leave to canter. He'd missed too many suppers—and breakfasts and lunches—with Morna already, and every single one still left to them was precious.

"Down you go," Graham said, hands around Morna's waist.

Morna hardly needed the assistance dismounting, but the pleasure of grasping Graham's shoulders, then hopping off her horse to find herself more or less in his embrace, was too tempting to pass up.

He grinned down at her, then kissed her. A sweet, good-morning buss that lingered for only a moment.

Morna leaned against his chest. "We're supposed to be inspecting the boundary walls."

"My boundary walls are crumbling by the moment. Besides that,

Peter has been conscientious about inspecting the walls in spring and autumn. Said Grandpapa would have expected that of him."

Graham's arms were around her, his embrace loose, his hand cradling the back of her head. A sense of feasting after famine overcame Morna whenever they touched, of being granted a heart's desire that might all too easily be snatched away again. They had been as distant as two people who cared for each other could be, and to have Graham back now, back and *close*, was ineffably precious.

"Why the sigh, Morna mine?"

"Because you brought me here simply to enjoy the view and made up that bit about inspecting the walls to guard your dignity. I will always prefer your company, Graham. Given a choice, I will be with you, inspecting walls, sitting by the Tay with an idle fishing pole, or calling on the vicar."

That chore yet awaited them, but Morna would take it on gladly, provided Graham accompanied her.

She felt him absorb her words, consider them, and store them away. That distance, that hovering memory of long and difficult separation, would haunt them both.

"We don't take each other for granted," Graham said. "A good thing, I suppose."

Good, but dearly earned. Morna stepped back. "The view is magnificent."

Many yards below, the Tay crashed and roared in spring spate over boulders and rapids. Far beneath the overlook, a deep pool hinted of deceptive calm. Across the river, soaring pines in majestic ranks mounted a steep hillside, and a canopy of celestial azure overarched the whole. An oak bench, silver with age, tempted any passerby to tarry a moment and admire the view.

"We should put a railing up here," Graham said, taking her hand. "A good, stout rail. The bench invites people to linger, though the drop is dangerous."

"You'd be accused of disrespecting the legend."

Graham peered down at the river below. "The water's deep

enough, if a man jumps at exactly the right spot. He'd have a good chance of surviving, provided he wasn't submerged in that cold for long."

Morna shuddered at the thought. A local lass had supposedly fallen in love with a crown officer. The lady's Jacobite brothers had taken exception to her choice and chased the unfortunate officer to the edge of the precipice. He'd leaped and lived, and the lady had subsequently eloped with him.

A triumph of love over national grudges, which wasn't the typical outcome for Scottish romantic ballads.

"Build the railing," Morna said. "John's fate will be reason enough."

"Good thought. Besides, I'm the earl. I have both the right and duty to make myself the object of talk. Walk with me?"

She loved him for asking and hoped the day soon came when he realized he didn't need to. They collected the horses and took the path that wound back toward the castle.

"I had a thought," Graham said, and the very casualness of his tone suggested the thought mattered to him.

"About?"

"A sort of get-it-over-with thought."

"Get what over with?" Could he be alluding to desire? Morna's attraction to Graham was as physical as it was emotional—and growing by the day. She curbed her carnal urges with the certain knowledge that once that dam burst its banks, restraint would become yet still more challenging.

"I know what you're thinking, Morna MacKenzie, and that is another discussion entirely."

"We will have that other discussion soon, Graham, and it will be notably brief. I desire you shamelessly."

He muttered something short and impolite. "I am the most fortunate of men, then, because your regard is reciprocated tenfold, at least. My present concern is the parade inspection—of me. Dunkeld's aunties broadly hinted that my best course is to throw wide the castle doors, so to speak, and let all and sundry come to gawk. Calling on the neighbors one by one is time-consuming and boring. I know that much after exactly three afternoons of tea and chat. Why not invite the whole horde to the castle to look me over at once?"

A parade inspection... of *him*. Morna mentally kicked aside the images that term inspired. "Dunkeld's aunties are a pair of shrewd veterans of the social battlefields. They would not make such a suggestion lightly. Tell me about the boring part."

Graham glanced back at his horse. "They all ask the same questions, Morna. How was the journey? Am I glad to be back? Nobody wants to be rude, but the curiosity is obvious. I am an oddity. MacIver said it plainly enough: The young people never come back. They take ship and are never seen again. I came back, and it's as if every neighbor must pinch me in person and sniff my hair to see if I reek of brimstone. I hate it."

Visiting the neighbors required travel over a twenty-mile radius, leaving out those who bided in Perth, but a formal ball—even an informal assembly—would be an ordeal of a different sort.

"Let's think about it," Morna said. "The next full moon isn't for three weeks. We can take a day or two to consider supplies, accommodations, the menu. Spring isn't the easiest time to feed a hundred Scots in a celebratory mood."

"I figure closer to a hundred and twenty-five, because they'll all come, Morna. They'll come to have a gawk, and then, I hope, I can get on with what matters."

Morna tugged him to a stop and kissed him. "You are getting on splendidly, Graham MacNeil, and I like this idea of celebrating your return. Dunkeld's welcome toward you is common knowledge by now, so your invitations will be accepted. Now, before plowing and planting, with much of the lambing done, is an excellent time for a gathering."

He hugged her, and they remained close until Tempi shuffled an impatient hoof.

"You truly like this idea?" Graham asked, walking on and again retreating into studied casualness.

"The result will be to save you a lot of jaunting around, swilling tea, and being agreeable, despite the whiff of brimstone in your hair. We haven't had a celebration at the castle for ages, and I'm sure Dunkeld's aunties will help." Lanie would shudder at the idea of permitting an invasion of the castle, but Peter might jolly her past her reluctance.

"The aunties will run the whole maneuver," Graham said. "They were spouting off names of guests and buffet suggestions nineteen to the dozen. Let's talk it over with Peter and Lanie and see if they're game."

Considerate of him. Crowds were a challenge for Lanie. She managed well enough in the structured confines of a church service and put up with the churchyard routine, provided Morna or Peter remained by her side, but she was more at home in a quiet parlor or around a family supper table.

"Speaking of Lanie," Morna said as the edge of the woods came into view. "Might we tarry a bit?"

Graham paused. "We can tarry all day, though I'm rather looking forward to lunch."

"Lanie and I had an interesting discussion regarding the events surrounding Grandmama's death. You should talk to her."

"I haven't wanted to. I am reluctant to approach Brodie, too, but when it comes to Lanie... She was a child, Morna. A child already hurting, one life had treated harshly in many regards."

"Lanie doesn't see it like that. Yes, we lost our parents, but so did you and Peter, and we had each other. Yes, she lost most of her vision, but she has keen hearing, a keen nose, and protective family. She wants to know what happened to Grandmama, but she hasn't felt comfortable raising the topic with you."

Graham nodded once. "She thinks I killed Grandmama, however accidentally. That's what everybody was supposed to think."

The hint of frustration in Graham's voice suggested that the bold and brave plan he'd concocted as a younger man now struck him as precipitous, which it had been.

"Lanie cannot place you at the scene of the crime, Graham. She recalls Peter coming up with the nightly posset, but doesn't recall him leaving. He could chatter forever when he had a wiling audience, and Lanie simply fell asleep in her chair by the fire."

Graham studied the ground, a damp conglomeration of dead leaves, pine needles, rocks, and the occasional snowdrop.

"I vaguely recall Lanie curled up in the chair. I wouldn't swear to it. Peter wasn't on hand. The fire had burned down, so the room was in shadows. I was a bit late with the tray because I'd become involved in a hand of whist with Grandpapa."

He brushed the toe of his boot over the bracken underfoot. "I had to rouse Grandmama for her last cup of tea. She was fast asleep, which sometimes happened, but we'd agreed it was better to wake her for her medicine than have the pain rouse her an hour later and torment her all night. She barely woke up enough to finish her dose and was back to sleep immediately. I tucked Grandmama in and went on my way. The candles had already been put out, else I might have taken more notice of Lanie."

"Lanie reported being stiff and sore upon waking." Morna thought back, plagued by elusive details. "She said even the air felt wrong, and Grandmama was snoring. Lanie went across to her own room and woke the next morning to Grandpapa shouting."

"A not uncommon start to our day," Graham said. "I am not sure Lanie's recollections gain us any insights."

He would say that. "She can place *Peter* at the scene, Graham. You see that much."

"Peter would never have intentionally harmed our grandmother, and the nightly posset was his little job. Gave him an excuse to make his final report of the day to Grandmama and put him on equal footing with me in the sickroom. He would never wish the countess harm."

"We're beyond the point where intentions matter, Graham. Lanie wants to know what *happened*, just as you do, just as I do."

Graham resumed walking. "At what cost, Morna? I thought I would sail home, interrogate Ramsey, put a few pointed questions to the old cook, read John's diaries, and see a pattern of events. St. Didier was to abet that cause, but his sole contribution to the whole undertaking has been to suspect Peter. I cannot put upon my younger brother's shoulders both responsibility for Grandmama's death and blame for sending me off on a transport ship."

Morna fell in step beside him. "I certainly don't want to see Peter in the dock."

"Let's plan a party instead, then, shall we?" Graham took her hand. "I will think about Lanie's recollections and tell her my own, but the burning need to uncover every last detail is fading, Morna. I am more and more inclined to let mishaps be mishaps, be they here, in Edinburgh, or in London."

No, he wasn't. Graham would fret over Lanie's memories, ask her about them, and come to his own conclusions. He doubtless had St. Didier making inquiries in Edinburgh, and he hadn't left the castle grounds on his own since his most recent return.

He was putting on a show of good spirits for Morna's sake. The least she could do was return the favor.

"The ballroom will take days to heat," Morna said. "And we'll need a fortune in candles."

"And a fortune in libation. St. Didier can do some shopping for us while he enjoys Edinburgh."

For us. For the MacNeils and the MacKenzies, for Graham and Morna. *For us.* A cheering thought indeed. Morna left the woods determined to put the cheering thoughts foremost, even as she knew the past continued to haunt them all.

∿

"Why in the name of all that is fragrant are you shoveling sheep shit?" Peter asked, surveying the dim and malodorous confines of the stone byre.

Graham paused in his labors to take a pull from his flask. "Because it's Scottish sheep shit and, better still, *MacNeil* Scottish sheep shit. Then too, the work has to be done. It was this or cut peat."

Peter made a face. "Spare me. Old Lochie is fussier than a bishop with his wine collection when it comes to the peat. 'The hill isn't ready,'" Peter barked in a quavery tenor. "'The hill is too dry.' 'Work here; no, don't cut there.' 'That bank wants careful leveling.' 'Why can't you work any faster, laddie-o?'"

"But we have ample peat," Graham said, taking up the handles of the full wheelbarrow and running the load up a set of ramped boards into the waiting cart. "The lot of it is perfectly cured, and cutting peat gives all the young people a chance to flirt and gossip." Some parts of the job were considered women's work, others for the menfolk, but there was always work enough to go around.

"I heard some gossip," Peter said, shifting to stand upwind of the wooden cart. "Brodie says we're to have a formal ball with all the trimmings. No stated purpose other than conviviality."

Grandpapa would have made a comment of that nature—always mindful of the coin.

"Brodie's report is for once accurate." Graham remained in the sunshine, enjoying the sensation of the wind on his face—the particularly Scottish breeze that wasn't quite cold, but certainly not mild either.

"If I continue to do the pretty household by household," Graham went on, "I'll be an old man before I've called on even the nearest neighbors." Only a slight exaggeration. "Morna has approved the idea of a formal ball as my presentation to the shire. I wanted your thoughts on the notion before we started sending out invitations."

Peter wrinkled his nose. "Don't let Uncle Brodie near the ladies' punchbowl, whatever you do."

Little brother wasn't growing up. He *had* grown up, and that was both wonderful and sad. "You don't seriously think he'd spike the ladies' potation again?" He'd pulled that stunt at some assembly several years ago and caused such an uproar that even St. Didier had passed the tale along.

"Uncle's version of humor still has a bit too much of the naughty schoolboy about it," Peter said. "Morna threatened to banish him to Mull if he ever did anything like that again."

Mull was beautiful, but if Uncle pined for lively society a few miles from Perth, he'd be bereft on Mull.

"Brodie will behave," Graham said, glancing at the sky. "Auntie Hibernia has given me her solemn assurances that this will be a dignified gathering."

Peter took up one of the shovels leaning against the byre's outside wall. "Then dignified we shall be, but why not wait until the next assembly? It's not that far off. Let the neighbors count your teeth there."

"The assembly rooms would be too crowded for dancing." Graham pushed the barrow back into the byre, which was a three-and-a-half-sided stone structure with a thatched roof set at a low pitch. Half built into the hillside, the byre would be cool in summer and cozy in winter.

And in need of a good mucking out accordingly, though nothing would rid the place of the smell of sheep, manure, and dirt.

Peter began shoveling on the far side of the barrow. "The ballroom might well be too crowded for dancing. What's the real reason you're spending a fortune to put yourself on display?"

"I liked you better when you were content to play with toy soldiers and put frogs in my bed," Graham said, stabbing his shovel into the mat of dirt, rotting hay, and manure at his feet. "Why must every celebration have a reason?"

"Celebrations don't need reasons, but excessive expenditures do."

Grandpapa to the life. "We can afford to indulge. I want to get off on a positive foot and let all and sundry know I'm here to stay."

Peter worked with the steady rhythm of one familiar with a task. "Is this for Morna?"

"Partly. She's been running the castle for years. She deserves to enjoy being the hostess." Closer to the back wall, the going was heavier, and each shovelful carried a whiff of mold.

Scottish mold, though.

"Lanie will detest the notion of a formal ball." Peter jabbed his shovel at the ground hard. "I'm less than thrilled with it myself."

Not the reaction Graham had anticipated. "If Lanie's concern is an inability to waltz, tell her I can't either."

"But you can learn."

"So can she."

"She might learn to waltz, Graham, but she won't risk it in a crowded ballroom. Sighted people go top over tail on the dance floor all the time, and that's usually an occasion for hilarity. For Lanie, a spill would be unbearable."

"So don't let her fall."

Peter dumped a load into the rapidly filling barrow. "If a lady dances with one man, she must dance with all who invite her. Surely you didn't forget basic etiquette in Australia?"

"So Lanie sits out with me and the other wallflowers." Except Graham knew that for a young lady to sit out wasn't the same as for the host or the chaperones to sit out. "We could limit the size of the sets."

Peter resumed shoveling. "That might work for the dancing, but what about the ladies' retiring room? I can't be with Lanie there, and neither can you."

Why would they need to be? "Peter, what am I missing here? Lanie is the dearest of young ladies, and though she might be a bit reserved in the churchyard, I am certain allowances are made."

Peter jammed his boot down on the shovel. "Then you would be in error. Lanie is envied, she is excluded, she is gossiped about, and nobody does anything to stop it." Real anger colored his words. "The vicar's oldest daughter is the worst, and her mother knows it."

Vera Conroy had tried to attach herself to Graham's arm in the churchyard, but he'd feigned a cough and wrenched himself free, then waved a handkerchief about when she would have taken him captive again. Morna and Uncle Brodie had been vastly amused.

"Why has nobody said anything to me about this before now?"

"Probably because it's old news. Lanie is shy, and some people take that for haughty. Two years ago, she discouraged Nevin Bodeen from paying her his addresses, and Nevin was not best pleased. She was supposed to be flattered that he'd consider marrying a blind woman. The whispering has been worse since then, and Lanie can hear whispers quite clearly."

Lanie wasn't shy. Lanie had been the first to greet Graham, pelting across the cobbles to hug him when she couldn't properly see him. She spoke her mind, and her insights were often keen.

"All the more reason to host a ball," Graham said. "You and I will dote on our Lanie. St. Didier will do likewise. Bodeen will mind his manners, and Vera Conroy had best behave, or she will find herself figuratively visiting Mull."

Another large shovelful went into the cart. "She'd hate that."

"Mull is lovely in springtime."

Peter worked away in silence for a few more minutes, and soon the barrow was full again.

Graham dumped the barrow and arched his back. "Hard work is supposed to be a tonic. Whoever said that never mucked out a byre."

Peter joined him in the chilly sunshine and rested the shovel against the wall. "Or cut peat. I know what you're doing, Graham."

"Earning myself a hot bath?" A long hot bath, with plenty of hard, fragrant soap. "I used to dream about Grandmama's scented soaps. All I had was tallow, lard, and lye when I first got to Sydney, and that was hard enough to procure."

"Graham, you didn't go with the peat crew because you seek the jobs that leave you isolated. You wandered the boundary walls by the hour, you cut through the woods on foot to confer with MacIver, and now you're mucking out the far-flung byres, a job any farmhand ought to be doing."

To argue—to lie—or to cede what had apparently been obvious to Peter? Graham chose a middle course.

"I am concerned about the incident in Edinburgh," Graham said slowly. "I seem to be safe enough here at home."

"And the incident in London, and if you are safe enough, you are certainly giving any malefactors ample opportunities to render you unsafe. Does Morna know what you're about?"

Insightful, uncomfortable question. "She has forbidden me to travel alone to the distant properties, so she must assume I'm safe at home."

"Morna forbids you these days?" Peter seemed intrigued rather than amused.

"Aye, and if her reasons are sound, I accept her guidance. Are you forbidding this grand ball, Peter?"

Peter gazed off across the pasture, to the dark line of the trees beyond the stone wall. "I am not. I agree with you that home seems to be a safe place, but if I could find you simply by asking in the stable for your whereabouts, then anybody else could too. We all keep an eye on you, and that's probably a good thing, but it means you won't easily find cover if you need it."

Spoken more like a Jacobite rebel than an earl's heir. "You should know I intend to ask Lanie about the night Grandmama died, Peter. She doesn't even recall me coming by, and I barely noticed her asleep in the wing chair."

"Then what do you hope to gain by questioning her?" The anger was back, banked but fierce. "This harrowing old ground over and over has to stop, Graham. You did what you thought best. You're home now. Let's be grateful for that and *move on*."

"Tell me something, Peter. Were the candles lit when you brought Grandmama her posset?" Graham put the question as neutrally as he could, though his nape was prickling, and drawing a steady breath took effort. The conversation had lurched into the muck, not because the topic was the past, but because Peter was loath to discuss it.

"Yes," he said, scowling. "As best I recall—candles blazing. I could see Lanie in her chair, and I could see to set the tray on the sideboard. I am almost sure that the two candelabra on the mantel, the sconce above the bed, and the sconce by the bedroom door were all lit."

"Good to know." Disturbing, but good in a backhanded sense.

"The candles were out when you came by?" Studied casualness now filled Peter's tone too.

Graham nodded. "And I am sure, Peter. Lanie did not put out the candles, and you didn't. Some time between when you came around with your posset, and I stopped by to serve Grandmama her last cup of tea, somebody else was in that sickroom, and they stayed long enough to put out the candles."

Peter ceased inspecting the trees. "Please do not question Lanie further on this, Graham. I will take her away from here before I let you do that. She means everything to me. I would kill for her, blaspheme, or dance naked in the streets of Edinburgh, and when I say I will take her far from the castle, I mean it."

"Lanie might not appreciate being kidnapped."

"We'd kidnap each other. The English call it eloping. Brodie would approve."

"Morna would not, and thus you'll cease such talk. I won't question Lanie, then, but if she brings up the past, I will tell her what I recall. She clearly doesn't share your unwillingness to reexamine matters, Peter."

"Then she's not as sensible as I'd hoped she was, but none of us is perfect, not even Lanie." He strode off in the direction of his horse, who'd been cropping grass farther up the hill.

"See you at supper," Graham called.

Peter waved an arm and kept walking. Graham went back to the reeking shadows of the byre.

Why the unwillingness to examine the past? Why the near panic at any attempt to get Lanie's version of events? Was Peter protecting Lanie, or perhaps protecting himself?

The byre was thoroughly mucked, Graham's flask was empty, and his back was one burning ache, and still, his questions admitted of no certain answers.

CHAPTER TWELVE

"You've been avoiding me." Morna fell in step beside a freshly bathed and shaved Graham, one who exuded the pleasant scent of heather and the relaxed attitude of a man who'd put in a good day's work.

A day's work anywhere but at the castle, *again*. She hadn't exactly lain in wait for him, but she'd

enjoyed the view from the alcove across from the earl's quarters at length.

"I cannot avoid you," Graham said, taking her hand and patting her knuckles. "You're in my every waking thought and most of my dreams. I dare hope your thoughts similarly dwell on me."

They did, blast him. Her thoughts and her longings, both. "Spare me your flattery, Graham. I know what you're about."

"Falling in love? Wallowing in love? Please explain the situation to me, *mo chridhe*, because I am in an exceedingly pleasant muddle."

My heart. "You've stooped to endearments. Next, you will be admiring my bonnie blue eyes. Graham, you needn't bother."

Morna stopped outside her own apartment, a modest configuration of sitting room, bedroom, and dressing closet that had been hers since she'd put up her hair. Lanie dwelled directly down the corridor, while Peter and Brodie had quarters on the other side of the main staircase. The countess's old suite was vacant, an unused guest room in the middle of the family accommodations.

"Your eyes are gorgeous," Graham said, sounding slightly bewildered. "Are compliments no longer an aspect of courting?"

"Now you're doing the humble suitor bit. You needn't bother with that either." Morna opened the door to her apartment, hauled him in by the wrist, and closed the door behind him. "I'm taking you to bed. I would like to take you to bed, rather."

His smile was equal parts puzzled and bashful. "Now?"

"Yes, now. Peter and Lanie are working on a pianoforte duet in the music room, which is a glorified excuse to sit nearly in each other's laps. They will rehearse until the third supper bell. Brodie is reading the Society pages while he indulges in his pre-pre-supper tipple, and that invariably ends in him snoring. We have privacy and time. Let's be about it."

Before I lose my nerve.

Graham studied her, then seemed to come to some sort of decision, because he locked her sitting room door.

"You find me irresistible," he said, "and your days are a torment of yearning. Though I haven't even properly proposed to you yet—the ritual wants a ring, as best I recall—I am supposed to presume on your virtue and pleasure you witless in the process. Do I have that much right?"

He'd somehow grown more imposing as he spoke—also more serious.

"I haven't any virtue to presume on. You should know that."

Graham led her to the sofa, in the opposite direction of the bedroom door.

"Your previous encounters are none of my business, Morna, provided you were a consenting adult at the time. As far as I am concerned, you bristle with virtues." He came down beside her, inches away and yet subtly remote too.

"You make me sound like a hedgehog. I was a curious, restless, foolish adult. He was kind, I suppose you'd say. Knew I wasn't smitten, and neither was he, but I wanted to know..."

"We all want to know. That's normal and healthy. Did he break your heart?"

To discuss this with Graham in the broad light of day was both unnerving and a relief. "Heavens no. He was the marquess's guest. He went back to Kent at the end of the summer, and last I heard, he'd married an American. He was a pleasant, canny, good-looking devil, but, Graham..."

Why was it necessary to delve into the details?

"Just say it, Morna. In case you've forgotten, lovers are supposed to trust each other."

Lovers. Well, yes. "He wasn't you."

Graham nodded. "You and I were cheated. I spent months plotting and planning how to advance my campaign in your direction, but then Grandmama died, and my hopes with her. What might have been has haunted me, Morna, and I don't want to bungle with you this time around."

"You are," Morna said, stifling the urge to pace. "Bungling, that is. Off you go at first light to march the boundaries, but I know what you're truly about."

"Mending wall?"

"Avoiding me. You have resumed your plotting and planning, considering all possibilities, and still fretting that some coach will come thundering out of the woods to flatten you. Do you propose to me and put me in danger too? Do you write me sweet little poems and leave flowers on my pillow? Do you marry me and see about filling the nursery because titles come with responsibilities, and Peter longs to build steam engines?"

"And kiss Lanie."

"That too, and she wants to more than kiss him. You are ruminating and brooding when you should be kissing *me*. If, heaven forbid, you should be struck down by a runaway team or bad eggs or the spring ague, I don't want to spend the rest of my life *wishing*,

Graham."

That sentiment—selfish, honest, and more than a little desperate —wasn't the worst admission Morna could have made, but it was bad enough.

Graham wrapped an arm around her shoulders. "I am supposed to argue with you," he said, "to insist that vows be spoken first, or at least promises exchanged."

"Please don't. Words uttered for the sake of propriety don't change how I feel. I want the words, and I appreciate them, but more significantly, I want you."

"When I ask you to marry me, Morna, will you say yes?"

"Of course."

He was sitting beside her, his half-embrace warm and secure, and Morna waited. She was so damned tired of waiting—for spring, for the next letter from St. Didier, for *Graham*.

"I think," Graham said, "we are allowed to be anxious, you and I. We worry that we'll be cheated again, maybe the next time cheated forever. We're together now, but we both know life has a way of inflicting the unexpected and even the tragic on the undeserving. I don't want to lose you either, Morna."

"You won't." He had, though, put a delicate finger on the part Morna wasn't willing to admit out loud: She was haunted by a now-or-never fear, by the certain knowledge that what had been snatched away once could be snatched away again.

"I could have lost you," Graham said. "That handsome, witty fellow from Kent could have wheedled you into marriage. The bad eggs could have been served to you, and illness is no respecter of persons. I worried, too, Morna, and I've acres of cleared ground outside Sydney to show for it."

"Acres?"

"Cleared ground, fences, a tidy little cottage. I worked myself to flinders because that was the only patent remedy available. 'What if I lose her? What if I've already lost her?'"

The rabbits dancing about in Morna's middle quieted. "Wait

until you see the Christmas linens. Lanie says I went needle-mad the first winter you were gone. And the second, and the third."

Graham apparently understood that she was still a bit mad, and—what a thing to share—he clearly was too. Still haunted by separation and loss, still fearful that the next parting could become permanent.

"We'll take each other to bed, then," Graham said. "If you're sure?"

"I am now."

He stood and offered her his hand. "You weren't before?"

"I was certain of my goal, not as certain of the strategy for achieving it."

Graham drew her into his arms. "A word of caution, darling Morna. If you announce an intention to take me to bed, you are soon likely to be sharing a bed with me."

He was utterly, absolutely in earnest.

"Good to know. Graham MacNeil. I would very much like to take you to bed."

"Then,"—he beamed at her—"let's be about it, shall we?"

Morna had seen what Graham had been trying to ignore. He had honestly been concerned with renewing his acquaintances among the neighbors, and he'd been making a staked goat of himself to any enemy willing to set foot on MacNeil land. He'd also been pondering the past and making what inquiries he could to shed light on Grandmama's death.

And all the while, he'd been keeping his distance from Morna. Since their outing to the overlook, when Graham had been ambushed by thoughts of trysting *en plein air*, he'd retreated to figurative high ground. The future Countess of Dunhaven deserved better than lovemaking against the nearest handy birch tree.

How did a man court lightning? How did he romance a female

tempest of intelligence, common sense, wit, and passion? How did he make up for years apart and find his way back to a shared future?

The answer that came to him as Morna led him into the bedroom was simple: He undertook the vast privilege of wooing his prospective wife *slowly*. He paused when he wanted to plunder and listened when tempted to shout.

He drove himself half barmy, in other words, or completely barmy if need be.

"I should have built up the fire," Morna said, closing the bedroom door.

"But that would have been tempting fate, inviting disappointment. We'll be warm enough under the covers."

Graham perched on the raised hearth to remove his boots, something he'd done in Morna's presence any number of times. He'd seen her bare feet too—wading in the shallows of the Tay, drying off in the summer sun—but the thought of those bare feet now had him staring at his stockings.

"You're sure?" he asked again. He was sure, desperately sure.

"I have been sure since the day you carried Lanie into the river and let her dip her toes into the water until your teeth were chattering."

Graham peeled off his stockings. "I'd forgotten that. She longed to go wading, but didn't trust her balance. I thought she'd never let me take her back to dry land."

"You were so sweet and so determined, and Lanie was so happy."

He set his boots on the far side of the vanity, away from the fire, and sat next to Morna on the mattress.

Her bedroom was unique in that its appointments sported no plaid. Her preference was flowers—red roses and purple irises patterned both the wallpaper and the carpet. The bedspread was quilted with the same adornments, and the green velvet curtains and bed hangings supported the floral theme.

A respite from blue and green plaid and a lovely setting for the lady herself.

"I fell in love with you regularly," Graham said. "When I came home after university, I finally recognized the symptoms for what they were. You tore a strip off Uncle Brodie for teasing Peter, laid into him in English and Erse. Said he had no business criticizing Peter's scholarship when he himself had excelled only in drinking, wagering, and vexing Grandmama. Grandpapa was positively jolly for the next week."

"Brodie has mellowed since. He fancied himself a frustrated satirist, but picking on children is never humorous."

Nor would Morna ever overlook such a transgression. Graham loved that about her, loved her forthright, shy, brisk, fierce, tender-hearted ...

"I love you," Graham said. "I want to get that out now, while I can still manage complete sentences."

"I love you too," Morna said, toeing off her slippers. "Though I may burden you with a repetition of that declaration at odd moments."

"Because for years, we could not say it, we could not write it, we hardly dared think it. I love you, I love you, I love you."

She bumped him with her shoulder. "Unfasten my hooks, please."

"I'll love doing that too."

The next part, which could have been awkward, was simple. Clothing piled up on the chest at the foot of the bed—one stack for him, another for her, though Graham hung Morna's dress from a peg on the bedpost.

Morna disappeared into the dressing closet while Graham used the warmer on the sheets. She returned wearing a dressing gown over her shift—more green velvet—and waited while Graham peeled down to his riding breeches.

She held up one foot swaddled in a thick gray wool sock. "My feet are always cold. I sleep with socks on."

Graham poured a glass of water from the carafe sitting on the vanity. "I set out two glasses of water for myself every night, and they are always empty in the morning, but I seldom recall taking even a sip. I sleep-drink."

They smiled at each other, then Morna hung the dressing gown on another bedpost and climbed beneath the covers.

"Don't be shy," she said. "It's only me."

"Not shy," Graham said, unbuttoning his falls. "Modest." Also half aroused and self-conscious with it. Did she expect him to leap beneath the covers, saber at the ready? To have kept all erotic thoughts at bay?

Something in between would have to do.

"Graham." Morna was sitting in the middle of the bed, cross-legged. She drew her shift over her head and threw it at him. "You are stalling."

He caught the linen against his bare chest, sniffed it—roses, his favorite flower forever—and draped it atop his shirt and waistcoat.

"I am taking my time, because the one thing I do know about how matters should proceed from here..." He paused to step out of his breeches. "Is that haste is to be avoided."

Morna visually inspected him while he worshiped the sight of her from a distance of six feet. Pale breasts, rosy nipples, a slender waist, and a houri's smile.

Haste was to be avoided. A flying leap onto the bed would likely be unwise as well.

"Stop showing off," Morna said, though her tone lacked its usual decisiveness. "Half the ladies in Australia must be mourning your absence."

"Not half," Graham said, climbing onto the bed. "Not even one." He arranged himself over her on all fours. "They weren't you."

She wrapped arms and legs around him, kissed him witless—slowly—and drove him mad with the sensation of fuzzy socks rubbed along his flanks.

"Graham," she panted, a small, exquisite eternity of arousal later, "it's not haste if you're simply getting on with the business."

"It's not?" He positioned himself against her heat. "Are you certain? Where exactly does the line between haste and passion, between a direct—ye gods, Morna."

She'd taken him into her body with an expedient roll of her hips. "This is lovely," she said. "This is quite lovely."

"If it's only lovely, I've some work to do." He went about his appointed rounds silently and slowly, keeping a tight rein on desire and a close eye on Morna. She was exercising similarly determined self-control, and that would not do.

Graham changed the angle of their bodies, heard a small gasp near his ear and then a sweet, soft sigh.

Got you at last. Morna yielded graciously, accepting what he offered until Graham felt her pleasure transform into satisfaction. Her hold on him loosened, and the soft socks brushed his flanks one last time.

"Worth the wait," she said, patting his bum. "Absolutely worth the wait."

Had he been capable of speech, he might have agreed with her. Instead, he began moving again and mentally vowed that his beloved would always have a vast supply of thick, soft socks to keep her feet warm.

The family parlor was cheerier, the smell of peat smoke more pleasant, and even the portrait of the first countess seemed to be smiling. Graham was still debating whether he deserved a tot to steady his nerves when Brodie joined him.

"Damned rain," Brodie said, going straight to the sideboard. "Civilized countries have seasons. Now it's summer, very pleasant if a bit hot. Now it's autumn, time for harvest. Scotland has *weather*, a fickle, fiendish procession of sunshine, hail, bitter cold, rain, and more sunshine, but nothing predictable enough that a man knows which coat to wear. We'll have a lambing snow tonight, mark my words."

Graham watched as Brodie poured himself a generous serving of brandy. "You can learn to miss snow, believe it or not." To miss familiar birds and fish, to miss the particular quality of a location's sunshine.

"I do not believe it." Brodie finished about half his drink at one go. "I also cannot believe that you chose to return to this drafty old pile, but I suppose the title was a rather compelling argument for the defense."

The title hadn't figured in the decision *at all.* "If I could make you the earl, Uncle, would you want me to?"

Graham sampled his drink and resented the burden of making small talk. He'd rather bask in the glow of becoming Morna's lover in more than name, rather enjoy the memory of her spent and sleepy in his arms.

"If I were the earl," Brodie said, scowling at his drink, "I would look in here at the castle for about two weeks in high summer and spend the rest of my time in cultured surrounds. The average Perthshire formal dinner gathering wouldn't know witty repartee if it was brought to the table on serving trays between the soup and the fish courses."

Uncle was in a mood, but then, he was often in a mood. "If you are so eager to enjoy more sophisticated company, then pack your trunks and go," Graham said. "You will always have a home here." Grandmama would have expected at least that for her brother.

"Easy for you to say." Brodie finished his drink and poured himself another. "You will likely be off to London by midsummer. I'm surprised you came home without tarrying for a time in Mayfair. That lot would overlook a bit of murder in your past, now that you're the earl. They might not offer you their daughters with all the trimmings, but they'd invite you for the novelty factor."

"Not murder, Uncle. Involuntary manslaughter. If you must bring up painful memories, at least do so accurately."

Brodie shrugged and went to the window to stare out at the rainy darkness. "My sister died—call it what you will. I call it a sad accident, but perhaps you did her a favor. Poor thing was in agony, but she had to drag herself to table and to divine services, and there was old Dunhaven, encouraging that foolishness."

Part of the reason Brodie had been able to tease Peter so relentlessly was that Peter had, for the longest time, risen to the bait. This discussion was baiting—and the last topic Graham wanted to air in his present mood.

And yet, needs must. "Uncle, what do you recall about the night Grandmama died?"

Brodie shot him an unreadable look. "Not much, having done my usual best to appreciate the libation at supper and afterward. You lot were on your assigned maneuvers with possets and remedies and whatnot. I left you to it, as usual. Just because I was her ladyship's only surviving blood relative on the premises was no reason to entrust me with the smallest aspect of her care."

Peter, John, and Graham had all been related to the countess by blood. "You generally avoided her ladyship's apartments, as I recall."

"Damned right I did—avoided her sickroom. I hated to see her like that, and she appreciated that I kept my distance. The rest of you would have done better to leave her more privacy. A woman reduced to slurping gruel doesn't need or want an audience."

Grandmama had never been *reduced to slurping gruel*. "So why bide here?" Graham asked, joining Brodie at the window. "If you have such unhappy memories of this place, if you're so miserable here, why not lark off to Paris or London? Heaven knows, Edinburgh has its share of wits, poets, and pundits."

"I promised my sister I'd keep watch over you youngsters, and I've kept my word. What do you suppose is delaying the others? I'm famished."

An abrupt change of topic from the family raconteur. A bit odd. "Peter and Lanie were still at the pianoforte when the second bell rang. If they needed to change for supper, they might be a few minutes yet. What do you hear from your correspondents in London?"

Brodie launched into a recitation of elopements, duels, and

phaeton races undertaken by people he'd never met in a city he hadn't visited for years. Brodie had regularly jaunted off to London and Edinburgh in Graham's youth, collected a new arsenal of quips and *on dits*, then returned to the castle to fire off his witticisms at any who'd listen.

Over and over. Grandpapa had taken a dim view of Brodie's peripatetic pleasures, but Grandmama had argued the merits of a respite from her brother's company.

"You then have no specific recollections of the night Grandmama died?" Graham asked when Brodie had refreshed his drink for the second time and recounted his famous wager at White's for the thousandth.

"I recall losing my sister," Brodie said on a sigh. "I miss her. But as for the sound of John's unsteady tread passing my door, a muted scream, drops of blood on the carpet, or any other such Gothic excesses, of course not. I would have informed the sheriff's man of same, except that I had nothing to tell him. My sister was dead, at peace at last, and that was that. If Peter goes to his reward before you do, perhaps you'll spare a thought for your old uncle and the sorrow visited upon him that night."

"I certainly will."

Lanie joined them before Brodie could start another round of when-I-was-in-Brighton. She looked radiant in an ensemble of blue merino that complemented her MacNeil plaid shawl wonderfully.

"I heard you and Peter practicing," Graham said. "You're better than he is."

"I'm better because I must pay closer attention. Morna plays through the pieces for me so I can hear them, and then I look over the score as best I can, holding the music at a very odd angle. Then I try to replicate what I heard and saw, and that takes concentration. Peter just skims through the notes, and he's quite good at it."

Lanie's smile suggested that she, too, was savoring precious memories, and that warmed Graham's heart. Old Brodie's problem was loneliness, and one could not blame him for that.

"I was just asking our Graham," Brodie said, "when he plans to quit the castle. As quickly as he travels, he could still enjoy the Mayfair Season or even pop over to Paris."

Half the glow in Lanie's eyes disappeared. "Why would Graham leave the castle? He just got here, and we've already done the pretty in Edinburgh."

"I don't plan to leave the castle," Graham said. "Uncle is teasing. This is my home, and I've spent quite enough time away from it."

"You'll grow bored," Brodie said. "Trust me on this. You've seen the world, albeit from the deck of a transport ship. You won't be content to muck out stalls and chat up rustics in plaid. You cannot imagine leaving this place ever again, but you never imagined traveling to Australia as a convicted felon, did you?"

Brodie was determined to be disagreeable, and if pressed, he'd say he was simply being honest or plainspoken, and one must not hide from the past.

What was Brodie hiding from? Because the poor old sod was definitely bedeviled by something. Before Graham could ask—plain speaking did have its uses—Morna arrived arm in arm with Peter, both of them looking like cats who'd found undefended barrels of cream.

Nothing like practicing duets to put spring in the air. Graham handed drinks around and silently toasted a day full of exceedingly precious memories. By the time he was escorting Morna in to supper, the rain had turned to sleet, suggesting Brodie had got at least one thing right.

They'd have snow overnight. With any luck, a pretty morning would melt into a mild, sunny afternoon. St. Didier would return from his errands in Edinburgh, and Graham could get a ring on his beloved's finger before sunset tomorrow.

CHAPTER THIRTEEN

"You look like you were to the plaid born," Morna said. "But what is a St. Didier doing in the MacKenzie tartan?"

"My grandmother was a MacKenzie," St. Didier replied as the fiddles lilted along. "I saw this kit ready-made in Edinburgh, had the tailors do a few alterations, and here I am."

"Here you are," Morna said softly, "still keeping watch, though nothing happened while you were off on the laird's business." Nothing except some wild, tender lovemaking, some long nights of sleepy affection, some cautious discussions of the future. In the past fortnight, Morna had allowed herself every possible liberty with Graham, knowing full well they were both trying to make up for lost time.

Maybe in twenty years, their intimacy would be less limned with rejoicing and wonder, less motivated by what they'd nearly been denied—assuming fate granted them twenty years.

"While I was in Edinburgh, spring arrived." St. Didier took a sip of punch that Uncle Brodie had not doctored—yet. Morna had assigned the first footman to monitor Uncle's behavior. Brodie had circulated in polite society very little in recent years, and a formal ball would doubtless tempt him to mischief.

"Spring arrives every year," Morna said, foot-tapping with each downbeat. "Good heavens. Vera Conroy's dancing master has failed his office."

Miss Conroy's steps were correct, her sense of rhythm adequate to the challenge, but she was pressed against Peter like a stray bit of wool clung to a thorny blackberry cane.

"How fortunate that Miss Lanie can't see the vicar's daughter making a cake of herself. Peter is comporting himself like a gentleman, though. I don't suppose you'd like to dance, Miss MacKenzie?"

The supper waltz was just beginning, and couples were still drifting onto the dance floor. Morna caught sight of Graham, Aunt Hibernia on his arm by the open veranda doors. He looked magnificent in full kilted regalia, Aunt Hibernia a mere sprite wrapped in a Royal Stewart shawl at his elbow.

Graham had been right to put himself on display like this. The neighbors were having a good gawk, and Morna was too.

"I'm sitting out for now," she said. "Lanie cannot dance, Graham cannot waltz, so Peter has had to uphold the honor of the castle. I am about half a wee dram away from telling Uncle Brodie that Vera Conroy fancies him."

"The poor young lady doesn't deserve that. Somebody needs to take her shopping in Edinburgh."

"She's been, which is why she's so consumed with jealousy toward Lanie. Lanie lives in a castle, Lanie has the latest fashions, Lanie's settlements are quite generous. When Vera goes to Edinburgh, she goes as a vicar's daughter, not as an earl's cherished relation, however distant. What, by the way, were you doing in Edinburgh for better than a fortnight?" Morna asked because Graham had all but told her St. Didier had been dispatched to retrieve an engagement ring.

Morna had regarded engagement rings as an extravagant affectation, but now that she was engaged, or as good as, she found the gesture touching and generous. Still, it didn't take two weeks to pick up a ring.

"I was sent to retrieve goods not suitable for entrusting to the mail," St. Didier said. "I also tried to find the former cook, Mrs. Theobaldia Gibson. I was unsuccessful."

The past, again. Always trying to intrude on present joys. "Graham set you at that task?"

"He did. Mrs. Gibson, who was quite mature at the time of the countess's death, emigrated to Boston when she left the castle. I did find her sister, who claimed Theobaldia's decision to leave Scotland was made abruptly, though Boston apparently agrees with her well enough. The sisters correspond, and Mrs. Gibson has never explained why she left a prestigious post here to skin rabbits in the wilds of Massachusetts."

"Mrs. Gibson claimed old women weren't safe in their beds at the castle." Morna nodded to Aunt Maighread, who had engaged old John MacIver in earnest discussion by the door to the cardroom. "The post was prestigious when Mrs. Gibson took it, but scandalous when she left."

"Scandalous by English standards, perhaps, but I gather local sentiment ran against the sheriff's man and Dr. Ramsey, not against the MacNeils."

He gathered correctly. "Graham came home referring to himself as a felon nonetheless. I hate that."

St. Didier took a perhaps dilatory sip of his drink. "Because he's innocent?"

As the waltz wound on, Morna considered her answer. "Because he's more than innocent. He took punishment that either should never have been meted out, or should have been meted out for another."

"Which theory do you favor?"

The question was serious. St. Didier sought her honest opinion. "Graham told you about the candles?"

"Somebody was in the sickroom between when Peter brought up

the posset and the present earl came by to see to the countess's medicinal tisane. Could it have been a maid or a footman?"

"Not likely. The family tended to her ladyship in the evening.
We each had our little jobs, and putting the candles out would have
been Graham's responsibility if her ladyship was ready to sleep
following her last dose of the day."

"Then whoever blew out the candles wasn't familiar with the
sickroom routine, were they?"

In the whole castle, who would *not* have known the nightly ritual
designed to give the countess enough company, enough nourishment,
enough medicine, but not too much of any of the foregoing? The
kitchen certainly knew the particulars, which ruled out Mrs. Gibson.
The housekeeper, maids, and footman, most of the family...

"Frustrating," Morna said, "to have no answers after all this time,
and when we think we have an answer, we have more questions
instead. Aunt Hibernia is quite bold."

The old dear had just kissed Graham's cheek.

"She is doubtless congratulating him in anticipation of his good
fortune. Might I escort you to the buffet?"

The music slowed to the final reprise, the dancing couples eased
apart, and Peter looked like a man who'd survived Waterloo. His
smile was wooden, while Vera Conroy chattered brightly at his side.
When he'd delivered his partner to the vicar's wife, he decamped
with observable dispatch.

Nevin Bodeen took Peter's place in less than three seconds.

"Graham has insisted that he'll see me to the buffet," Morna said.
"Besides, you owe the local belles a chance to interrogate you. Unlike
Uncle Brodie, your recollections of fashionable London date from the
present century."

St. Didier smiled, and Morna realized with a sort of dismay that
he could be *attractive*. Too serious, too observant and quiet, but when
he allowed himself a glimmer of humanity, his looks took on an
appeal that Morna would not have believed possible absent the
evidence of her own eyes.

"Escort Aunt Hibernia," Morna said as Peter made his way toward them through the throng. "She will have more intelligence to share with you than Wellington's best spies ever gathered behind enemy lines."

"I'll do that. Peter, good evening. Your gentlemanly forbearance does you credit. In your situation, I might have been tempted to engage in a judicious bit of tripping on a lady's hems."

"I didn't think to trip over her hems. Forewarned and all that, for next time. Morna, a question."

"Of course."

"Where's Lanie? I searched before the supper waltz, which I wanted to sit out with her, but then Vera the Limpet got hold of me, and now I can't find Lanie anywhere."

"Shall I check the ladies' retiring room?"

"She'll go up to her apartment rather than brave that brood of vipers, but the footman at the landing said she hasn't gone up."

The footman was stationed on the landing to stop misguided guests from wandering into the family wing.

"Let's have a word with Dunhaven, shall we?" St. Didier suggested. "He's been by the veranda door for the past quarter hour. Perhaps he saw her slip out of the ballroom."

Morna took a quick inventory of the guests not yet heading across the corridor to the buffet in the gallery. Vera Conroy was still in earnest discussion with Nevin Bodeen, and the lady looked entirely too smug for the occasion.

"Let's have a word this instant," Morna said. "Lanie would not have absented herself voluntarily right before supper without telling me."

"Fetch John MacIver," Graham said quietly, though the urge to bellow was nigh choking him. "Fetch him discreetly."

"Lanie is missing," Peter retorted. "Nowhere to be found, and you want to chat up the gamekeeper?"

Morna glowered at Peter and then slipped away in the direction of the corridor.

"Does MacIver have scent hounds?" St. Didier asked.

"He does, and they are well trained," Graham said. "He's also loyal."

Peter looked from Graham to St. Didier. "Loyal to the MacNeils?"

"Loyal to me," Graham said, "and the castle. We'll need something that bears Lanie's scent, preferably something she was wearing this evening. Peter, get you to her apartment and find us a shawl or dressing gown, even a pair of slippers or a shift, if she's worn them recently. St. Didier, we'll need warm cloaks. and you'll want to change into boots. I'll meet you at the back terrace door."

The ballroom emptied while Graham stood near the grand staircase and pretended to admire the decorations. Antique chandeliers glowed with hundreds of eight-hour beeswax candles, pennants hung from the minstrels' gallery, and pots of daffodils and ferns graced the ballroom's perimeter. While the guests dined, the footmen would sweep up the original chalk pattern decorating the dance floor and apply new, and fresh ice sculptures would be brought up from the cellars for the punchbowls.

The stags had long since lost their antlers, and Graham would soon lose his mind. Two eternities later, Morna glided into the ballroom, the picture of serene good cheer, John MacIver at her side.

"Laird, good evening." Craggy old MacIver in full Highland kit was an impressive sight. "A fine spread you're puttin' on."

"We'll see that you get a heaping plateful," Graham replied, "as soon as we find Miss Lanie. She's not in her room and not in the castle that we've been able to discern, though we'll do a quick inspection upstairs in the next quarter hour. I'd thought to impose on your hound for assistance with the search."

MacIver studied the fancy ghillie brogues laced about his feet. "Bit nippy to go for a stroll."

"Nippy, dark, and dangerous for a blind woman. We fear she might not be out strolling voluntarily. We need your discretion as well as your best tracking dog."

"Then I will need me boots, Laird, and something from Miss Lanie's wardrobe that she's worn recently."

MacIver's response eased the tiniest morsel of Graham's worry. "I can send a groom to fetch the hound, and we'll find you a pair of boots. You'd best eat now while you have the chance. This could be a long night."

"Aye, and cold. We'll find her, Laird. If she's on the property, we'll find her."

MacIver strode off, a groom was dispatched with all possible speed, and Graham was left with Morna in the deserted ballroom.

"You take the family quarters," Graham said. "I'll do the guest wing. I'll meet you back here."

Twenty minutes later, Graham was out of breath and out of patience. "No Lanie," he said when Morna joined him in the ballroom. "I've asked the aunties to make a discreet perusal of the music room, library, and so on. Peter is having a gander belowstairs."

Lanie's shawl lay over the newel post at the foot of the grand staircase—another carved stag.

Morna took up the shawl and sniffed it, then rolled it into a ball and waved it at Graham. "Don't say it, Graham MacNeil. Do not say this is your fault. Lanie might well be napping in some alcove."

"The whole castle is too noisy for somebody with her sensitive hearing to nap, and we've looked in the alcoves. Somebody has taken her."

"She would set up a hue and cry if somebody tried to abduct her." The confidence in Morna's tone was belied by a glance toward the terrace doors, which still stood open.

"A hue and cry," Graham replied, "that we wouldn't hear while two hundred feet are stomping on a wooden floor and Perthshire's best fiddles are trying to be heard above that racket. The staff is going full tilt in all directions, and Lanie would easily have been tricked into showing somebody a portrait in the library."

From there, she could have been spirited out the French doors and into the night. The work of a moment.

"Then somebody is a kidnapper," Morna reported, "and that is not your fault. We've had criminals in Scotland since before the Flood, I'll have you know, and we had them even when you were off in Australia."

How dear, stubborn, and wrong she was. "Morna, somebody is making a point: I can hide on the family estate all I please, but I and the people I love are not safe as long as I dwell here. Perhaps if I'd not asked so many questions about the past, Lanie might still be safe."

"You don't know that. God in heaven, Graham, Lanie might be having a good cry because she can't waltz with Peter while Vera Conroy was trying to count his ribs with her own."

That observation offered a glimmer of both hope and dread. "Miss Conroy was in earnest discussion with the Bodeen twit immediately after the waltz. Bodeen offered for Lanie, didn't he?"

"And she turned him down flat, showing the good sense for which we all treasure her."

A footman signaled Graham from the terrace doorway, and Graham nodded acknowledgment. "MacIver's hound has arrived. Let's find our gamekeeper and meet St. Didier by the terrace door."

"I've already changed into boots." Morna held up the hem of a lovely velvet ballgown to reveal the toes of a pair of very practical, substantial boots. "The latest in Scottish fashion, that's me."

Graham kissed her, for courage, and because, for his sake, she was trying to remain calm in the midst of disaster.

"No dancing slippers for me tonight," Graham said, taking the shawl from her and leading the way to the corridor. "I've warned Peter we'll be gathering by the terrace door. Drat and blast, it's snowing."

"The hound won't care about a dusting of snow." Morna swept

past him, and they were soon at the door to the back terrace, where MacIver, St. Didier, Peter, and a panting canine met them.

"Lanie's shawl," Graham said, passing over the ball of wool. "She wore it earlier today. One of her favorites." His voice shook as the thought assailed him that Lanie might never wear it again. "How the hell do we start, MacIver? We've thousands of acres, and now it's damned snowing."

"Barely," St. Didier said, passing Morna her cloak. "A few stray flakes. I'd suggest a perimeter search first."

Peter pulled on a three-caped greatcoat. "What does that mean?"

MacIver stroked a hand over the hound's head. "Yon Englishman is thinking that if Miss Lanie was led away from the premises on foot, then we'll pick up her trail by making a loose circle around the whole castle. We'll come upon her line of scent, and we can follow where it leads."

"No carriages have come or gone in the last hour," St. Didier said. "I asked the groom who brought the hound. Unless somebody lifted Miss Lanie off her feet, threw her over his shoulder, and carried her away without provoking her to screaming, we stand a good chance of picking up her trail."

Graham searched for his new cloak among the garments hanging from pegs along the dimly lit hallway, lost patience with the exercise, and grabbed the countess's old cloak. Morna passed him a scarf and wrapped one about her own neck.

"Lanie might need a cloak," Peter said, taking one off a peg. "And I might need to kill somebody."

"We'll find her," Graham said with a calm and confidence he did not feel. "MacIver, you're in charge."

"Then you will all stay well behind me. Give the beast time and space to do his job. He's the best in the shire, if not in all of Scotland. Come along, Hamlet. We're off for a wee stroll."

Hamlet, the doomed prince. Lovely.

Graham allowed everybody else to file out into the night behind MacIver before bringing up the rear and closing the door. The front of the house had been resplendently lit with torches, while the back was lit only by the rising moon. Flurries drifting down on a chill breeze shone like diamonds, probably the last of the season, and tonight of all nights.

As Graham tromped along behind the others, Morna dropped back and took his hand.

"We'll find her, Graham. She wants to be found, she's quite sensible, and we're determined."

All true, but little comfort, so Graham squeezed Morna's fingers and kept silent. Twenty minutes later, nobody was saying much of anything when the hound stopped, sniffed more slowly, and looked up at MacIver.

The gamekeeper merely stood still while the dog resumed sniffing, then broke into a trot, nose down, and headed for the dark line of trees twenty yards ahead.

"The woods," Peter muttered. "Lanie would never have gone for a walk in the woods at night by herself, much less by day. Somebody wants to die a slow and painful death."

"The Leap is that direction," Morna said. "Threaten violence later. Find my sister now."

The hound let out a yodeling whuffle, and MacIver responded with a command in Gaelic.

Graham dropped Morna's hand and broke into a run.

Morna caught up to Graham only when he'd stopped ten yards short of the precipice.

"Who's there?" Lanie asked, two words laced with more anxiety than annoyance. She sat on the old bench, knees drawn up and skirts tucked over her feet, a small, dark shape in a large shadowy night.

"Lanie, it's Morna. Graham is with me. Peter and St. Didier are coming right along, and MacIver and his hound are with us too."

Lanie stood up, not six feet from the drop, and Morna nearly screamed.

Graham ambled toward the bench. "Stay right where you are, Lanie. You're about two yards from the Leap, and we wouldn't want you starting any new legends. I do believe that's my cloak you're wearing."

"It's too long on me."

Graham reached her, enfolded her in a hug, and soon had a lachrymose female in his embrace. "You're safe, Lanie. We'll get you back to the castle, find you a toddy and a warm fire. You're safe."

"I want P-Peter." A wail from the heart as Lanie slipped from Graham's arms.

Morna wiped a tear on her sleeve and shoved Peter forward.

"I'm here, Lanie," Peter said, sounding surprisingly calm and cheerful. "I've brought your old cloak."

Lanie was shivering despite the warmth Graham's cloak afforded. Peter wrapped the second cloak around her. "Let's get you out of these woods."

"I knew I was at the Leap because of the noise from the river and the knots in the bench, but the falls below made it hard to listen for the violins."

"The violins are silent now," Morna said. "The guests are enjoying the supper break." Somebody had timed this kidnapping very carefully, somebody who knew of Lanie's acute hearing. Graham's thunderous scowl told Morna he'd reached the same conclusion.

"You can tell us how you came to be here when you're warm," Graham said. "Because everybody is focused on the buffet and the gossip, few will even have noticed that you were absent."

"I am so cold," Lanie said, leaning into Peter.

"Let's get you home." Peter wrapped an arm around her shoulders. "Follow the sound of MacIver's panting hound, to whom I promise a diet of juicy steak for all the rest of his days."

"He'd rather chew on your boots," MacIver said, "but the steaks would suit me quite well."

Morna wanted to hug the old man for providing a pragmatic touch of humor and hug the dog for preventing a tragedy.

"He told me to stay on the bench, and I'd be safe," Lanie said. "People can freeze to death. I thought I felt some snowflakes on my cheeks."

"You did," Morna replied. "Did you recognize the voice, Lanie?"

The only sound for the next few moments was the dog snuffling along as he led the party in the direction of the castle.

"I did not. I assumed he was a man, but he whispered, and his accent was odd. English, but not from the Borders or Yorkshire. He smelled like Graham, and his hold on my arm was quite firm."

Morna could *feel* Peter growling and *hear* Graham silently swearing vengeance, which wouldn't yield them any answers.

"How did this person trick you into leaving the ball, Lanie?" Morna asked.

"He smelled like Graham. He was wearing Graham's cloak. I realize that now. The new one, from Edinburgh. He whispered to me that if I'd come along, somebody had asked to meet me on the terrace. Then it was 'just a bit farther' until I began to struggle and demand to be returned to the castle. I realized Peter would never ask me to rely on a stranger out of doors in the dark, and my escort didn't walk like Graham. Besides that, Graham would never give me cause to worry by playing blind man's bluff games with me or whispering like some truant schoolboy."

"Damned right I wouldn't."

The abductor knew which cloak was Graham's, knew that Lanie identified people by scent, and further knew that the cloak would be redolent of Graham's heathery fragrance.

"How did you find me?"

"Peter tried to locate you before the supper waltz," Morna said. "He was waylaid by Vera Conroy, then he sounded the alarm at the first opportunity." And that blasted waltz had gone on forever.

"Graham summoned MacIver," Peter added, "and we had old Hamlet fetched, and here we are. I am personally ready for a go at the buffet."

Was Peter trying to comfort Lanie by mentioning food? To calm himself? To pretend Lanie hadn't been abducted from amid a crowd of neighbors in her very home?

"Some things had best be discussed now," Morna said, "while Lanie's recollections are fresh."

"That's up to Lanie." Graham took Morna's hand and gave it a squeeze. "She can decide if she'd rather eat, talk to us, do both, or rejoin the crowd in the ballroom and put off the rest until later."

Morna wanted to argue, but Graham was right. Lanie's needs came first.

They emerged from the woods, the back of the castle looming before them against the night sky.

"Not far to go now," Peter said. "We're out of the woods, Lanie."

"I know. The smell is different, and we're no longer walking on leaves and bracken. My feet are blocks of ice."

Good God, she was wearing heeled slippers. Graham and Peter muttered curses.

"You are all too quiet," Lanie said. "If you want to know my preferences, I'd like to return to the ball, enjoy supper with Peter just as we'd planned, and make sure Vera Conroy sees that I'm on hand and enjoying myself."

Vera Conroy lacked the wits to orchestrate this crime. Nevin Bodeen was mean enough to consider this a prank, but he'd have needed an accomplice from within the castle.

"If nobody objects," St. Didier said, "I'll find a footman to take the hound back to his hearth."

MacIver passed over the leash, and St. Didier headed across the garden toward the sunken steps that led to the pantries.

"St. Didier will feel responsible," Lanie said. "He's like that. He thinks he's supposed to keep everybody safe all the time."

Graham sighed. Peter was muttering again, this time in the Erse.

"We think," Morna said, "that you deserve to be safe in your own home."

"I'm all but blind," Lanie retorted. "I will never be safe when the rest of the world is for people who can see well. I am hungry."

Morna wished she could pry Lanie from beneath Peter's arm and hug her and shake her and hug her. Lanie was trying to be brave—more brave than usual—and that she had been victimized yet again, not by a disease, but by a person acting willfully, was abominable.

"You'll need dry shoes and stockings," Morna said, rather than curse and rant and kick the potted tulips. "Let's get you up to your apartment."

"I want to take a tray in the study," Lanie said. "The study will be warm, and I can eat in peace there with Peter. By the time the fiddles are tuning up again, I shall be smiling graciously where everybody can see me, and you lot can watch for who acts surprised."

Graham and Peter exchanged a look, and then it was Peter's turn to sigh.

"If that's what you want, dearest Lanie," he said, "that's what will happen."

With profuse thanks to MacIver, who looked to be standing at least three feet taller in his kilt and boots, the party broke up at the back terrace door. Morna went to fetch dry slippers and stockings, Graham took up impersonating a jovial host, and Peter escorted Lanie to the warmth and safety of the old earl's study.

Only as Morna was sorting through wool stockings in Lanie's dresser did she realize the full impact of the night's mischief. Lanie was shaken—they were all shaken—and might well come down with a lung fever as a result of being kidnapped.

Peter was furious now, but likely also hoping to pass the whole matter off as a prank taken too far.

St. Didier was off to sort suspects and evidence belowstairs.

And Graham was, without doubt, planning to leave, to go far, far away for a very long time, once again taking the blame for a crime he did not commit.

CHAPTER FOURTEEN

"None the worse for her little adventure, then?" MacIver asked, stroking a hand over the hound's head.

Graham had found the gamekeeper and his familiar enjoying the midmorning sunshine on the porch of MacIver's cottage. The cottage had been built back in Queen Mary's day and had often housed a large family comfortably.

Now, one old man, a few hounds, and a lot of memories were left to fill the entire space.

"Miss Lanie is bearing up," Graham said, settling on the wooden porch steps. "Like Peter, she prefers to put bad days behind her. I bring her thanks as well as my own, Miss Morna's, and Peter's for your help."

"Part of my job, Laird, and part of Hamlet's job. I wish we could track the bastard that pulled this trick."

The dog raised his eyebrows, his chin remaining on his paws.

"Can you find him?" Besides conveying personal thanks, this was the other purpose for Graham's call. "You know where to start casting for his scent, and he was wearing my cloak." Until the wretch had tossed it at Lanie and strode away, apparently, leaving her shivering on a bench under a dark, frigid sky. The dusting of snow had been gone an hour after sunrise, while Graham's ire remained unabated.

"That's the problem," MacIver said, pulling the hound's ear gently. "He was wearing your cloak. Fine wool, velvet lining. It would reek of you for donkey's years and mask the other fellow's scent to a significant degree. If Hamlet were to follow the smell of the trail itself—the broken vegetation and footprints and such—he'd simply take us to the Leap and back to the castle. If I were your villain, I'd have rejoined the festivities, which hosted both a crowd of guests and a crowd of footmen and maids lent by our neighbors for the night."

MacIver lowered himself gingerly to sit one step higher than Graham. "I am sorry, Laird. Somebody deserves a good hiding, at the least."

Somebody deserved to be left alone in the dark, unable to see, six feet from certain death.

"We might not have found her but for you and your hound, MacIver. I don't mean to insult you, but you could ask anything of me now, and I'd be delighted to make your wishes come true. Steaks for the dog don't half begin to show our appreciation."

"Can you bring my Nan and her weans back from Nova Scotia?"

"I'll fetch her back on a chartered sloop if that's what you want."

MacIver snorted with what might have been amusement. "Don't you dare, laddie. She's happy there, if her letters can be believed."

Letters MacIver doubtless read over and over, until the ink faded and the creases began to wear through.

"If she's not to come home, then why are you still here?" Graham asked, giving the hound a scratch about the ears. A thick tail thumped a couple times in response.

"Where would I go?"

"Nova Scotia, of course. Take your hounds and set sail. The coneys will rejoice until Michaelmas."

Nobody would rejoice if Graham returned to Australia—Graham least of all—but somebody might stop threatening the lives of the people Graham loved.

Might.

"If I lark off across the sea, who will keep your game, Laird?"

"The braw, bonnie laddie of your choosing, that's who. All the local men know how to read sign, set snares, and fill a game bag thanks to you. Those skills served me well in Australia, I'll have you know."

Graham had not come here to talk MacIver into retirement, much less emigration, but the old man seemed to be giving the notion some consideration.

"I love my home," MacIver said. "That's the Scot in me, and here, I have my post, a roof over my head. Responsibilities. *Respect*. If I trade that for a chair by Nan's fire, I'll turn into another version of that wretched fool Brodie, a teller of tales—and boring tales at that. They'll start calling me Back-in-Scotland, as we used to refer to Brodie as Down-in-London. Not a flattering way to end one's days."

Brodie had behaved himself at the ball. He'd refrained from spiking the ladies' punch and avoided the near occasion of duels or slaps to his face. He'd been least in sight at breakfast, and Graham had yet to tell him of Lanie's abduction.

MacIver, who'd had the more taxing evening, had doubtless been up before the sun.

"Firstly, you'd have your pension. You've long since earned it. Secondly, you would not sit by Nan's fire for long. You'd be out in the woods, showing her lads how to catch a coney with their bare hands. And the stories you have are the ones they need to hear and the ones Nan longs to hear again. If your sobriquet becomes Back-in-Scotland, it will be bestowed with respect and affection."

So many stories in Australia. Injustices, christenings, sprees, miraculous coincidences, journeys, and silly mishaps. The stories had done as much to fortify the transportees as any ration of grog ever had.

Why didn't Brodie's stories have the same quality?

"Brodie is a cautionary tale," MacIver said. "Always has been. 'Don't be like yon ass,' my wife used to tell the lads. Never paid his wagers, always dodging off to avoid some angry papa or broken-hearted female. London was welcome to him. If you were to leave again, we'd miss you, Laird."

Canny old hound. "What makes you think I'm contemplating another journey?"

"You've had trouble since you came home, despite your watchful English ghillie, if one might use a contradiction in terms."

English ghillie. St. Didier would be flattered. "Some trouble. I didn't expect everybody to welcome me with open arms. I was judged guilty of a serious crime."

"Bollocks to that, laddie. The countess was old and frail, and you would never have wished her harm. We knew that. All I'm saying is, you'd be missed. We'd understand—we understood last time—but you'd be missed."

"Go to Nova Scotia," Graham said, rising. "I'll stand you to a first-class ticket, and that includes as many hounds as you'd care to travel with."

The thought of another sea voyage... Graham felt sick at the very notion, but not as sick as he'd felt when Hamlet had started on the trail to the Leap.

"First class is for idiots like Brodie. The company is much better in second and downright convivial in steerage."

"Second, then. I'm serious, MacIver."

"You're worried, and with good cause." MacIver rose as well, not a hint of stiffness in his movements. "A person who will put a blameless and blind woman in danger is cursed with a black heart indeed. Think carefully, Laird, before you decide on next steps."

"Good advice. Again, our thanks, MacIver."

"No need. No need a'tall."

There was every need, and yet, one did not argue with old John MacIver.

Graham cut through the woods on the way back to the castle, forcing himself to sit on the bench at the Leap and consider options. Leaving was one choice, but far from ideal. Lanie had nearly come to harm at the ball. Morna had nearly come to harm in Edinburgh. St. Didier might have been stabbed in London.

Somebody was very determined and very well informed. "I could spend three more eternities in Sydney and still not stop them from whatever mischief all this crime is in aid of."

The river roiling below made no reply, save for its relentless roar.

The old fears crowded in next: What if the determined somebody was Peter? Always willing to leap over the past, to change the subject, to lighten the conversation, but having faced many difficulties in life and as capable of anger as the next man.

Though Peter, even to hide his own past misdeeds, would never countenance risk to Lanie.

What if the somebody was Peter trying to protect Lanie—for reasons outlandish or genuine—and Lanie had acceded to his schemes?

"I'm going daft," Graham muttered, getting off the bench and considering the swirling water far below. Not quite full spate, but still frigid and dangerous. Looking into those waters, he felt again the sheer terror he'd experienced the previous night.

"What comes after daft?" Graham asked the brisk morning air. "Something awful."

As Graham left the woods, he was sure of only one thing: The time had come to talk very honestly to Morna. He did not want to leave the castle, no matter how relentlessly some scheming bounder pushed him toward that course.

More significantly, Graham did not want to leave Morna, and he was incapable of seeing past that reality.

The decision to confer with Morna for a consideration of all possibilities, no matter how outlandish didn't exactly settle Graham's nerves, but it did feel right. He'd made a weighty choice before without consulting her, and look how that had turned out.

Graham was halfway up the garden steps when he heard Uncle Brodie shouting out a window at the footmen hauling the torches off the back terrace. The hour was nearly noon, half the day gone and brilliantly sunny, and Brodie expected silence to aid his slumbers.

"Down in London, nobody stirred before noon, you damned louts! A proper morning call was made at two of the clock. How is a man supposed to recover his humors with the racket you make?"

He shook a fist and banged the sash down, leaving the footmen to exchange patient grins. They caught sight of Graham, bobbed shallowly in his direction, and went back to stacking the torches in a barrow.

Down in London…

Peter's comment, about fearing to become like Brodie, haunted Graham anew. A cautionary tale, MacIver had said. Graham was still staring at Brodie's closed window when St. Didier sauntered down from the terrace.

"You look gobsmacked, Dunhaven."

"I am… in possession of an insight. A truth. If I return to Australia, or make my way to India, I will end up exactly like Brodie." Far better to end up like old John MacIver—knowledgeable, respected, patient with human foibles, capable of great sacrifice on behalf of loved ones, and always ready to put his experience in service to others.

"End up like Brodie?" St. Didier studied the footmen wheeling their barrow down the row of torches. "You'll spend your days flirting with widows and avoiding creditors?"

"Not that part, the part about boring stories. I'll cling to an endless lament about when I was back in Scotland, and the Scottish have a saying, and the best food in the world is to be had in Scotland. Boring stories from a boring old man who has nobody's respect."

The rest of the insight clobbered him like the cold, salty deluge of a huge sea wave breaking over the bow of his life.

Blessed Saint Andrew, *no.* Graham took off across the terrace at a jog.

"Dunhaven, where are you going?"

"To talk to Morna. Keep a close eye on Brodie if he condescends to leave his apartment before supper, please."

"If I must."

"You must. You absolutely must." Graham didn't take an easy breath until he found Morna, hale and whole, in the music room.

"Where are Lanie and Peter?" Graham asked, closing the music room door.

Morna rose from the piano bench, surprised at his preemptory tone. "Why?"

"Humor me, please. Recent events have left me a bit unnerved."

He didn't sound unnerved. Lanie might say he sounded determined and formidable. "They're counting the silver in the butler's pantry. The senior staff has the day off, and that will be one less job for them to do. Graham, what's bothering you?"

"Has Lanie said anything more about last night's abduction?"

"Not to me. I hope she's putting Peter's friendly ear to good use." Lanie had certainly been clinging to Peter's friendly hand last night and had insisted on sharing her meal with Peter exclusively. The pair of them had then sat among the potted palms for the rest of the evening, until Lanie had pleaded fatigue. "How is MacIver?"

"He's planning a remove to Nova Scotia. He just hasn't quite settled to the notion yet. How are you?"

Morna took a seat on the stool behind the great harp. "Worried. You are in some sort of swivet, and you won't tell me what it's about. The last time I felt this way, matters did not resolve themselves to my satisfaction." Graham had left Scotland, taking secrets and half of Morna's heart with him.

He pulled up the piano bench and sat facing her, nearly knee to knee. "My less-than-sanguine mood is caused by the need for some plain speaking."

"You are not leaving for Australia, Graham MacNeil. I forbid it."

Morna should have trembled to deliver such an ultimatum. "You aren't leaving without me, that is."

Graham sat back as if slapped. "You cannot come to Australia with me." He stood, sat down again, and used a finger to coax an incongruously gentle glissando from the harp. "What I mean to say is, would you truly consider leaving Scotland with me?"

"Try to stop me, but I don't favor that course. You belong here."

He took Morna's hand. "You are daft, you know. I've always fancied that about you. Since I've come home, somebody has indulged in kidnapping, assault, and an attempted tragic accident to make me rethink my return. I've considered everybody but you as a possible suspect."

He was apparently in deadly earnest, suggesting daftness was catching. "Why not me?"

"The notion that you'd use minions and subterfuge, much less put Lanie in harm's way to send me off is laughable. Besides that, I love you, so even if you did want me gone, I'd not believe it."

"You love me."

"Madly. But we cannot have any more abductions, Morna, or worse. I've considered Peter or some combination of Peter and Lanie as our culprits. I've even tried to pin the mess on St. Didier."

Morna laced her fingers with his. This was plain speaking indeed. "I've done likewise, but unless St. Didier poisoned Grandmama and hopes to keep you from further investigating the past, he has no motive for the present mischief, and he had no motive for taking Gran's life in the first place."

"That's my Morna, always practical. I reached the same conclusion, and I also considered Dr. Ramsey again, but he had every reason to keep Gran from her celestial reward."

"I know. Graham, where are you heading with this?" Not to Australia, thank heavens.

"I can't make accusations without some proof, Morna, and for that I need to talk to Lanie. Peter can disown me, you can disown me

—though I hope you don't—but it's time Miss Lanie and I put our heads together."

"She didn't kill Grandmama, Graham. She would never do such a thing, and she was just a child and would have no idea..."

Graham took Morna's other hand in his. "She had survived a bout of measles and knew all about being dosed with patent remedies. Her eyesight was better then, and she might have been simply following Grandmama's instructions without realizing their import. I am more focused on the fact that somebody besides me or Peter blew out the candles, and Lanie was the only person whom we know to have been in the room at the time."

Morna's whole being rebelled at Graham's suggestion, and yet... what few facts they had fit this hypothesis.

"You have to be wrong, Graham."

"I expect I am wrong. I suspect Lanie is blameless, and another party entirely is behind the entire ball of trouble, but Lanie alone can support that conclusion with evidence. I propose that she and I have a private chat—no witnesses, no eavesdroppers, and the less Peter knows about the whole business, the better."

"You're asking my permission to talk to Lanie?"

"If you want to put it like that, yes. I did not consult you before I signed away my freedom following the countess's death. I thought I'd protect you with distance and silence, rather than have you trying to exonerate me and putting yourself in harm's way. I am sorry for that, Morna, and I hope you've forgiven me. I'm consulting you now, and I will be guided by your counsel."

What had it cost him to put the reins in Morna's hands? "I could have made you talk to me. I didn't even try, Graham. I nursed my injured pride and then embroidered my fingers numb with regret and resentment."

"I broke sod. Australian sod is ungodly tough."

He smiled at her, and Morna leaned forward to put her forehead on his shoulder. "I never want to lose you again, Graham MacNeil. Talk to Lanie. Get to the truth."

He circled her shoulders with one arm and spoke close to her ear. "And if the truth lets all manner of demons out of the box with it?"

"The demons are already free, driving coaches and leading Lanie into the woods. To banish them, you and Lanie must clear the air."

"You're sure?"

"I wish I had even the slightest doubt. Peter will be furious."

Graham kissed Morna's temple. "He thinks he's protecting her, and she probably thinks she's protecting him. Fools in love. A common problem. Can you have Lanie meet me in the study?"

"Give me half an hour, but whatever she says, Graham, you know she'll tell Peter of the discussion."

"That will be her choice."

Morna indulged in a long, fortifying hug, denied herself the pleasure of kissing Graham, and went in search of her sister.

"I love this room," Lanie said, inhaling the aromas in the earl's study as if she were in a blooming garden. "Our whole story is in here, with the scents of the leather, the books, and the peat; the portraits, the ledgers, the furniture that's been in the same spots for ages. I hate when somebody moves furniture on me. Detest it bitterly."

"Lanie, you needn't be nervous," Graham said. "I don't want to talk about last night." Graham, oddly enough, wasn't nervous. He'd spent too much time being unsettled, anxious, frustrated, and bewildered, as had they all. The time had come for answers.

"I'll talk about last night," Lanie retorted, "though not in front of Peter. He isn't always the pleasant, easygoing fellow he wants us to believe he is." Lanie put out a hand, connected with the back of a wing chair, and sidled around to take a seat.

Damn the blindness, but Graham was counting on the backhanded gifts that blindness had bestowed.

"Peter was threatening to kill whoever abducted you. Nobody

chided him for it. I think you know who the culprit is, or you have a strong suspicion."

Lanie toed off her slippers, tucked her feet up, and pulled the plaid blanket from the back of the chair to drape over her legs.

"It was dark, Graham, and if I'm to see at all, I need strong sunlight. The whole neighborhood was on hand, and that creates a confusion of scents. Even Hamlet apparently needed some time to sort out what he was sniffing."

"Right, but we aren't concerned at the moment with last night. Lanie, talk to me about the night the countess died. I know you and Morna broached this topic, but you and I have never discussed it."

She nodded once. "Because it upsets Peter. He thinks discussing the past upsets me, and I am apparently too delicate to bear such a burden. The past does hold some unpleasant memories—ask anybody who's been cursed by measles about that—but what truly bothers me is not knowing what happened."

"Though you have a theory. I have a theory, too, Lanie, and while you are bothered, I am nigh obsessed with the same riddle. I believe all the recent difficulties—the reckless coach, an attempted assault on the London docks, your abduction—are an effort to drive me from my home. I've asked too many questions, but I haven't asked the right questions."

"Or you haven't asked the right people. Ask me, Graham. I'll tell you what I know."

Graham mentally hugged her for her fortitude and hoped her honesty was up to the challenge. "I know you kept Grandmama company on her last night, as had become your habit. Peter brought her a posset as usual and noticed you dozing in the chair by the fire. The candles were lit at the time, but when I came by later—again, keeping to my routine—the candles had been doused."

"Peter mentioned that, but I wasn't sure of the signif—oh. You wonder if I doused the candles, but I don't recall doing so. That wasn't a job for a blind girl. I might have knocked a candle over, or left one burning by accident, or burned myself blowing them out. I could toss peat onto the fire safely enough, but I left candles for others to deal with."

"I assumed as much, so we know somebody else was in the room between Peter's visit and mine. Lanie, what scents do you recall?"

She pleated the hem of the blanket, unfolded it, pleated it again. "My recollections are muzzy, Graham. I was muzzy, for that matter. I'd been deeply asleep, for some reason, though I seldom slept well then. It's hard to get physically tired when you can't go hiking through the woods at will or take your pony out for a hard gallop."

So much Graham hadn't considered about Lanie's realities, though Peter was doubtless keenly aware of these facts.

"Morna said when you woke up to return to your own room, you didn't feel right. What was off, Lanie?"

This part was delicate. Graham didn't want to suggest memories into existence, but he wanted every crumb of truth Lanie could part with.

"I told Morna even the air felt wrong. What did I mean?"

"What did you smell, Lanie?"

Her hand went still on the blanket. "Cedar—that was your preferred fragrance at the time. Balsam—that was Peter, even then. The lemony-cinnamon aroma St. Didier prefers wasn't in the mix, and neither were Morna's roses, but..."

Lanie went silent.

"Tell me, Lanie. The evidence won't be enough for a conviction, but justice doesn't always mean involving the courts."

"Cigars. The stink can't be obliterated by more pleasant aromas, and it lingers forever. Graham, I smelled cigars."

Graham felt no sense of triumph or vindication at this revelation, only the relief of a sad hypothesis confirmed.

"Uncle Brodie," Lanie said. "Why would he end his sister's life? Could it have been an accident? He would not have known the sick-room routine, would he?"

"He would, if he'd asked any footman or maid." Or if he'd asked

Mrs. Gibson. "Lanie, is there any doubt in your mind about what your nose told you?"

She stroked a hand over the soft wool of the blanket. "I think I knew without knowing, Graham, which is why when Peter told me to let it go, I was willing to heed him. He thinks I killed Grandmama, doesn't he?"

"He might, and his reaction has been to protect you rather than sort out the past. Will you tell him what you've recalled?"

"I want to. You believe me, don't you? I smelled Brodie's cigars, and that's why the air felt wrong."

"I believe so, and other evidence points to Brodie's guilt."

For three ticks of the clock, they sat in silence, and then Lanie folded up the blanket in her lap. "What now, Graham? Will you challenge Brodie to a duel? Peter says they're going out of fashion. Besides, you're a peer, so you can't challenge a commoner."

"And Brodie is very much a commoner. Have you been brushing up on the *Code Duello*, Lanie?"

"Peter read it to me. Don't tell Morna."

"May I tell Morna about what we've discussed?"

Lanie gathered up the blanket, shoved it behind her, and rose. "You may, but what will you do about Brodie?"

Graham got to his feet as well, but he could not let Lanie leave quite yet. "You smelled cigars last night too, Lanie, didn't you?"

She scooted around the chair, putting it between them. "I did. I noticed that my escort had brandy on his breath—that rank, been-at-the-decanters sort of breath, and when I realized that, I knew he could not be you. You were keeping a clear head, as the host, according to Peter."

"As the main attraction," Graham said. "And this fellow did not walk like me, and you also smelled cigars?"

"Yes, and I told myself I did not want Peter killing Brodie, and Brodie has never known when a prank isn't funny, and I came to no harm, and... I thought about asking Morna what I should do, but Peter does have a temper. I lean on Morna for much, and on Peter, and sometimes I think I will never have any independence unless I insist on thinking for myself. Does that make sense?"

"Lanie, you are more independent than many sighted women, and I am walking evidence that too much thinking for oneself can cause serious problems."

"You'll marry Morna, won't you? Peter says you have to marry her first before he and I can tie the knot."

"I dearly, dearly hope to marry Morna, and I'm delighted to hear that you and Peter are engaged. Right now, though, I'll settle for talking to Morna with Peter, and with St. Didier on hand as well. If you'll join us, we'll have the first MacNeil counsel of war in at least a hundred years."

"Good. I never cared for Uncle Brodie, and Peter doesn't much like him either."

"Make yourself comfortable, then, and I'll fetch the others, but, Lanie?"

"Graham?"

"Lock the door behind me and admit no one whom you don't recognize by voice. Brodie has to be getting desperate, and precautions are in order."

Precautions, a counsel of war, and then—at long last, the truth aired in the full light of day.

～

"We'll be late for the noon meal," Peter said, preceding Graham through the study door. "Lanie, I thought you and Morna were counting linens." To Morna's eye, Peter looked displeased to find Lanie someplace other than the linen closet.

The two brothers stood side by side before Grandpapa's enormous desk, the elder a bit taller and more muscular than the younger, but both balanced on the knife edge between caution and battle.

"The linens can wait," Morna said. "Graham has invited us here for a family discussion, and now it only needs..."

St. Didier paused just inside the door. He'd put aside his kilt and reverted to the attire of a typical English country gentleman, and he, too, bore a watchful air.

"What's *he* doing here?" Peter asked, folding his arms. "He's not family."

Lanie held out a hand. "And you, dear Peter, are not normally rude. Come sit by me and stop fretting."

Peter crossed the room and perched on the arm of Lanie's chair. He looked fretful nonetheless. Morna was certain that where Lanie was concerned, some part of Peter would never stop fretting.

St. Didier shoved the hassock closer to the hearth and took a seat. "A footman conveyed a summons to me. A novel experience, and here I am. Dunhaven, your brother is right: The noon meal awaits. Why not take the conversation to the dining room?"

Graham half sat, half leaned on the desk. "We'll eat soon enough. First, I'd like to put a theory before present company and ask each of you for your best effort to prove or demolish my theory. The matter has to do with Uncle Brodie."

He summarized Lanie's recollections regarding the countess's death, and sometime during that recitation, Lanie took Peter's hand.

"I don't care for Uncle Brodie," Peter said slowly, "but why would he kill his sister? To put it crudely, wouldn't that have been like killing the goose who laid his golden eggs? Brodie could lark around London and Edinburgh, cut a dash as a handsome bachelor, and then retreat to the castle when he was out of blunt. Grandmama was his patroness, more or less."

Morna found it encouraging that Peter was applying logic rather than fists to the situation.

"Brodie came into a competence upon his sister's death, didn't he?" St. Didier asked. "Coin of the realm has motivated more than one violent crime."

"He did," Graham said, "and Grandpapa had promised Brodie a home for life, so Grandmama's death would have put Brodie ahead financially."

"He doesn't seem to be ahead financially now," Morna said. "He's either become the quintessential pinchpenny old Scot, or he's as skint now as he perpetually was in his youth."

"Maybe he's spent his funds," Peter surmised. "Stupid wagers, a ransom to the tailor and the bootmaker, horse races, fashionable apartments, light-skirts, begging the pardon of present company. He also must have his pretty snuff boxes."

"Possibly," Graham said, "but by the time Grandmama died, Brodie was sporting about London and Edinburgh less and less. I suspect his debts had become pressing, perhaps mortally so. Until I speak to him, we don't know if Grandmama's death was an accident, but we do know Brodie is responsible for abducting Lanie last night."

Peter kissed Lanie's knuckles when Morna had been braced for him to explode.

"I knew you were keeping something to yourself, Lanie dearest," Peter said, caressing her fingers. "You caught the stink of Brodie's cigars last night, didn't you? When I put Graham's cloak about your shoulders, I thought I might have smelled the same thing, but I dismissed the notion. The whole house reeked of beeswax, the card-room was smoky, and the peat fires were roaring. I couldn't be sure."

"Leading me into the woods wasn't a prank," Lanie said quite firmly. "That was an attempt to frighten Graham into leaving, which he must not do."

Peter scowled at his brother. "The coach in Edinburgh?"

"And," St. Didier said, "the footpad on the London docks. Brodie still has old connections there, and some of them are apparently in low places. If I were Dunhaven, I'd be very cautious about everything I ate or drank."

"I have been," Graham said. "I don't order any trays sent up from the kitchen, and I eat only what's prepared for the whole family at meals. Peter, I suggest you do likewise."

"Why?"

The truth landed in Morna's awareness like a lit Congreve rocket. "Because if Brodie seeks wealth, Graham's death and yours would bring him closer to that goal. Scottish titles can often be preserved through the female line, and even if Brodie could not inherit the title, he could inherit Graham's personal wealth, as well as your own, or a good portion of it."

"I've left it all to Lanie," Peter said. "Took care of that the day I turned one-and-twenty."

"Morna is my heir," Graham said, sharing a bashful smile with his brother. "The legalities required a trust document and some weaseling words, but the lot of what I own goes to my dearest."

"I hate that we're discussing Uncle Brodie like this," Lanie said. "We have only the evidence of my nose and a lot of conjecture to convict him, and yet, convict him we have."

"The evidence of your nose," Morna said, "is more than enough for me."

"That's not all we have," St. Didier said. "You, Miss MacKenzie, made Dunhaven aware that Dr. Ramsey remained in correspondence with Brodie. I found that odd after all these years. When Dunhaven suggested I have a chat with the physician, I asked some pointed questions about that correspondence."

Morna sent Graham a puzzled look. "You thought Dr. Ramsey was holding something back, but you didn't press him."

"I was too anxious to get us all back to the castle," Graham said. "Besides, St. Didier has an uncanny knack for encouraging people to air their guilty consciences. Ramsey had more to say, none of it flattering to Brodie, but by no means evidence of murder."

"I'm told St. Didier is a credit to a kilt," Lanie said. "A dangerous man, if he's also prone to wheedling confessions from the unsuspecting." She emphasized her accent on the final word in the phrase a dangerous *mon*.

"I'm feeling dangerous myself," Peter said. "I'd like to murder Brodie in his bed, but I suppose a duel will have to do."

Lanie unwrapped her hand from his. "Not funny, Peter."

"Not joking, Elaine Marie."

"No duels," Morna said, causing all heads to swivel in her direction. "Injury in a duel is considered an assault, and any violent death can be prosecuted as a murder. I will not support activity that could see somebody I love transported or hanged."

"Nor will I," Lanie said.

"I wouldn't kill him," Peter muttered.

"Not on purpose," Graham replied, "but you don't want to take the risk of him flinching or—more likely—firing early, do you?"

That Graham also disapproved of a duel was more relief.

"Dunhaven, have you a plan?" St. Didier asked. "Brodie might well show himself at supper, and one wants to know one's lines."

"I have some ideas," Graham said, "but they want refining. My general thoughts are as follows."

Morna detested his general thoughts. Peter and St. Didier were intrigued by them. Lanie had some general thoughts of her own, and before lunch was served, the workings of a plan were agreed to, though Morna didn't care for the proposed scheme one bit.

On a more encouraging note, Uncle Brodie would positively loathe Graham's plan, *if it went well.*

CHAPTER FIFTEEN

Both at lunch and in the discussion that had preceded it, Morna had said far too little for Graham's liking. Discretion had been necessitated at supper by the footman at the sideboard, and thus St. Didier, Lanie, and Peter had carried on a conversation focused on planting, shearing, and Graham knew not what else.

He dragged the brush through his hair one more time. "You're not going to Almack's, laddie," he informed his reflection in the cheval mirror. "You're off to the library to fetch a book."

The library lay in the opposite direction of Morna's door. A detail. He gave the sash of his dressing gown a yank and sallied forth.

Only to be greeted by Morna in similar dishabille halfway down the corridor. "You couldn't sleep?" he asked. "Off to fetch a book from the library?"

"From the study."

Which lay in the opposite direction from Graham's door. "The fire is roaring in my apartment," he said. "We can discuss literature, if you are so inclined." He winged his arm. Morna gave him the slightest hint of a smile, and his whole being eased.

He waited until they were behind the locked door of his sitting room before taking Morna in his arms.

"You're worried, dearest lady. You go quiet when you're anxious." And she'd been quiet for hours.

"You're worried, too, or you should be. I don't like this plan of yours, Graham."

She burrowed closer, which Graham liked a bit too much. "It's not my plan, it's our plan. Shall we sit?"

Morna drew back and glowered at him. "I came here to scold you. To admonish you to be careful, to take every precaution, to rehearse and review and... If this scheme goes awry, I will follow you into hell itself to take out my wrath upon you."

He glowered back, or tried to. "Perhaps we've spent enough time in the outer reaches of perdition, Morna. After tomorrow, that will all be behind us."

"Good. Because I have no intention of dwelling any longer in such an insalubrious location."

Her words were right. Morna's speech was intended to convey that she was in high dudgeon, poised to call a halt to the whole campaign, but her tone was pleading rather than demanding, and her gaze...

She wasn't merely worried, Morna was frightened, and that tore at Graham's heart. "I will take no risks. I will stick to the letter of my marching orders. I will blow retreat at the first sign that I've misread the situation."

"Do you promise me all of that, Graham? No heroics, no martyring yourself for the sake of the castle, no committing crimes that could get you entangled with the law again. Promise me."

"Morna MacKenzie, would I lie to my affianced bride?"

The smile came again, knowing, a bit impish, enough to drive a strong man to raving.

"Have I missed something, Graham? A proposal possibly? A formal request that I consider marrying you?"

The lady had a point. Not a detail at all.

"Come along, Miss MacKenzie." Graham led her by the hand into the bedroom and from there into the dressing closet, which was illuminated by a single sconce. The ring was exactly where he'd left it, nestled in a corner of the jewelry box.

"You don't have to kneel," Morna said when he went down on one knee.

"I'm not doing this twice, Morna. I'll kneel if I please to."

She sank onto his dressing stool, looking a little bewildered and a little amused. "Proceed, then."

Part of Graham was aghast. He was proposing in a *dressing closet.* Speaking the most important words of his life not amid the gorgeous Scottish outdoors, or surrounded by the books Morna loved, but amid boots, shirts, and jackets. Not even clean boots, given the pair in the corner.

The scent of leather and starch blended with the fragrance of heather, and the single candle cast more shadows than light. Wrong, wrong, all wrong.

And yet, the moment was right. He had Morna completely to himself, and they had peace and quiet in abundance. What's more, she had as good as given him permission to propose, and that had to be a good sign. For himself, Graham wanted to go forth the next day secure in the knowledge that he was her betrothed.

For her, he wanted to give her everything he could give her, most especially the heart he'd left with her years ago.

"Morna MacKenzie, I have loved you forever and will love you forevermore. Will you marry me?"

"Yes."

He rested his forehead on her knee, an enormous weight falling away as Morna stroked his hair.

"You worried I'd refuse you?"

He sat back. "I did not dare make assumptions. I will try never to make assumptions with you."

"Assume that I love you, too, Graham, and always have and

always will. I like to hear the words, by the way. They embarrass me, but from you, I do like to hear them."

"All my love," Graham said, holding out the ring. "Always."

Morna slipped it onto her finger. Thanks to a stealthy raid he'd made on her vanity, the fit was perfect. "That stone is the same color as your eyes, Graham MacNeil. A sapphire?"

"I bought it in Siam. They know what they're about in Siam when it comes to precious stones. The color reminded me of home skies and of you."

"You bought it...?"

"On my way home." He shifted to sit on the cedar chest so they were knee to knee. "I'm supposed to say the purchase was whimsy on my part, but I hoped even then, Morna. I've been hoping for years, until I'm consumed with it."

Hoping and fearing.

"I told a small fib," Morna said, head bowed.

She was so dear when she was being brave. Also when she was trying to be meek. "Agreeing to my proposal of marriage had better not be part of your dissembling."

"No part at all. I told you I came here to scold you."

"And I am duly scolded." Scolded, and formally engaged and nigh bursting with that joy, despite all the circumstances weighing against both hope and joy.

"I said I would follow you into hell if this plan tomorrow fails."

"It won't fail." Graham would not fail. He could not fail, or... well, he could not.

"I will make good on my threat, Graham. If you can't pull this off, I will be deeply, deeply disappointed, angry even."

"We will pull it off. You and I, ably assisted by our loyal familiars. We, Morna. The same we that should have thwarted Brodie's pernicious nonsense all those years ago."

She leaned against his shoulder. "Be patient with me."

He slipped an arm around her waist. "We'll be patient with each other, or try to be. I can get loud when I'm trying to be patient."

"I recall that about you. Graham, what I meant was... I will follow you into hell, but I would also, if you are so inclined, follow you into bed."

Bed. The sensible half of Graham's mind tried to go off on a flight about offers made under extenuating circumstances and perhaps when tomorrow's business was behind them... His heart slammed the door on that nonsense. They were *engaged to be married.*

At long last, they were to be married. "I am so inclined." He scooped her up and carried her across the dressing closet threshold into the warm, airy confines of the bedroom. That wasn't quite how the tradition was supposed to go either, but it moved the proceedings into the bedroom, which was close enough to the spirit of the customary ritual.

"You're sure, Morna?"

"Stop asking me that, and please see to warming the sheets."

"I love it when you give me orders in the bedroom." He was rewarded with that smile again, the half-secret, half-amused cross between tenderness and humor.

"Then get out of those clothes, your lordship, and help me out of mine."

Regret refused to be shed as easily as Morna's dressing gown. Like the thick wool socks wrapped around her feet, regret joined her in bed. While she snuggled beneath the covers with her woeful feelings, Graham did her the courtesy of tending to his ablutions before the fire.

By taking such care with soap and water, Graham was being either considerate or diabolically shrewd. Morna would have bet her second-favorite shawl—her most favorite was one Graham had given her for her sixteenth birthday—that Graham had bathed thoroughly before he'd gone prowling the corridors. His scent, when he'd embraced her, had been as fresh and airy as a Highland meadow.

Morna had indulged in a good soak as well, but her thoughts had bounced from wanting to drown Uncle Brodie in a horse trough to sheer wonder that Graham had willed his entire personal estate to her. Was that encouraging? Terrifying? A woman could lose her wits trying to fathom Graham MacNeil's motivations.

Her heart was already a lost cause.

He half turned so the line of his thigh, hip, back, and shoulder caught the firelight just so.

"If you spend any more time with that flannel and basin, Graham, I will soon be snoring. This bed is exceedingly cozy." And exceedingly large.

He straightened, and Morna's heart beat faster. Gracious heavens, he was magnificent.

"Morna, if you keep looking at me like that, the bed hangings will go up in flames the moment I set a knee upon the mattress."

"I've always delighted in a roaring bonfire."

He set the basin on the hearth, as casually as if he were fully attired rather than sporting about in the altogether.

"I'm contemplating something more in the nature of a volcano, Miss MacKenzie." He stalked across the room. "Or one of those comets that illuminate the entire firmament. Budge over."

Morna shifted twelve inches away from the center of the bed. Graham climbed aboard, making the mattress dip. Now came the difficult part, the part where she had to have self-possession and competence when, in fact, she was all at sixes and sevens. Their previous encounters had been lovely, but those occasions hadn't been overshadowed by the knowledge that their enemy was family.

Tomorrow would be dangerous, and Graham was choosing to confront that danger personally.

"I'm feeling a bit befuddled," he said, drawing the covers up. "But then, I've never been betrothed before, so we're exploring *terra incognito*. Perhaps you'd like to lead the expedition?"

He lay flat on his back beside her, and such was his sheer mass that Morna was rolled into his side.

"What I'd like," Morna said, "is to be eighteen, with Grandpapa and the countess still with us, John still wandering about muttering in law Latin, and Lanie still in possession of more of her sight. I am so angry, Graham, at what has been taken from us. Why didn't we see what Brodie was up to when we could have prevented so much heartache?"

Hardly an impressive sortie into the wilds of passionate abandon.

Graham slipped an arm beneath her neck and cuddled her close. "We don't know precisely what Brodie got up to, Morna. We have hunches and suspicions and theories. We will know more tomorrow, if luck is with us. What I tell myself is that if you and I had been allowed to pursue our interest in each other all those years ago, we might well have ended up together—I was certainly intent on that goal—but there's a significant chance I would have been less appreciative of my good fortune."

"I would not have needed much pursuing, Graham. I was rather determined to be your good fortune and to have you as mine."

"So we lost years, but we gained wisdom. As a younger man, I would have been proud to marry you, and—you will agree—a bit arrogant about taking you to wife. The arrogance got transported right out of me, I hope. The sadder, wiser fellow in bed with you now will hold to his vows with every particle of his honor and determination, Morna. Not simply the part about fidelity. That would have been yours regardless. I can promise you now that you'll also have the rest of it—the patience, humor, loyalty, trust, and respect. You are getting a better bargain now than you would have years ago."

At some point in that recitation, Graham had taken her hand and laid it flat on his stomach just beneath his waist.

Sadder and wiser, yes, and also—Morna's hand drifted lower— more fierce, more determined, braver, humbler, and irresistibly more attractive.

"We cannot be trifled with," Morna said slowly. "You are right about that. I wanted the castle to be in good working order if you ever returned. I got it into my head that if I could keep things organized here, you were more likely to return. I took up the reins and to blazes with anybody who tried to question my authority."

"Trifle with me all you like, Morna. Just go gently."

She did not trifle, though she did a bit of tickling. She explored the impressive bits and their oddly vulnerable near neighbors, and the curious, warm, slightly crinkly surrounding terrain. She sniffed, she fondled, she listened to Graham's heart and rode the rise and fall of his breathing with her hand.

Morna still had regrets, but to admit them, to know Graham understood and shared them, meant she could keep her socks on and let those regrets slip away.

"If you were to kiss me now," Graham said, "you would preserve me from begging. Your future husband's dignity is at stake, Morna."

She further imperiled her future husband's dignity by swinging a leg over his hips and straddling him before granting his request.

"Will you merely lie there while I do all the work?" Morna asked, scraping a fingernail across a flat male nipple. "What of my dignity?"

Graham shaped her breasts through the linen of her nightgown. "What of your pleasure?"

His hands were warm, even through the fabric. Warm and knowing and inventive. "I like that." An understatement.

"Kiss me, prospective wife. You'll like that too."

"Somebody very recently urged me to go gently, prospective husband. My body says let's leap into the inferno. My heart says I have missed you for so long, and I still need to savor what you offer if I'm to believe you are truly mine."

"The same for me." He gently urged her down with a hand on her nape, and the kissing recommenced.

Morna kept the reins for a time, until she realized Graham would let her equivocate all night if she needed to.

"One request," she said, brushing a hand over his chest. "Don't leave me."

At some point in the proceedings, Graham had rolled with her so he was above her, braced on his elbows.

He peered down at her. "I will never leave you. Perish the thought. Damnation be to him who—"

"No, I mean..." She patted his bum, and a fine bum it was too. "Don't *leave* me." A few strokes and a squeeze ensued. "Always before, you've withdrawn, and I understand the prudence and courtesy involved, but we are betrothed now."

He rested his cheek against hers. "I'm trying to think. Betrothed is not wed. That's as far as ratiocination takes me. You will be impressed that I managed such a big word. A dozen syllables or thereabouts."

Bless him, he was trying to decide whether to leave the reins in her hands on this decision as well.

"Betrothed means we shall be wed. We shall." Morna ceased stroking his backside, though the self-denial involved in that sacrifice was prodigious. She was asking a lot of Graham, asking him to trust that fate—never their ally thus far—would allow them the time and safety to wed.

"You'll wear my ring?" Graham asked, kissing her nose. "Tomorrow?"

"Tomorrow and for all the rest of my born days, Graham MacNeil, unless I'm swimming in the Tay or kneading bread dough."

Another kiss, this one to her forehead. "That's all right, then. Do you have the least comprehension how distracting a wool sock caressing a man's calf can be?"

"Yes. Do you have any idea how desperately I desire you at this moment?"

He lifted his hips a telling few inches and began the joining. "I have an inkling or two. You said you needed to savor our lovemaking rather than leap into the inferno."

She moved with him, and all the heavens began to move as well. "I was lying."

"Such a propensity for falsehoods you're developing. I love you, Morna MacKenzie, soon-to-be Lady Dunhaven."

Ye gods. Lady Dunhaven. She hadn't even considered that part. "I love you too, Graham MacNeil, and that is an eternal verity."

He did not leave her, and she would not have allowed him to if he had made the attempt. They fell asleep exhausted, replete, and entwined. Morna's feet were warm despite a lack of socks, and her heart was at peace.

When she woke in the morning, she was nonetheless alone in the bed. Some nincompoop was humming in the dressing closet, and the sun pouring through the window was wretchedly bright, while Morna was nowhere near as well rested as she ought to have been.

Which thought caused her to smile.

"I left the bed curtains open," Graham said, emerging from the dressing closet, "the better to feast my gaze upon your wondrous, snoring beauty. Good morning, beloved."

He wiped a spot of lather from his cheek, one of the most prosaic actions a man could take in the midst of the thoroughly boring job of finishing his morning toilette. He tossed the towel back into the dressing closet and surveyed her, his hands on his hips.

"No," Morna said, sitting up and patting the place beside her. "No, you are not going down to breakfast just yet. I have plans for you."

Graham unbelted his dressing gown. "Just as well. I have plans for you too."

They missed breakfast altogether and instead shared a midmorning tray in the study, where Morna pretended to look for a good book while she also rejoiced—and worried.

"I kept Brodie up playing whist until well past midnight," St. Didier said. "He cheats, but not excessively."

"How much?" Graham asked, leading True along the path that led to the geldings' pasture. The afternoon was brilliantly sunny and almost mild, which was the least boon a newly betrothed man deserved.

"Two pounds. I considered that a reasonable donation to the objective. I made him work for it."

"Is it work if the task is undertaken before a roaring fire while swilling French brandy and keeping the kitchen awake to send up sandwiches on the hour?"

True ambled along behind, a horse in charity with the world now that spring grass had come in.

"You're angry," St. Didier said. "You're entitled, but today might not be the day to unleash your wrath."

"Justice and wrath can bear a close resemblance." Graham had pondered, between kisses and cuddles, the years Morna had spent managing the castle, though she had no rank, no seniority, and only the most attenuated family connection. She'd doubtless sailed through any number of tempests, and all because Uncle Brodie...

All because Uncle Brodie might have accidently poisoned his sister?

Graham opened the gate for True and commended him to the company of the other geldings, who, to a horse, were munching grass and swishing their tails at the occasional fly.

"So peaceful," St. Didier said, taking up a lean against the post-and-rail fence. "So bucolic. You must have missed this when you were away."

"Scotland sparkles," Graham said, fastening the gate. "The grass in the morning, the skies, the waters of the Tay... It's all nearly magical." Like Morna's smiles and laughter, like the steady rise and fall of her breathing when she'd been loved to exhaustion. "Australia has much to recommend it, but it could never be home to me."

"How long did it take you to realize that?"

"A quarter of an hour at least, but then, I was staggering with fatigue by the time we made port and suffering a touch of the headache. Stop fretting, St. Didier. We'll confront Brodie, and he'll have choices to make."

"Don't trust him, Dunhaven. He wasn't playing cards last night like a man whose schemes have been foiled."

"Let's get back to the stable. One doesn't want to be late for a meeting." One wanted the meeting over, the whole mess with Brodie resolved, and the shadows banished from Morna's eyes for all time. "How was Brodie playing cards last night, when he wasn't cheating?"

St. Didier strode along in silence for the length of the fence. "Brodie has another plan," he said. "He fancies himself clever, and he's already shown us that if one scheme fails, he'll come up with another. He's already fashioned that next scheme and is relishing its implementation."

The most recent plan—hauling Lanie into the woods—had been fiendishly cruel. "Then we'd best not keep him waiting. You go first. If any of the grooms are malingering, chase them off and tell them to loiter in the servants' hall until given leave to get back to work. They'll adore you for it."

"They'll adore the undercook's ankles. You be careful, Dunhaven. Be damned careful, and don't turn your back on Brodie for any reason."

"That's why you'll be there. To guard my back." Morna had insisted, as had Peter and Lanie. Graham decided to be touched rather than insulted. Besides, the whole undertaking wanted a witness, and St. Didier—an English gentleman of impeccable repute —was the most disinterested party available.

St. Didier consulted his watch, an elegant gold affair that winked brilliantly in the afternoon sun. "We have thirty minutes. I'm off to take up lurking in the shadows. For the last time, be careful."

Morna had said the same thing when she'd kissed Graham following the noon meal. *Be careful.*

In Brodie's case, Graham would have preferred to be violent, providing the facts supported Graham's theory of events.

St. Didier took a nip from his flask—more winking gold—and saluted Graham with it. "We happy few and all that. A man who will cheat a guest at cards and leave Miss Lanie shivering in the woods is a creature without a conscience."

"He's likely in want of coin as well. One takes heed, St. Didier. Away with you."

Graham remained in the sun, watching the horses, considering what Brodie's next moves might be, because St. Didier was doubtless correct—Brodie was concocting another scheme, probably worse than all his previous mischief put together.

And Morna had spent years placating him and managing him and ignoring his snide asides, only to see her sister menaced in return —and her prospective husband.

Waiting thirty minutes was difficult, but well-laid plans proceeded on an agreed-upon schedule, according to St. Didier. Thus, when Brodie appeared in the deserted stable, Graham had just taken up a bench, with the saddle, rags, and leather soap arrayed at his side.

"You summon me to the stable," Brodie said, "and I find you doing the lowliest lad's work. Since when do earls clean saddles?"

"I'm hiding," Graham said, taking up the cloth and applying it to the cantle. "The festivities the other night rather wore me out, and I'm not up to ledgers, inventories, and callers today. One isn't as resilient in later years as one was in one's youth."

Brodie remained on his feet, while Graham sat, trying to exude grumpy harmlessness.

"Do I take it your friend St. Didier will be leaving us now that the grand ball has been endured?"

St. Didier ought to be in True's empty stall at that moment, listening to every word and ready to leap into any ensuing affrays.

"Our guest has not confided any such plans in me, but then, he's not much for confiding anything in anyone. How much did he take you for at whist?"

"I took him," Brodie said, rocking up on his toes. "Five pounds, if you can believe that. The man ponders every card in every hand, and he's too predictable by half. Is this where you tell me you'll be returning to Australia?" He extracted a flask and held it out to Graham.

Graham set aside his cloth and accepted the offering, though toasting his uncle's lies sat ill with him. "Why would I return to Australia? I just got home."

"Because you aren't welcome here, my boy, if I might indulge in a bit of avuncular blunt speech. I heard about that business with Lanie at the ball. A nasty prank at best. Somebody is trying to let you know that you are *persona non grata*, and I shudder to think what form the next message might take. Do drink up. That's the latest cherry brandy, all the rage in Paris. More fire than cordial and a pleasantly complicated finish."

Graham uncorked the flask and held it to his nose. "You don't attribute Lanie's mistreatment to village spite?" The first footman had confirmed that Brodie had disappeared in the direction of the men's retiring room, and been gone nigh three quarters of an hour.

"Village spite should never be underestimated," Brodie said, strolling along the rows of empty stalls, "but based on what I've managed to pick up from the staff, Lanie was all but kidnapped, and that is a hanging offense. We can attribute ill-will to the vicar's daughter or to the Bodeen imbecile, but not the requisite boldness. They are sly creatures, that pair."

Graham put the flask to his lips and reached not for boldness, but for prudence.

"Valid point. Still, I won't be returning to Australia. The place is dangerous, and Morna would rather bide in Scotland."

Brodie chuckled and, when Graham would have returned the flask, waved it back into his keeping.

"Drink up. Hair of the dog that bit you." Brodie reversed course just before reaching True's empty stall and returned to the doorway. "So Morna has wasted no time getting her hooks into you? I can't blame her. She's been the unpaid housekeeper for years, and she'd be a fool to pass up a chance to wear a tiara, even the somewhat tarnished article you could offer her. You might as well finish the brandy, I have a few more bottles in my stores. Very decent stuff, and you won't find its like easily."

Graham put the flask to his lips again rather than bash Brodie over the head for referring to Morna with anything less than respect.

"I have it on the authority of MacHeath's aunties that a little banishment adorns all the best Scottish peerages, but that's not what I asked you here to discuss."

"I would look after the place in your absence, you know." Brodie glanced behind him, as if that offer somehow merited discretion, but remained standing with his back to the sunshine at the end of the barn aisle. "I *have* looked after the place, in fact. Morna kept the maids in line, but reminding the steward and tenants of their obligations, listening to their laments, and keeping them from taking advantage, that all fell to me."

No, it had not. St. Didier had taken a hand, Peter had done his best, and even the ruddy London solicitors had provided epistolary reminders of when the rents were due. Morna had doubtless shown the flag on every tenant property and kept track of who was due for a new ram or who had a son who could apprentice to the castle's farrier.

But Brodie's offer revealed his entire hand. He wanted the castle and its revenues for himself, and that required Graham to decamp once more, leaving the family wealth in Brodie's ever so willing hands.

"Then I owe you my thanks," Graham said, "for all your selfless hard work and loyalty. Nonetheless, I won't be turning the castle over to you any time soon, Uncle."

"You'll want somebody keeping an eye on the place during your wedding journey, surely? Peter can't keep two thoughts in his head for the duration of a minuet. The boy is as flighty as my late sister. I'm not saying he's foolish, but he is young, and in case you hadn't noticed, he's smitten with poor, blind Lanie."

Poor, blind Lanie. Graham nearly tossed the flask at Brodie's head. He put it in a pocket instead, the better to keep his hands free.

"Lanie's eyesight is poor, I agree, but she has other skills that compensate for what she lost to measles."

"I would like my flask back," Brodie said, "though you must finish the contents if they appeal to you. My sister gave me that particular article. She called it elegant. I call it plain, but serviceable, and full of sentimental value."

He held out his hand, and Graham ignored it. "Lanie has an excellent nose too," he went on as if Brodie hadn't spoken. "She, in fact, discerned that her kidnapper, despite wearing my new cloak, reeked of cigars. Careful interviewing of the staff confirmed that while Lanie was being abandoned in the woods, not two yards from a precipice, you were absent from the ball, Uncle. What have you to say for yourself?"

CHAPTER SIXTEEN

Brodie's slouch against the barn doorway shifted to an upright stance. He'd taken the tactically superior position, with the strong afternoon sunlight at his back, so Graham assumed the place across the wide doorway from him.

"Do you accuse me of mistreating Lanie?" Brodie asked.

"I accuse you of kidnapping her, putting her at very great risk of harm, exposing her to the harsh night weather, and upsetting her sorely, and you did this while you wore my new cloak. I haven't decided if you were trying to mislead any staff who saw you getting up to your tricks, or you were clever enough to try to deceive Lanie's nose."

"Lanie's nose is very frequently stuck in the air, and you clearly left half your wits in Australia. Why would I seek to harm a blind girl whom I regard as family?"

Not a denial, and some part of Graham had been hoping for a denial. "Two reasons. First, you are trying to banish me again, and second, because Lanie was in the room when you gave your sister a fatal dose of laudanum. Even if you could not frighten me all the way back to the Antipodes, you could certainly throw a bad scare into Lanie." And, by extension, Morna and Peter.

"You accuse me of murder now? How droll. A bit late for that, isn't it? The culprit of record—who stands before me, I might add—has been caught and punished, subsequent to his own confession."

Again, not quite a denial. More in the way of a deflection. Graham was abruptly weary of the discussion.

"Lanie detected the stink of your cigars in the countess's sickroom," Graham said. "As best I can piece together the facts, you poisoned the whole teapot—the blue one, always the blue one, which Mrs. Gibson probably told you—and thus when Lanie had a mere half a cup, she soon dozed off. The countess would have drunk the rest of the pot, finishing the last of it when I came along to administer one final dose of medicine. She was already drowsy and drugged, but I never thought to question her state. Your sister died because you saw to it that she was liberally overdosed with a powerful patent remedy."

"You can't verify any of that."

"Mrs. Gibson is thriving in Massachusetts. I suspect she also noted you tampering with the teapot, or making an unusual offer to carry the tray abovestairs, and you threatened to see her blamed for your crime."

Brodie stalked away from the barn door and down the aisle. "My sister was suffering terribly. Ask that quack Ramsey if you don't believe me. He's something of an expert on rheumatism. The countess would never have recovered. She would get worse and worse, lingering for years. The real question is how you lot could tolerate to see her enduring such agonies."

Graham turned away from the sun, mindful of St. Didier's warning to never give Brodie his back. "You stayed away from the sickroom generally to ensure suspicion would not fall on you, but you couldn't resist checking on the progress of your crime. That's why Lanie detected your signature cigar reek in Grandmama's bedroom.

Lanie will testify to that, too, though I'd rather spare her such an ordeal."

Brodie pivoted and smiled. "Very gracious of you. If Lanie isn't determined to see me in chains for being my sister's angel of mercy, then what is the point of this discussion?"

The smile was genial, while the eyes remained watchful. St. Didier had been correct: Brodie had more plans in train.

"You admit to hastening the countess's death?"

"Nobody else had the stomach for it, so yes. I ended her suffering. Purely as a concerned brother, I interviewed Ramsey regarding her prognosis. His own mother expired of the disease, and that was not a fact he wanted publicized when the countess went to her reward."

"Which is how you've been able to blackmail him all these years."

"My, my, my. You have been a busy little lad, haven't you? The trick to blackmail—you do not want to know how I come by this knowledge—is to demand a modest sum to be paid at regular inter-vals, like a mortgage. The victim will always reason that the price of silence is easily borne, while the truth if aired could be disastrous. An easy choice, and Ramsey is a sensible fellow."

A sensible fellow who, like Mrs. Gibson, would have made a logical suspect, except that Ramsey had been shrewd enough to sound an early, loud alarm on behalf of the expired countess.

"I thought of nearly everything," Brodie said, shaking his head. "I did not think of Ramsey getting the bit between his teeth, and God's judgment upon him for that recklessness. There was no need for any rubbishing inquiry."

"He is supporting a large family, and he's Scottish. You left him no choice but to guard his own reputation."

"Got back a bit of my own, though, didn't I? His little infusions of cash have come in handy. You have no idea what it's like to be told that the family's entire wealth, every spare groat, went into your older sister's dowry. Dunhaven would have wed her if she hadn't a pair of shoes to her name, but her settlements had to be worthy of her station. I was barely breeched when she wed, and nobody spared a thought for me or my prospects."

The afternoon was so pretty and peaceful, but inside Graham's heart, grief, rage, and sadness engaged in a roaring battle.

Brodie had been educated, clothed, fed, introduced to polite society, and given a haven to last him all his days, and yet, he saw himself as the injured party.

"I suppose you ran through the competence Grandmama left you?"

Brodie approached, letting his fingers trail against the iron railings that allowed horses to see out of their stalls and air to circulate.

"She left me a competence, true, but she also tied it up in a damned trust. I get a quarterly pittance. Can't touch the principal until I've reached my three-score-and-ten. Bedamned Dunhaven made her do that, but she could have warned me."

"Then Grandmama died for nothing." The worst possible outcome for a story that might have ended in a remorseful explanation of an accident. That Brodie wasn't dissembling, that he was nearly boasting of his wicked deeds, offered further proof that he had more trouble up his sleeve.

"Your grandmother died because her life was reduced to endless suffering. Then too, had I not been able to satisfy the worst of my creditors with regular sums, however modest, I might have been the one cut down."

"Because you borrowed from the wrong people, and they might have made an example of the pretentious swell who had neither means nor title. You chose to commit murder rather than ask for help."

Carriage wheels rattled in the stable yard. A damned inconvenient time for a neighbor to call. When Graham perused the conveyance, he recognized it as the venerable equipage available at the village livery. Sturdy enough to withstand a trip to Glasgow or Edinburgh and pulled by an unprepossessing team of chestnuts.

"I *had* asked for help," Brodie snapped. "Dunhaven lent me sums here and there, but he had no idea of the cost of maintaining the sort of style that would entice an heiress to the altar. I all but begged him for a bit more generosity, but he could not be bothered."

Nobody was getting out of the coach. "Did you kill Grandpapa too?"

"I didn't have to. Grief did that for me, but he still foiled me for a time. I could have managed John, but those solicitors were impossible. I bided my time. I excel at biding my time. You should have remembered that."

Graham asked the next question, despite not wanting to hear the answer. "What of John? Was he another of your victims?"

"Not as such," Brodie replied with a monstrous sort of modesty. "I did make sure his flask was full at all times, though, and that he had an ample supply of flasks. Nature took its course. Speaking of flasks, how are you feeling, my boy?"

"Furious." Also betrayed and bereft. How many people had suffered or died because Brodie hadn't been able to entice an heiress into matrimony?

"You should be a bit dizzy by now. I adjusted the dose to suit your dimensions, and brandy is a first-rate medium for enhancing the properties of all manner of soporifics."

Soporifics caused sleep rather than death. "You expect me to get into that coach, Uncle?" One driven by a skinny coachman in a black greatcoat.

"Indeed, I do, and when you are peacefully embraced by the arms of Morpheus, I will bundle you along to an East India Company vessel getting ready to set sail from Glasgow. I have a head for details, despite what you might think, and I've been setting matters in train since you failed to accommodate my efforts in London and Edinburgh."

The coachman tipped his hat. Edinburgh. The runaway team of bays. Of course.

When Graham's gaze returned to Brodie, a pistol had appeared in Uncle's hand.

"Into the coach, my lord. You will find the door handles have been removed from the inside, but the roads down to Glasgow are reasonably smooth. We'll have you there just in time for the midnight tide."

Where was St. Didier? "I don't care for sea voyages."

"Can't be helped, but you mustn't fret about the castle. My associate there holding the ribbons put me in touch with a fellow who excels at copying wills and other tedious documents. Yours was easy to duplicate."

Because a copy resided in the family safe, and Brodie had the combination. "You simply substituted your name for Morna's."

"When you make it that simple, one is helpless to resist. And then you obligingly took your own life at the Leap. Saw the tragedy myself from a distance. Could not believe my sorrowing old eyes, but of course, your ordeal in Australia robbed you of all sense. Now into the coach with you, and don't expect your English lackey to come to the rescue. I was rather more liberal with the dose I added to his flask. The medicine has no taste, I'm told, much like the English themselves."

Brodie grinned at his little slur while Graham calculated the distance between the pistol and his own heart. Too close. Morna would disapprove.

Fortunately, Brodie wasn't the only person capable of making alternative plans.

"Uncle..." Graham pretended to steady himself on an oak pillar. "You can't expect to get away with this."

"I can and I do, and we must secure you in the coach before you nod off entirely. Come along."

Graham stumbled, he reeled, he went down to one knee and braced himself on the dirt floor of the barn aisle.

"Not feeling quite the... Ruddy hell."

The gun barrel dropped an inch.

Graham came up fast, throwing a handful of dirt straight into

Brodie's eyes. The older man staggered and shook his head, the pistol still in his hand.

"Get away, you idiot. Get back, or I'll shoot."

The horses stamped at the commotion, while the coachman tried to calm them.

"Nice try, my boy," Brodie said, still blinking and wiping at his eyes. "But a failed try. Any more of that nonsense, and old John MacIver truly will find your corpse bobbing in the Tay, the self-inflicted wound to your temple explanation enough for any sheriff."

Brodie had apparently lost his reason while biding in the middle of the beautiful Perthshire countryside. "I didn't drink your damned poison," Graham said. "I knew better."

"You might wish you had. I certainly wish you had. Move." Brodie waved the pistol in the direction of the coach, just as a shadow emerged from the stable's overhang.

"Put the gun down, Uncle," Morna said. "This is not a parasol I'm holding against your back."

Thank heaven's most vigilant angel. "Set your pistol on the ground, Uncle," Graham said. "Gently. Morna, my thanks."

Brodie complied.

"Move away from the lady. Five steps in the direction of the coach."

The look in Brodie's eye suggested he was hatching yet another plan —to retrieve the pistol, overpower Morna, take her gun from her grasp, or simply flee. His schemes were thwarted by the coachman whipping the team into a trot and disappearing in the direction of the main gates.

"Give it up," Morna said as Graham retrieved Brodie's pistol and emptied it of bullets. "You've committed your last swindle, and by God, you shall pay."

"You heard?" Graham asked, accepting her pistol when she passed it over.

"Every word, as did Lanie and Peter. Now what's to be done with him?"

Fair question. "Make sure St. Didier yet breathes."

Morna ducked into the barn and returned a moment later. "No longer on his feet, but breathing and muttering curses."

"Then Uncle is in luck, of a sort. Lanie, Peter, show yourselves and help St. Didier get to his feet. Even muddled, he'll have useful counsel to offer."

"I'll leave," Brodie said. "I am not safe anywhere but on the castle's grounds, truth be told, and I will just damned leave."

"Wrong." Morna looked very severe as Peter and Lanie emerged from around the side of the stable.

"What does she mean?" Brodie asked. "If those damned fellows in Edinburgh get wind that I won't inherit, they will begin by breaking my legs."

"She means," Graham said, "you are no longer safe on castle grounds, and one refrains from arguing with a lady, especially when she's absolutely correct."

~

Peter, ably assisted by two of the largest footmen, escorted Brodie up to the castle.

"He killed her," Morna said, watching them go. "I cannot believe he killed her, all so he could play cards and bet on horse races and..."

Graham slipped an arm around Morna's waist, which was fortunate when her knees had grown unreliable.

"By the time Grandmama died," Graham said, "flirting and gaming were no longer the issue. Brodie had dug himself a hole as deep as a grave, and his creditors would have been only too happy to shove him into it. That sort depends on a reputation for ruthlessness, and Brodie really should have known better than to ever tangle with parties of that ilk."

Lanie squeezed Morna's hand with cool fingers. "We should have known better than to trust him. You were magnificent, Morna. 'This is not a parasol I'm holding at your back...' You promised him death. I heard that in your voice."

"Not death. I want him to suffer for years, as Grandmama suffered. I want him to know real want and privation of the sort Grandmama spared him. I want him to miss Scotland ten times worse than Graham ever did. If I'd killed him..."

Words were growing difficult. Brodie had planned for Graham a fate worse than death, a return to Graham's worst nightmares, another banishment by sea, and this one without any hope of a return. No resources, no way to let his family know his fate, at least not for a very long while.

"I should have killed him." Morna sagged against Graham, anger and sorrow blending with physical and moral unsteadiness. "He was miserable to Peter, nasty to the staff, never satisfied no matter how much he was waited on... I am crying. I hate to cry."

Graham wrapped her in a hug. "Saving my life entitles you to do as you ruddy well please, woman. Bawl so loudly they'll hear you in Edinburgh."

"St. Didier is coming," Lanie said, two instants before that good soul emerged from the barn, shaded his eyes, and proceeded into the stable yard at a careful pace.

"I missed all the fun?"

"The old wretch tried to drug me too," Graham said, arms still about Morna. "Peter is standing guard over the prisoner, whom my countess subdued easily. Lanie, if you would see St. Didier up to the castle, he'd probably appreciate a pot of stout black tea and some of Cook's shortbread. We'll be along soon."

Morna felt an awkward pat to her shoulder. St. Didier, apologizing perhaps for having literally fallen asleep at his post. She tucked closer to Graham and wished the whole world to the Antipodes.

"They're gone," Graham murmured near her ear. "Lanie is right. You were magnificent. Shall we find a bench? Or maybe you'd like me to carry you?"

Morna drew back. "Carry me?"

"Steadies my nerves to have you in my arms. All of you. Brodie held a gun, Morna, and he would have shot you before he fired at me."

Graham had seen Brodie's face while Morna had not. "Is my lord having trouble staying upright?"

He nodded, his eyes desperately serious. "We had a plan, and you holding a gun on Brodie was not part of that plan."

"You had a plan. You and St. Didier. I know I agreed to it, but then I thought about that coach in Edinburgh, and two heads are better than one, and Uncle would have never thought to consider me a threat."

Graham gestured across the stable yard to the path that led to castle. "No forced marches, please. I want to bellow and pace and shake my fist, Morna, but you are right: Brodie did not consider you a threat. He might have shot Peter, but he wasn't expecting you in any guise. Neither was I."

"You thought I was safely at my embroidery up at the castle."

"I thank you and all the benevolent powers that you were not."

"You aren't angry?"

They walked along, arms about each other's waists, and Morna's heart settled into a steadier tempo.

"I am ready to tear Brodie's head from his neck with my bare hands. He is a rancid stain on the family escutcheon and a bird dropping on the honor of the Scottish race. If we turn him over to the authorities, he is very likely to hang for blackmail alone."

"Because you are the earl, and you could ensure that outcome."

"Because, according to the law, he deserves that fate. As far as I am concerned, his fate is in your hands, Morna."

The castle came into view, a glorious sight on a gorgeous spring afternoon. Seeing it, Morna felt a little as Graham must have felt upon returning from exile. Home, safety, family, traditions, and a worthy future were all encompassed in one ageless edifice, but first, old troubles had to be resolved once and for all.

"I don't want him to hang," Morna said, a degree of certainty infusing her words. "Brodie is a killer, but I want no responsibility for his death."

"And if he kills again?"

"I see the difficulty. The world must be warned against him. Can you have him transported?"

"I like that," Graham said. "Has a certain symmetry to it. Transported for life, though, not a mere seven years. I don't know how much time he has left, but I want the entirety of it spent someplace far, far away from me and mine."

"As do I."

She eased away, but kept hold of Graham's hand. They made their way together to the castle, and when Morna had fortified herself with a nip from Graham's personal flask, Graham summoned the accused to the library, along with Peter, St. Didier, and Lanie.

"They heard you," Graham said, standing before the central hearth and looking all of a piece with the third countess's portrait above. "They heard you admit to causing Grandmama's death, admit to blackmailing Dr. Ramsey, and admit to leading Lanie into the night and certain danger. Have you anything more to add?"

Graham sounded so calm, while Morna's heart was back to imitating a slow war drum.

Brodie looked amused. "Am I supposed to apologize? You cannot prove I had anything to do with my sister's merciful demise. Lanie was perfectly safe, else how comes she to be here now? As for Ramsey, perhaps he sends small tokens of gratitude for all the kind words I put in various ears about his excellent services."

St. Didier examined his fingernails. "And perhaps he'll sign an affidavit to the effect that you threatened to disclose his mother's terrible struggle with rheumatism and his thorough knowledge of patent remedies used to treat it. Perhaps he'll also swear in writing that you further threatened him with false testimony to the effect that you saw him coming out of your sister's room late on the night in question. Who knows what he'll testify to in person, but we do know he's willing to testify."

If Morna was not mistaken, St. Didier had just engaged in a bit of fanciful embroidery himself.

Brodie's smile faded. "You cannot seriously... This is preposterous. Graham confessed. I cannot be blamed for the fact that he confessed. I could have seen Ramsey arrested, but Graham had to interfere and take matters into his own hands."

"Suspicion," Peter said through clenched teeth, "would have also fallen on 'poor, blind Lanie.' You were counting on that."

"And I would have had no alibi," Lanie said. "I would have only a muddled recollection of the whole evening because I was drugged, too, but I know what I smelled, Uncle, and you deserve to hang."

Her eyes glittered with tears, and Morna itched to throw something heavy and jagged at Brodie's head.

"Nobody would hang a blind girl," Brodie said. "This drama is all quite excessive and beyond tiresome."

"You are fortunate," Graham said, pacing before the hearth, "that Morna is not a great proponent of violence, else you'd already be dead, Uncle."

"Listen to him," Lanie said. "*Listen to his voice.* He means it. You'd be dead if Graham's wishes prevailed, and I'd rejoice to know you burned in hell. I could hear the River Tay, damn you, taunting me to set a single foot off that bench, hectoring me to take the smallest, shivering risk. I will never forgive you for that, for making me afraid in a place I love. Perhaps we should shove you off the Leap, Uncle. That might be justice."

Brodie's expression became uncertain.

"We have your attention," Graham said. "And don't think to bolt out the French doors, because we've posted footmen at all the exits who will be only too happy to catch you and thoroughly *subdue you*, with my blessing. You will stand trial on felony charges. If you plead guilty to blackmail, I will urge the court to show you the lenience of transportation for life. You may take one trunk and such cash as you can legally lay your hands on, but you will depart Scotland, never to return."

"Or," Peter said, "you could stand trial for murder, kidnapping, *and* blackmail. Graham deserves to be exonerated."

Morna could have hugged him for that observation. "Bear in mind," she said, "I am becoming more of a proponent of violence by the moment. Lanie's suggestion has very strong appeal."

Brodie looked about the room and must have seen that nobody would object to summary judgment at the Leap.

"I'll take my snuffboxes. They are worth a great deal, and—"

"No," Graham said. "You will take such snuff boxes as remain when enough have been sold to make Ramsey whole. Restitution is a vital part of justice and good for the conscience, assuming you acquire one. For every objection you make to this plan, we'll send one of your snuffboxes to Vicar for the poor box. Is there more to be said?"

Lanie walked up to Brodie, drew back her arm, and delivered an unerring blow to his cheek. "'Poor, blind Lanie' has decent aim, Uncle. Who knew?"

She departed with the dignity of a queen.

"Lanie speaks for me," Peter said. "If fate is just, you will never live to blight the shores of Australia. Consider yourself belatedly disowned on behalf of my grandparents." He followed Lanie out the door, leaving Brodie to stare at the floor.

"St. Didier," Graham said, "if you and the footmen would see to confining the accused in an empty pantry, I'd be obliged. My lady, a word with you, if you can spare me the time?"

Morna took one last look at the man who'd nearly shattered her family, the man who'd valued jeweled snuffboxes above love and honor.

Pathetic. Utterly, unredeemably, hopelessly pathetic. She said not a word of farewell, but took Graham's offered arm and commended Brodie to a far kinder fate than he deserved.

EPILOGUE

"Are you managing?" Morna asked as seagulls wheeled and cried, and children darted up and down the quay.

Graham wished he and his lady weren't wearing gloves, but an earl and countess on an occasion of state must dress the part—and Morna was his countess. Had been for nearly three deliriously happy, occasionally exhausted, and thoroughly loving months.

Sometimes he held her hand out of sheer affection. Sometimes he held her hand because any excuse to touch her was a good excuse. Today, he held her hand because he needed her steadiness and calm.

"The occasion is not sad," he said as the guest of honor arrived from the inn, Hamlet and his consort trotting along with him on the end of fine leather leashes. "Seeing Brodie onto the transport ship was worse in a way, but also a relief. The sea can do with him as it pleases, and Scotland gets the same bargain where I'm concerned. I am more than content with that arrangement. This is a happy occasion, and the River Clyde is not Cape Horn."

The River Clyde was in fine fettle, sparkling beneath the summer sun, the picture of riparian beauty. Peter and Lanie were, as usual, in deep conversation, with Peter gesturing up and down the quay, and Lanie listening intently. They held hands too.

Perhaps all newlyweds were prone to the habit.

"MacIver is truly leaving," Morna said. "How did you talk him into it?"

"Home is where we're loved, and John MacIver loves his family and his hounds. The first batch of canines is probably already gamboling about the fields of Nova Scotia, and his royal highness and friend will found a dynasty there under MacIver's watchful eye."

"Who is to be our gamekeeper?"

"MacIver's youngest nephew, who also has a way with a hound. I believe you're supposed to make some sort of speech, Countess."

MacIver strutted down the quay with his canine retinue, shaking hands and tolerating hugs. The whole village had turned out to see him off, and Graham had put every farm wagon, cart, and carriage he possessed at their disposal, lest they walk the distance from the castle.

"The speech to be made is yours," Morna said, easing her fingers from his grasp. She glided forward, kissed MacIver's leathery cheek, and murmured briefly into his ear. The kiss hadn't mortified him in the least, but Morna's parting words had the old man looking bashful.

Graham strode forward, his hand extended. "A cheer for our John MacIver, off to the New World to see that his family's stewpots are always full and their woods free of the presuming coney. You take our thanks, our best wishes, and a piece of our hearts with you, MacIver, and if you don't send regular reports, my countess and I will know the reason why."

"Mind you lot look after the puppies," MacIver said with mock fierceness. "And keep an eye on his lordship and her ladyship too. They are new to their honors and will want careful minding."

Hoots and laughter followed as MacIver's hounds sniffed the gangplank then made their way onto the ship, MacIver muttering to them and pausing for a final wave from the rail. The requisite roar went up in response, and the moment was over.

"I'm standing a round in honor of MacIver," Graham called. "All hands to the Happy Hare!"

Morna leaned close. "Generous of you."

"Strategic. They will linger, drinking, reminiscing, and laughing, while we make an early escape and have the road to ourselves. I could do with a pint first, to be honest. I will miss MacIver. He was the first to truly welcome me home. Perhaps we should name our firstborn after him."

Morna gazed out over the sparkling river. "John is a family name and worthy of respect. I like Joanna as well. I expect we will need to have settled on a name by about the first of the year."

The sunlight, or something, shone too brightly in Graham's eyes, or maybe the breeze chose then to pick up. "Morna?"

"Possibly by Yuletide. Why do you look so surprised?"

"Stunned, pleased, agog." Right there before the milling crowds, the seagulls, and the River Clyde, Graham scooped up his beloved and wheeled with her in the morning sun. "By Yuletide, she says, or at the New Year. Ah, Morna."

He pressed his nose to her cheek, and a fierce, mighty joy settled upon him, a homecoming, a peace, a rightness. "I'm glad you told me here and now. We begin a voyage, you and I. One I undertake with hope and love. Thank you."

Morna repaid his thanks in her own way, and for reasons best known to the occupants, Lord and Lady Dunhaven's coach made only leisurely progress on the return journey to the castle, where in accordance with custom, the earl and his countess found the pennant flapping merrily in the summer breeze.

They named their red-haired first born Joanna, and she had the most uncanny knack with hounds, rabbits, cats, and horses.

Printed in Great Britain
by Amazon

62671648R00136